Cast Doubt

Leila Kirk

rowanvale books

First published 2022
by Rowanvale Books Ltd
The Gate
Keppoch Street
Roath
Cardiff
CF24 3JW
www.rowanvalebooks.com

A CIP catalogue record for this book is available from the British
Library.
Paperback ISBN: 978-1-913662-95-0

Foreword to Cast Doubt:
The Book with a Metalworking Fluid Mission

James Bond's Beretta made me do it. No, I wasn't held at gunpoint, but this good idea had the same effect. Last year, in an address to the British Occupational Hygiene Society, Bill Cassells urged us hygienists to think outside the box. We needed to increase awareness of hazards to health, to get it across to health and safety managers, process engineers, employees. Well, everyone really.
To find out more, visit www.bohs.org.

Currently, the big nasties that are shortening lives of employees in the UK are metalworking fluid mist, crystalline silica and welding fume. Occupational hygiene is the profession that strives to keep people at work safe from threats like these. We want workers to enjoy retirement, not to have it shortened and spent confined to a chair with oxygen pipes stuffed up the nose. To find out more, visit www.hse.gov.uk.

So, that's where James Bond comes in. As a teenager, I could roll Beretta, Colt, Browning and Kalashnikov off my tongue simply from following 007's exploits in grubby, dog-eared paperbacks. 100W-filament moment: why not make factory hazards the backdrop to a corny thriller... with a sabotaged aeroplane... a beautiful factory inspector... a BMW car chase... a Transit van with Nürburgring history... a race to save a sister? Maybe a bit of torture and being locked in a foundry oven, but we'll gloss over that for now. To find out more... dive in!

And if you like to collect interesting facts about jet engines—this book is for you too.

Chapter 1

Riddle of the Hands

Squadrons of gleaming CNC machines, each the size of a large van, hummed and pumped, whirred and squealed. Coolant gushed. The air was warm, sweet, oily. Production at Gauge Precision was relentless.

Familiar sights, smells, sounds—but there was something very wrong. The hands of the operator of machine number seventy-six had erupted into a volcanic mass of cracks and open sores. It was my job to prevent ill health. Evidently, I had failed.

Barry, the machine's burly operator, showed me his sore hands. Blue-ink Union Jacks defaced by tender, red, swollen skin. Painful splits across thumbs and knuckles wept clear yellow fluid from crusted cracks. *Bloody hell! Work was doing this to him?* But how had this happened? What had caused it?

Involuntarily, I gasped and glanced up. The man flushed and turned away, hastily covering his hands in nitrile disposable gloves.

Behind my shoulder, a torrent of creamy liquid suddenly splattered, loudly battered, a window.

"Woah!" I jumped.

"Changing tools." Barry's eyes creased in amusement.

"Ah!" I nodded with a rueful smile.

The whirring of rotating shafts and spindles in the machine was replaced by metallic clunks and the hiss of pneumatic air release. The door window drained, revealing the cutting head spinning next to the grey metal of the aerospace casting being milled.

The blade inched closer; metal ripped. Coolant lubricant poured from orange nozzles over the whirling dance and smashed between the metal partners into a grey mist, blurring the scene through the window. The whirring, whining noise resumed, increased to a high-pitched crescendo for a couple of seconds then abruptly cut off. The cutting head retreated to approach from a different angle. Speed, power, precision, like the aeroplanes these parts were destined for.

The answer to the cause of Barry's skin problems lay in there. Barry's hands could be reacting to the chemicals of the neat coolant, to the metals in the nickel alloy being milled, to bacteria living in the liquid. A skin reaction fuelled by Barry's natural allergic response could be triggered by touching the coolant or even breathing it in.

"Two and a half thousand revs," Barry reported with pride.

Pen held unnaturally upright avoiding his knuckles, he filled in his production sheet as the machine resolutely followed its programmed moves.

I jotted down the figure. The rotational speed confirmed there would be tremendous heat and shearing of the coolant into a very fine mist. *Could Barry be breathing in more mist than before? Is the machine running hotter on this programme? What substances are lurking in that coolant?*

"Hm." I looked up. "You reckon nothing's changed to cause this reaction?"

"No, nothing. It just come on about three weeks ago." The middle-aged man looked at his gloved hands with a frown. Swollen fingers strained the thin nitrile material.

I sighed, racking my brain for a reason for dermatitis to suddenly flare up.

The operators of the CNC machines were exposed to the liquid coolant and to the mist of the coolant in the air we all breathed in the factory. Somehow, the coolant must have changed. But just in machine seventy-six?

"You've worked here for, what, fifteen years?"

Barry put his pen down and peered into the machine's window. "That and more. Jim and me was here when it was Browns Aerospace."

"Oh, I see." I noted the long duration of his employment with CNC machines. "What was it like when it was Browns?"

"Much like it is now. It weren't the dark ages, if that's what you're thinking. We used a couple of manual lathes in production, but we moved them to the toolroom."

Could he have been exposed to high levels of metalworking fluid mist or oil mist in the past and only be feeling the effects now?

I considered Barry as he made an adjustment to the orange screen of controls. He was my height, around six feet, but of a heavier build. Dark hair and tattoos covered his forearms. Like all employees of Gauge Precision Engineering Limited, he wore a black polo shirt embroidered with the company logo.

"And how long have you been on machine seventy-six? Weren't you on the CNC grinders a couple of years back?" I gesticulated to the large blue machines in the centre of the factory unit.

"Just over a year. You was doing a noise survey then! Fancy remembering!"

He was right; it had been a noise survey. The company—through Philip Wheatley, the Health and Safety Manager—contracted me to keep on top of the noise, coolant and dust emissions that could otherwise harm their employees. Annually, I measured levels, identified sources, and generally did my best to help them reduce emissions. I was pretty good at remembering machines. Like the blue grinder. It was just luck that I'd remembered Barry with it. I felt a glow that he remembered me, though.

He cleared his throat with a short cough.

If Barry's skin is reacting, could his airways be reacting too?

"Got a cough?"

"Oh, it's nothing. Just a frog in my throat."

I persisted, dreading the answer, in case it was asthma. "I know this sounds odd, but do you get breathlessness, or a tight chest at night?"

"Funny you should ask that. I've woken around four the last couple of nights, with my chest feeling right heavy."

"That's not nice. So, what do you do?"

"Get up, get a drink. Don't want to disturb the wife; it passes off, and I go back to bed. Do you think that's related?" The man's good-natured face was trustingly searching mine, concern starting to tighten the skin under his eyes.

My heart sank. I had to get to the bottom of why Barry's hands—maybe the whole of Barry—were reacting so badly. I'd have to tell Philip my concerns, as much as I dreaded it. He would ask if the HSE needed to know. God, what a mess!

"Er, yes. Look, um, it might be related." I was only guessing. How much could I say without knowing the facts?

"Have I got asthma? Is that what you think?"

"Um, I don't know." I scratched a sudden itch on my scalp. "It's common in machine shops, and it can start with not being able to breathe at night."

"Can't you test me or something?" The pitch of Barry's voice increased in his anxiety.

I shook my head apologetically. "Sorry. I just test the air you breathe, not how well you breathe."

I realised I had caused him to worry. But if I hadn't asked, I would never have known about this possible escalation from dermatitis to asthma. I felt wretched, not knowing if I had done the right thing.

I dredged up a reassuring smile. "I'll have a word with Philip, see if we can't get you booked in this week with the occupational health people for a proper lung function test."

Machine seventy-six interrupted our conversation with a final staccato peppering of the door window. Barry looked at the time on his phone. "Break time. Do I still need to wear this?"

I had fitted a small black plastic IOM sampling head onto his lapel, attached to a quietly buzzing pump that was clipped on his belt. This was to measure how much coolant mist he was breathing in. The plastic head had a hole in it, like a single nostril, and held a filter that collected particles from the air going through it.

"Not if you don't want to. The buzzing'll be annoying in the canteen. I could do with running it while you're working for the rest of the shift, if you don't mind, to make sure we collect enough for the lab to analyse."

"Yeah, that's fine by me." Barry unclipped the sampling equipment.

"If you put it on your bench here and let the sample head just dangle in the air, it'll be alright. Then I'll help you put it back on after break."

We walked back towards the canteen. Around us, machines were quietly ticking over. There was the occasional sharp hiss of an airline. A contract cleaner in blue overalls on a floor washer left squeegeed contrails on the pale grey floor.

"Have you got family, Hal?" Barry asked as we walked.

"No—confirmed bachelor, me! I've got a sister in Wales. She's an engineering apprentice."

"You must be proud of her." He smiled and looked at me. "Younger than you?"

"Yes, er, to both," I replied. "How about you? You said you have a wife. Children?"

"The children are grown up. The wife and I, we're looking after the grandson at the weekend." He scrolled through a few photos before a little boy in a fireman's helmet popped up on his phone screen.

"Handsome little chap," I obliged. "Does he come over most weekends?"

I could sense this grandfather swelling with pride. We were nearly at the canteen, where men mingled around the lockers.

"Oi, Barry! Show him your bed!" called a man from the crowd.

"Just getting to it!" laughed Barry.

I shook my head with a smile, wondering what this was about.

Barry flicked back through a couple more photos and came up with a child's bed in the shape of a fire engine. He passed me the phone.

"Nipper's nuts about fire engines," he explained.

"You made that? It's brilliant!"

"It's nothing, really," he said modestly, peeling off his gloves and throwing them into the bin by the lockers.

Passing back the phone, a thought struck me.

"What adhesives and paint did you use? Could this have affected your hands?"

He shook his head. "I made it last Christmas, a good four months ago."

"Shouldn't be that then." Another dead end. I let out a sigh as I stood back. Time to stop putting off the inevitable. "That's a pretty mean bed. See you later. I'm off to have a word with Philip."

**

Philip Wheatley was the health and safety manager at Gauge Precision. He contracted my company, IDP—which was just me—to provide occupational hygiene services. He followed my advice to stay legally compliant and keep the workforce healthy. *And how well has that gone, Hal?*

Philip, a lean, lined gentleman in a grey suit looked up from his desk in the open-plan office. He stood to greet me, his hand outstretched.

I shook the proffered hand. "Good to see you again."

"Glad you could make it at short notice," he said.

I smiled and sat down.

He continued, "You got in this morning without any problems, then?"

Of course I had—and he knew it as well. Philip had, as always, planned the whole thing meticulously from the moment I'd told him I'd need to be in for all of Barry's shift. Over the years, I had found the presence or absence of a pen with the signing-in book was a pretty accurate guide to the standard of health and safety at a company. The signing-in pen at Gauge was securely attached by string.

"Absolutely fine, thanks. I was expected and the lads were helpful."

"Good, good." The blue-grey eyes focused on my face. "So, Hal, what do you think we are dealing with?" He waited, leaning back in his chair, arms folded, expression neutral.

I rubbed my forehead. "Seriously, I don't know." *Could have said that better!* "Bear with me a mo, if you will. Barry is definitely reacting to a substance at work. You verified that with his GP."

Philip's frown deepened. "Yes, go on."

"I fear he is developing an allergic respiratory condition."

"Asthma?"

"Mm. Asthma or deep lung hypersensitivity pneumonitis. He says he has a tight chest at night."

"And that's RIDDOR reportable, as well as industrial dermatitis?"

I gave a defeated shrug. "Yes. 'Fraid so. If that's what he's got."

Philip shrank before my eyes at the thought of reporting to the HSE. His long fingers strayed to his in-tray, from which he plucked a sheet of dirty-white government paper.

I took it, scanning the sections, the threat in them tangible. It was a computer-generated circular, informing the reader that the serious but preventable industrial diseases of asthma and hypersensitivity pneumonitis were caused by inhalation of metal-working fluid. It gave links to web pages defining controls the HSE expected to see and warned that the HSE were making spot inspections of all businesses using metalworking fluid coolant. Failure to follow guidance would result in enforcement action taken, fees for intervention and fines. Then, just to ram the point home, possible imprisonment of offending company directors. Signed Specialist Inspector Isobel Fleming.

Who was this Isobel Fleming? The tone of the letter conjured a picture of James Bond's enemy, the stumpy, middle-aged Colonel Rosa Klebb, with a severe bun. I shivered.

I looked up, determined to be upbeat. "That's okay. I know you follow all the procedures. Well, as best you can."

"But dermatitis and now asthma..." He trailed off. Barry was proof that we had a problem somewhere. There was no getting away from it.

"I'm confident something has changed. I'm going to investigate what that is." I uncurled my fingers, which had unconsciously dug into my palms.

Philip looked at me quizzically. "What do you propose?"

"As you know, we are dealing with an allergic condition. Something is triggering Barry's body to react. The only thing he is really exposed to is metalworking fluid—you know, the coolant. So, whatever it is he is reacting to has to be in the coolant."

"Yes, go on." Philip stroked his chin.

"The coolant contains neat metalworking fluid, water, and metals from the parts being machined. The alloys Gauge Precision machines here contain nickel, chromium and traces of exotic metals, all of which are known to cause allergic reactions. Also, I know you get the sumps checked every week, but if there were bacterial contamination, there would be endotoxin, and that could cause this reaction as well."

"Why has he had no problems up to these last few weeks, then?"

"Either the mist controls are failing, or he's doing things differently and his exposure is higher. Otherwise, the contents of the sump have changed. I'm taking samples for inhalation exposure on Barry and on the adjacent machine operators. After break, I'll take samples from the sumps of machine seventy-six and a few other machines on similar tasks to send to the lab for comparison. I'm also going to observe how much mist he is working in using the dust lamp."

"What about Barry's health? What do you think I should do?" Philip's eyes were earnest under furrowed brows.

"I'm really worried about him," I said. "You've got to send him home on sick pay until we know what's causing this and can be sure it's safe for him. I told him I'd see if you can arrange for lung function testing. Really, I'd prefer you to arrange a full medical with your occupational health provider, including allergy testing."

I checked my watch. End of break. I'd promised I would be back to refit the sampler onto Barry, and I'd better check the other samplers were all running too.

I left Philip contemplatively drawing red circles around the specialist inspector's name. Back to the factory floor.

***

"Time to wire me up again?"

Good-natured crinkling round Barry's eyes allayed my concern that maybe he was fed up with wearing the sampler.

I chuckled at his comment as I lifted the pump and dangling sample head off the bench. Barry stood for me to slot the air sampling pump into his belt at his back, wind the clear plastic tube under his arm and across his chest, and finally clip the sample head onto his polo shirt shoulder seam. *Lift the shirt; don't catch his skin!* The sampling head dropped down over his lapel, as close to where he breathed as I could get it while keeping it comfortable. I had read in a Jo Nesbø thriller that only close family enter your personal space within 20cm of your face, and here I was doing it every day with strangers. It never got easier. Odd job, really.

I stepped out of his personal space, released my breath and noted the time against the sample number in my notebook.

"Thanks for doing this. You okay to carry on with it for the rest of the shift?"

With good humour, Barry shrugged that it was okay and then said into the sample head, "Testing, testing, one two three. Over and out!"

I laughed. Barry carried on leaning through the open machine door, setting the machine for the next workpiece.

Time to check what's in that coolant.

"When you've got a minute when the machine's running again, could you show me the machine coolant in the sump and where you get it from for topping up, please?" I asked.

Would the fluid that flowed from the sump into those orange nozzles be well maintained, clean and creamy, or would I find frothing and pools of tramp oil?

Five minutes later, clutching a white plastic sample bottle and a plastic finger-length paddle coated in agar for sampling bacteria, I followed Barry around the side of the machine to the attached sump tank.

I opened the sump cover, and received an unpleasant shock.

Chapter 2
You Don't Want to Be Breathing This

I recoiled in momentary disgust at the smell that assaulted me. *Eau de rancid dog food!* The meaty body odour of millions of bacteria partying in the coolant of machine seventy-six.

"Barry!" I spluttered. "Have you not noticed this smell?"

"Yeah, vile isn't it! I put a card into maintenance yesterday."

"And they haven't been to see you or sent the oil man down? You don't want to be breathing mist of this stuff!"

"Short-staffed." Barry shrugged.

Thin blue nitrile gloves on, holding my breath against the smell, I scooped out samples of the offensive liquid into my plastic bottle and swirled the agar-coated paddle in the murky grey coolant under the scum.

This was bad news—or good news, in a way. Endotoxin from the bacteria was the likely cause of Barry's chest tightness. Maybe the inflammation it provoked had exacerbated his skin reaction too. But the skin reaction came first... *Hal, you've got to keep looking!*

What was this cocktail of metals, oils and endo-toxin doing to Barry? To everyone here?

I visualised swollen, pitted, weeping pus-laden lungs in the same state as Barry's hands. All from breathing in droplets of this turgid industrial soup.

We moved on to the neighbouring machines. The sump contents were clean and creamy-white in each one. I photographed them all and took notes.

Barry showed me the green-and-red 205-litre drum of neat metalworking fluid that was watered down for the machine coolant by an automated pump. It was the same make and product I had seen here for the last few years. I looked at the pure gold liquid shimmering inside. Nothing untoward here.

The problem has to be at machine seventy-six. Maybe metals from the parts machined?

Back at machine seventy-six, I picked up a casting from the blue plastic tray. It looked like a matte gunmetal-grey fan blade. The tip was thin, the stub end a solid lump. I compared it to the finished parts, which stood on foam supports in another blue tray. The parts from Barry's machine had steps cut into the stub end.

Curious, I walked over to a trolley of trays. There were other blades, some bigger, some smaller, and a number of shiny, rectangular fixtures. Different parts doing different jobs in the plane. What was Barry machining, and what was it made from?

"What is this part that you're milling, Barry?" I asked.

"It's a turbine blade for an aero engine."

I noted that down and had a thought. "You don't know who you're machining these for, by any chance?"

"Not really, no. Why?"

"Just curious because my sister works for an aero-engine company."

"Your engineer sister? That's cool! Which one? What does she do?"

"Er, Sterling Ace Aerospace. I don't really know what she does." Shame flooded my answer, and with a hot face, I changed the subject back to the investigation. "Is this different from the ones over there?" I pointed at the adjacent machine from which I had sampled clean coolant from the sump.

"No, that's the same turbine blade. We've both been on them for the last month. That's the part number on the top of the sheet. If you want something different, Glen on machine forty-five is doing a batch of tail actuators."

I started writing down the thirteen-digit number: *HP-774SFT303X9.*

"So, these were what you were working on when the dermatitis started?" I confirmed.

"That's right."

"Could you be breathing in more mist than a month ago, perhaps?"

"I don't think so."

"Do you mind if I shine a bright spotlight next time you open the machine's door? I want to check the delay is long enough for the extraction to clear the mist. You'd only see it in the torch beam, so you might not have noticed."

"Go ahead." He consulted his orange screen. "This cycle finishes in five minutes."

I pictured my high-power torch still in the front footwell of my pickup, connected to the charger. *Damn!*

"I need to grab my torch from the pickup," I told him. "Is it okay to leave my book and the sample bottles on the side here?"

"Yeah, no problem!"

"Cheers."

I marched swiftly through the factory, skirting other CNC machines, and out through the employees' entrance. As I walked across the car park, my trouser pocket buzzed. I pulled out my phone, and it reconnected to the world. Missed call notifications pinged in, thick and fast. Two of them stopped me in my tracks.

My sister Catrin. I had never known her to call at work.

I called her back. It rang until the answering machine jumped in with a laughing Welsh voice. "Hi, this is Catrin. I'm glad you called but I'm doing something important, so please leave a message."

I tried again as I crossed the wet tarmac to my pickup.

I reached into the truck and pulled out the big, bright-yellow spotlamp. Heart hammering, I tried Catrin's phone again but still, she did not answer. I tried to reassure myself. *Surely she would have left a message if it was really urgent. Observe Barry's machine now. Must be close to five minutes.*

Just in time! A final spray of coolant noisily spattered the machine door window, heralding the end of the cycle. I angled the blinding torch beam across the door so it would highlight any fine spray escaping from the opening.

Barry waited thirty seconds and then slid the door open—good use of the door delay. No mist was visible in the torch beam. Satisfied, I made a note that the machine's extraction had cleared the mist before the door was opened.

Focused on his job, Barry leaned in through the doorway and took out the machined part. He put the fifteen-centimetre blade with its sparkling silver, newly-stepped shank on a piece of absorbent matting to drain. Barry's gloves were glistening with coolant. His arms appeared to be dry. I made notes that so far, Barry's inhalation and skin exposure had been minimal.

Next, he reached under the door for a blue airline with an attached chrome-plated airgun. He used the loudly hissing gun to blow swarf off the jig in the machine. Swirls of fine, dancing dots of coolant mist escaped around him in the torch beam. Glowing orange bullets to the lungs. I hated those airguns!

Barry intently carried on the job with the airline. Just as I thought he had finished, he picked up the drained part and blew the remaining coolant off that. The holes made the mist spray back into his face as he tried to clear them, and they screamed at him with an ear-splitting squeal. I sighed in frustration. Why had they found no alternative to airline blowing? At least most of the coolant had drained out of the part first and would not be made airborne.

Ten seconds later, all was quiet, no speckles. Barry placed the machined part on a short rack and then took another casting and fixed it to the jig in the CNC machine. He tapped the screen to set the programme, closed the door, and the machine started its twenty-five-minute cycle once more. I knew how this was going to end.

I made a quick calculation in my head for the number of parts machined per shift. Would this little routine eight or ten times a day be sufficient to cause sudden illness? I doubted it. The answer lay in the sump. For that, I would have to wait for the lab analysis.

While Barry performed quality checks on the part, I continued to ask him questions about the work he was doing and whether anything had changed. Nothing jumped out as significant.

By two o'clock, at the end of the shift, I had pages of handwritten notes, as well as air sample filters and bottles of sump contents to send off to the lab for analysis. I was ready for a serious discussion with Philip Wheatley.

"Hal, take a seat. All done now?" Philip rose in greeting, then slumped back on his chair. His thinning grey hair was mussed up, as though he had been running his hands through it. He gave a tired smile and tapped a tidily written list on a spiral-bound notebook in front of him. "I think we've got everything you asked for."

I was impressed but not surprised that Philip had taken action so swiftly. "That's good. So, what's happening then?"

He chewed on the end of his pen as he contemplated the first item on the list.

I waited patiently while he ordered his thoughts.

"HR will be giving Barry sick leave on full pay for a maximum of four weeks," he said eventually. "Our health provider is coming over to speak with me tomorrow, and they have put in a request for Barry to see a specialist dermatologist in Birmingham for allergy testing."

"To be honest, that's a real relief to me. We've got breathing space to find the cause."

"You said that you suspected the sump on machine seventy-six. Should we just not use that machine for now?"

I adjusted myself on the chair, uncrossing my legs, and leaned forwards.

"The sump should be emptied and the machine disinfected. What I would like to happen is a short training session—you know, a toolbox talk for all the machinists so that if anyone else is made ill, they will recognise and report it straight away."

"I'll see to that. You will write all this in a report?"

"Yes, yes, of course."

"And if we have another case of dermatitis or breathing problems?" I could see in his eyes and the tension around his mouth that he was expecting the worst.

"We close the factory until the cause is found. There's no excuse for another Powertrain."

"Powertrain?"

"Powertrain in Birmingham. Bacterial contamination of the sumps led to eighty employees being admitted to hospital with breathing difficulties. The HSE had a field day!"

Philip nodded with a raised eyebrow, then stood, hand out, ending the conversation. "Well then, Hal, we had better find the cause."

As we shook hands, my tight smile must have mirrored his.

"I'll get the report to you as soon as possible after I get the lab results back."

***

As I was signing out at reception, my pocket buzzed. The little screen berated me with another missed call and now a voice message from my sister. *Oh God—is she alright?* I dialled the message service and waited for the phone to connect while I sat in my pickup cab in the grey April afternoon drizzle. *Please be okay, Catrin.*

"Message received today at one forty-four p.m." Then my sister Catrin's voice, reassuringly healthy with a strong Welsh accent: "Hal, when you get this, call me. Please. It's Catrin and it's, er, Friday, quarter to two."

I released my breath with relief and tapped hash to connect to Catrin. I couldn't relax yet, though. Something serious could have happened at home—maybe with my mother or my stepfather, Gareth.

On the fifth ring, Catrin picked up.

"Hiya, Hal. Can you talk?"

"Hello, you. Yeah, I'm just at a factory. You alright?" A rivulet of rain trickled down the windscreen.

"Yes, yes."

"Mum and Dad?" Unseen forces of gravity and surface tension pulled the trickle this way and that.

"They're fine."

Phew! "What's up then?"

"I need you to come to the awards dinner at work. I only ever see you at Christmas. You haven't seen where I work, or what I do, or who I work with. I really want you to come. They want final numbers."

"Slow down a minute!" I laughed, covering the guilt that had been growing since my confession to Barry. My guilt about not knowing what my sister did at work tore through my mind like a rampant triffid.

"I understand you don't like crowds and don't do parties, but it won't be like that," she continued. "You'll find it interesting. You'll be with family. I'll introduce you to my friends. You'll enjoy it!"

"I don't know." I wavered, familiar unease about crowds retaliating valiantly.

I was already twelve when Catrin was born. Right from when she could walk, she had been a happy, helpful little blonde person. She was far more extroverted than I could ever hope to be and had always enjoyed being with friends. I knew she would be right in her element at this event. It would be churlish to spoil it.

The drip stalled, going nowhere.

"Please, Hal, it's really important to me. You are the only one who could understand what I am doing at work."

Was that true? I didn't even know what a turbine blade was until just now.

Four years ago, Catrin had nearly left school with many of her friends when she was sixteen. Her school friends were getting office and shop jobs and she was desperate for independence and cash. I had remembered that teenage feeling and the advice Gareth had given me when I was quietly rebellious at sixteen. It was all about choice and control of destiny. The better you did at school, the more chance you had of doing what you wanted, controlling your destiny and finding what you were good at. I had tried to repeat it to Catrin on one of my infrequent visits back. Whether this was instrumental or not, I'd never know, but Catrin stayed on at school and two years ago was accepted onto the degree-level aerospace engineering apprenticeship at Sterling Ace Aerospace. Pride did not do justice to the heart-swelling awe I felt.

Gravity won, with the trickle making it to the bottom of the glass.

I gave in with a guilty sigh. I couldn't say no.

Chapter 3
Family Values

It was the weekend. A day off from factories. I wound my way around horseboxes on the top of a grassy hill to the start of the cross-country course. A small area was roped off with timing equipment at one edge, ready for the next rider. About to start was Aunt Miranda, wearing a purple and gold cross-country top and matching hat silk. She was riding Teddy, her muscle-bound bay gelding. The horse's coat shone like burnished copper. The pair looked professional, tough, experienced.

The powerhouse of a horse pranced with excitement. His nostrils flared as adrenaline kicked his flight instinct into gear. He was ready to run. To jump. This animal would face any obstacle. On top, the familiar, quirky, one-sided smile momentarily etched on my aunt's weathered face vanished as she stiffened in disapproval. I could see the horse thinking "uh oh!", and obediently, he stood still. A headmistress–pupil relationship if ever I saw one!

Miranda let the psyched-up equine athlete move off when she was ready. She was a fearsome woman, close to sixty, highly respected as an international journalist and as a rider. She did not tolerate bad behaviour.

I wanted to pick her brains about my sister's company. That would have to wait.

"Good luck!" I called.

"You can watch him in the lake. You never know, we may take a ducking for your amusement!" Miranda walked the horse on. "Must go. Talk later."

Off my aunt rode, Teddy's long, athletic strides taking her to the start of the cross-country course.

The day after my Gauge Precision visit, I'd had a text from my Aunt Miranda saying she had a competition in the area on Saturday, and would I like to meet up? She was competing at Weston Park Horse Trials, a cross country course in the parkland of a stately home in Staffordshire.

Aunt Miranda was more than just family. She was my sounding board. With her being a business journalist, I thought I'd see what she knew about Sterling Ace Aerospace.

I had seen her last at the fizzing, top-end-of-society New Year's Eve party she had held with her partner, Prue, in their large, converted Surrey farmhouse. As usual, their guests were an eclectic, wealthy mix of horse-world and journalism, with interesting headline-makers thrown in for good measure. Miranda had put me on drink topping-up duties and insisted on introducing me to everyone—single and beautiful, male and female. The atmosphere had been vibrant; we cheered in the New Year without fireworks because of the performance horses stabled behind the house. Everyone drank a toast to good health and competition success. They were that kind of people. I doubted any had been in a factory or had seen how things are made.

It was a lot easier to be in a social gathering if I had a job to do; Aunt Miranda understood that. My chest felt tight at the unknown void of Catrin's awards dinner. I could not picture it. I would know barely anyone there. I did not know enough about aerospace to hold a conversation. A chasm. *Catrin will be ashamed of me.*

The day was mild, countryside and horses doing their own thing, making no demands on me. Sky, wide over rolling parkland, lifted my spirits. My thoughts gratefully reset to the present as I ambled down the gently sloping parkland towards the lake. Two riders fell off into the shallow water—though not specifically for my amusement as Miranda had joked. The felled tree-trunk fence with a drop into the lake was catching riders out.

I spotted the purple and gold colours in the distance, rapidly increasing in size as they thundered towards me. Teddy's ears were pricked forwards, on a mission. To my mind, the foam-flecked horse was coming in too fast for the drop fence. Hooves pounded on the turf, the rhythm slowing momentarily. I watched him fly over the log, forelegs extended as he braced to land in the water below. A splash. Aunt Miranda gathered up the reins, urging her mount across the lake. Teddy sprang up the bank, and off they galloped. With a satisfied sigh, I turned and sauntered back to the lorry. One never doubted Aunt Miranda.

The air smelled of crushed grass and horses. It reminded me of early childhood with Miranda and Prue. I walked with a light heart over the short, springy turf towards the horseboxes. The competitors' area was roped off from the public routes, more to prevent the public from being run over than for the security of the equine athletes. I ducked under the rough sisal rope and looked for the huge purple and gold Volvo lorry. I saw Prue first, short grey hair escaping from a baseball cap, olive padded gilet and straight jeans tucked into wellington boots. Looking round the hay net she was tying to the lorry, she waved.

"Henry, dear, how good to see you."

I felt a rush of fondness for this lady. "Prue, how are you?" I called.

As I got closer, Prue came over, blue eyes twinkling over ruddy cheeks. She had to be close to seventy but looked far healthier than many of the people I worked with in factories.

"I am very well, thank you. How have you been since we saw you last?"

I smiled at how Prue spoke: kind of old-fashioned and correct.

"Fine, thanks, nothing special to report. Oh, Catrin wants me to go to her work's awards dinner," I threw in. *Should I tell Prue that I really don't want to go?*

"What fun! Jet engines, were you telling me? You must be very proud of her." Prue smiled as she turned to pick up a bucket.

"Mm." I faltered. "Would it be really wrong not to go?"

Prue put the bucket down and looked at me, her head tilted to one side. "I think you know the answer to that. Be brave. Let your sister know you are proud of her."

"But I won't know anyone. I don't know anything about jet engines. I won't know what to say. Catrin will be ashamed."

"Nonsense!" Prue scolded. "You just need an ice-breaker plan."

"What?"

"When you are introduced to someone you don't know, ask them a nice, easy question."

"What, like 'What do you think of the weather?' Oh, no. Too embarrassing."

"Henry, now you are being feeble!"

"I suppose I could ask if they have come far or had a good journey."

Prue nodded and picked up the bucket again.

"You must excuse me; I have one coming back in that will want sponging-off before the showjumping."

"Sorry, Prue, I was miles away. Anything I can do to help?"

Prue handed me the empty bucket, indicating a 25-litre water container. "Just half full, please." She pushed a stray curl of grey hair back under her cap. "So, tell me, how are you really?"

With the heavy, white container supported against my legs, I poured water into the bucket, The turbulent liquid sloshed, almost upsetting the bucket. "I'm fine, honestly." I put the water down and straightened up.

"What happened to Carla was tragic, but you can't run away from relationships forever."

"Prue!"

This side of my family had none of the difficult noise of complaints, gossip and idle chat of other people. It was so much easier when speech, opinion and emotion were purposeful.

At that moment, my phone rang. I pulled it from my jeans pocket. Darren from Dustco. He repaired the dust extractors that ultimately controlled how much dust factory employees breathed in, so we met at factories pretty often. I flapped a hand at Prue and took the call round the other side of the horsebox.

"Alright, mate. I haven't disturbed you, have I?" The warm voice was tinged with amused cheekiness.

"Darren, it's Saturday!"

"So? You, who never takes a day off, is telling me it's Saturday?"

"I'm out today. What do you want?"

"Ooh," came the falsetto reply. "Who is she, then?"

"I'm at a horse trials with my aunt."

"The scary one? You've gotta get a life, mate!"

I laughed. "Cheeky sod. My life's perfectly fine, thank you. So, what did you ring me for? Anything good?"

"I just wanted your thoughts on a silica job we're quoting. It'll wait till Monday."

I agreed to give him a call.

"If you're passing," he said, "pop in for a brew."

"Will do. Have a good weekend."

I reappeared from round the end of the horsebox, still amused by Darren's call. Prue had been joined by a white horse. Its flanks steamed under the sponge with which she was washing off sweat.

Prue updated me: "Sally's horse. She's gone to collect lunch. Miranda's due back any minute."

***

Lunchtime at the horsebox. I perched companionably at the top of the ramp with Aunt Miranda, Prue and a bottle-blonde woman in riding gear, younger than me. Wrappers full of steaming chips and burgers were spread across our laps. The smells made my stomach rumble in anticipation.

Miranda made the introductions. "Sally, this is my nephew, Henry. And Henry, Sally is my training protégé. We are aiming for Burghley this autumn."

I inclined my head. "The international three-day event? Impressive."

Sally eyed me up speculatively. "Miranda!" she laughed. "You never told me you had such a handsome hunk in the family!"

I smiled at the ground, my cheeks on fire.

She would have been pretty if she just wore less makeup. As it was, her skin was caked to a matte finish, her eyes black-rimmed.

"Do you ride, Henry?" she asked.

Mouth full of chips, I shook my head. I *could* ride but hadn't in quite a while. *Too complicated.*

Sally's toned thigh pressed against mine, under the meagre cover of a polystyrene chip tray. I choked in surprise. *Do women chalk up conquests? Bet she does!*

While I coughed, Prue decided to tell Sally about me anyway. "Of course he rides! Henry was a dear boy, with the naughtiest pony imaginable, which we kept at our stables. He would spend every hour of the day with that pony."

"Was this in Surrey?"

I concentrated on my burger.

"Oh no, dear. Miranda and I lived on a farm not far from here actually, near Cannock. Miranda's brother—Henry's father, God bless him—and his family lived across the twenty-acre field, in the village."

The burger stuck in my throat. *Oh no, don't go there. I can't talk about my father. Go back to horses!*

I jumped in. "Cracker wasn't naughty—he just liked to go fast!" Even now I could feel the thrill of galloping up that twenty-acre field, wind whistling, hooves pounding, mane flying, free, not a care in the world.

I felt a burst of relief when Prue stuck with horses. "Yes, you rode everywhere at speed! You were always making up games with imaginary foes. Miranda, do you remember that day Mick returned from harrowing the fields, reporting he'd seen Henry up to no good, galloping up to trees and fence posts and hitting them with sticks!"

"Hitting trees with sticks?" Sally laughed incredulously, using the excuse to lay her hand on my arm.

"I was a knight in shining armour..." I smiled indignantly and took Sally's fingers off my arm and ceremonially held them by their bitten nails. "...defending the beautiful princess!" before putting them back on her lap.

Other days, I'd been an intrepid explorer searching the stream for giant alligators, a Red Indian on the warpath with a bow and arrow, a battle-hardened soldier and his trusty steed taking supplies to the front.

"Oh, I see. I did that too as a kid, playing battles on horseback," said Sally with a companionable pat. "And who was Mick?" she asked, pulling me back to the present.

Miranda replied, "My eldest cousin. He farmed the land while Prue and I ran the stables. He moved into our old house when we moved to the stables that you know, in Surrey."

I vividly remembered the angry man. Mick would shout and cuss at me and Cracker if we got in his way or rode on the crops. I had been frightened of the red-faced farmer.

"Mick had a soft spot for you, Henry."

"But he threw a broom at me, more than once!"

Mum had left me with Prue and Miranda for three years after my father had his accident. Then my mum sold Cracker and took me to Port Talbot in South Wales when she had found a new man and started her new life as a nurse.

"I wish I had grown up with you and Miranda, Prue." Sally sighed. "It sounds idyllic, freedom to ride whenever and wherever I want."

Horse girl through and through—a no-strings relationship could get everyone off my back, I thought. *And she lives miles away…*

"It was lonely for a little boy, Sally," Prue cautioned. "Henry's school friends did not live in the village. Many times, we would find him sitting in the straw of Cracker's stable, his nose in a book."

"I never thought I was lonely, Prue." I protested. "I had a great time with you." *The best time of my life really. Apart from Carla, but she was taken too.*

Prue scrunched up the burger wrapper with finality. "We enjoyed having you, Henry. But look at you now: an important man with your own business, keeping factory employees healthy."

"Talking of factories, I'm going to Catrin's works awards dinner. Miranda, is there anything I should know about Sterling Aerospace?"

"I was going to ask you about that. Their PR company sent me a press release that they were having an awards evening," Miranda confirmed, her deep-brown eyes frowning. "It used to be a very good, solid, family-owned company. I'm sorry, but recently they have been making a few business errors under their new CEO. Their share value has dropped steadily over the last two years since he has been there."

"But how can they afford an awards dinner?" I interrupted.

"Investment to promote the company. That's why they issued the press release about it."

Aunt Miranda knew what she was talking about. She was worrying me about Catrin's future there.

"I hope that doesn't disappoint you. I am sure the company will be fighting for their place again," she reassured me. She checked her watch and stood up, ending the conversation. "Young Catrin will be fine."

***

Later that week, on the way back from site one evening, I called in at Darren's industrial unit. Dustco's filter servicing contractors were a great bunch of lads; they did a professional job and they passed testing work to me, and I passed repair work to them. They were good for a laugh and were always there with industry gossip.

"How do, take a pew," indicated bearded, middle-aged Darren with one burly arm outstretched. "Want a beer?"

"Did the silica company agree to a HEPA filter in the end?" I asked, cracking a can of lager. "You were right to be worried."

"Yeah, he was fine with it. I told him what you said about silicosis."

"Well done! By the way, you did a good job on the dust filter units at the refractory ceramics place."

"Cheers. We had a right struggle opening them up. Set like concrete inside. Took three of us two days to do five units." Darren exhaled hard, emphasising the struggle.

Things continued like always, sharing gossip about the goings-on in the world of extraction systems and fickle customers. They had the servicing contract at Sterling. My breath caught when they mentioned a rumoured takeover. They hoped it would give them access to the buyer, maybe Rolls Royce or General Electric: a big player with multiple sites.

"The engineering manager—what's his name? Stuart something?—he would see we got a look in," said Darren seriously. "Known him years and he's always treated us okay. Asks us for a price, never a problem getting a purchase order and a day to do the work."

"He reserved a parking space in the factory so we could unload, and he makes us tea. Good bloke," remembered the other middle-aged partner, Nigel.

"We'll get you in there, Hal," Darren promised earnestly.

"My sister works there," I offered.

"Never! What a small world! You never said you had a sister." Nigel's interest was genuine.

"How old is she—is she a looker?" Darren asked.

"You wouldn't have a chance," I laughed.

Darren was currently separated from his abusive alcoholic wife. Despite his banter, he was a good-hearted, honourable man in whom I had total trust. He would give #metoo no concerns.

I found a photo of Catrin on my phone and showed it round.

"What a smasher, but she's just a kid," Nigel said. "You say she works at Sterling?"

"Yes, she does engineering."

"You gotta be joking—a little bit like that? Well, good luck to her, I say."

"If we see her next week, we'll say hello." Darren looked at the year planner on the wall. "That's right, isn't it, Nige? It is next week?"

"Got a booking for fifteen filters to be delivered week tomorrow," confirmed Nigel, checking the online calendar.

Darren looked at me with an expectant beam on his chubby face. "Well, did you not see my van outside then?" He gestured to the window. "Got me new alloys. Bought them for a song, had them done up round the corner. Put them on this afternoon."

"Can't say that I noticed really, sorry. Show me now?"

We traipsed out to inspect the green crew-cab Transit van. Pitted tarmac contrasted with the silver stripe on the smug style-icon with its front splitter and side skirts, and now diamond-cut alloys to match. Alloys that complemented the tattoo every well-dressed speed-freak automobile wanted: a Nürburgring sticker.

I laughed, pointing at the sticker. "You haven't!"

"Oh yes we have!"

"You've seen my GT3?" said silver-haired, goateed Nigel, starting what was obviously a well-worn tale.

"The Porsche? Yeah," I replied slowly, already relishing the promise of half an hour of track-day talk.

We walked back into the cramped office of the industrial unit. Darren gave me his seat, while he perched on a table.

"We trailered it to the Nürburgring, but because of the ferry, we got there early," Nigel reminisced, leaning back. "My time slots weren't booked until the next day."

"So, we unhitched the trailer," prompted Darren with a grin.

"Got a lap ticket." Nigel chuckled.

"And I drove the Transit round before it closed." Darren beamed.

"That has got to be the greatest—it was on two wheels on the corners," added the third contractor, a well-muscled man around my age.

"You threw up after," taunted Darren.

"You'd chucked us around."

"And it was only two minutes slower than your Porsche!" crowed Darren to Nigel.

"That's because you don't care about the van as much as I value my Porsche," retorted Nigel.

"You could have killed us!"

We comfortably shared sports car stories of track days and derring-do. They had approved of my fast Ford Focus RS but made fun of the L200 pickup truck.

"Get a van," they said.

We chatted some more, as usual returning to clients who didn't pay and bad work done by their competitors, then dispersed off homeward.

Chapter 4
The Big Day

Over the following few days, as April turned to May, the weather steadily improved, and my regular factory visits continued without problem. I was busy enough to have put the problems at Gauge to one side, pending sample results from the lab. I had called Philip for updates. Barry was going for tests and convalescing at home. The HSE still had not visited. Philip was on edge. Not all that reassuring, but without test results, there was nothing more I could do now.

I was still torn about whether to mention Aunt Miranda's doubts to Catrin. At least I was no longer wavering about going to the awards dinner. I put off the call yet again and decided to wash the truck. Standing outside in T-shirt and jeans, with the hosepipe running, I bit the bullet and called her.

"Hiya, Hal," came her chirpy Welsh voice.

"Hiya yourself!" I sprayed water over the dusty bonnet, psyching myself up.

Before I could bring up the shares problem at Sterling, Catrin butted in. "You couldn't do me a big, big, big favour, could you? Please, pretty please?"

I gave a pantomime sigh. "Okay, what do you want?" Let off the hook, I dropped the hose and picked the soapy sponge out of the bucket.

"I need glittery makeup for the awards evening."

Soapy smears smudged the truck's windows.

"What do you mean, need? Oh, never mind! Is this special makeup?" I stretched over the bonnet, wiping it clean. "Don't they do it in Wales?"

"It's MAC and they don't stock it in Neath, but they do have it at their store in Birmingham Grand Central, above New Street Station."

Bubbles on the headlights.

"So, how do I know it's the right stuff?"

"Tempting Fate!"

I dropped the sponge. "What?"

"The eyeshadow is called Tempting Fate."

Oh God, do I tell her about the company now? No, that would be bad.

"That sounds a bit risky! Anything else?"

"Pink glitter, please."

"Does that have a name too?"

"No, silly, it's just pink glitter. It comes in a jar."

I returned the sponge to the bucket and hosed off the bubbles. The spray bounced back, soaking my T-shirt. It was cold.

"Ach! Er, yep, I can do that."

"What are you doing, Hal? You sound like you're doing something outside. I can hear water."

"Washing the truck."

A peal of laughter reached me. "*That's* what it sounded like. Did you just spray yourself?"

"Just a bit, can't let the truck have all the fun."

"Idiot brother."

"Tell you what, I'll bring your stuff down with me on Friday. I'll come an hour before we need to set off for the do."

"You're a lifesaver!"

Missed my chance. I couldn't ask her now, not with her being so excited.

"Bye, little sis. See you Friday. Take care. Love to Mum and Gareth."

"Will do—you're a star! See you Friday!"

I finished cleaning the truck, pondering how to, or even whether to, broach the shares issue again.

***

I sprinted up the everlasting tarmac ramp, bursting my lungs to catch the Birmingham train waiting at the top. *Stupid green imbecile box of a ticket machine refusing to print out a ticket!* Rain flattened my hair and seeped through my trainers.

Heavy clunks. *Too late—they're shutting the doors! Keep running in case they see you!* As I arrived on the platform, the small green train glided away. Hands on my knees, I caught my breath, too winded to stand up for the moment.

I needed to set off for Port Talbot at noon, and here I was racing to get into Birmingham and back before then!

I stood up and read the schedule flashing round on the illuminated platform sign. Half an hour until the next train. It would mean changing at Walsall, but I could still make it in time. The MAC shop was in the station complex. I could catch the first train back.

Anxiously, I waited for the next train. The late-spring rain eased off and I started drying, but I was still chilled to the bone. My knuckles took on a purple hue. I paced up and down to keep warm, all the time keeping an eye on the sign. *Don't be late, train.*

I checked emails on my phone, but there was nothing from the lab. *Call Philip? There's nothing else to do.*

I dialled Philip Wheatley's extension. He answered after a couple of rings.

"Philip Wheatley."

"Hello, Philip. I just wanted to let you know that I'm still waiting for the lab results. How is Barry?"

"Ah, I have some news on Barry. He requires further tests to determine whether he has asthma or a viral chest infection. The dermatitis is definitely healing, and he wants to come back to work."

"But he can't! It might happen again." I protested, surprised.

"Well, here's the thing. He had the allergy test results and they were positive for nickel and cobalt. I thought we could put him in the toolroom unit down the road. They only deal with carbon steel. Do you think that would work?"

"Mm, I see where you're coming from. It's worth a shot. He's sensible enough to let you know if he starts to feel his skin reacting again, don't you think?"

"The next train to arrive on Platform One is the Walsall train, calling at..."

In a thankful panic, I zoned out of the Tannoy message and peered up the track, where a green shape was taking form.

"Got to dash. I think that's a great idea, Philip. I'll be in touch on Monday."

"Have a good weekend, Hal."

"You too, bye."

This time, I jumped on the train the moment the door opened. I was greeted by a wet-dog fug, steamed-up windows and muddy footprints on the lino floor. At Walsall, I made sure I caught the New Street train, which delivered me to the station with no further ado.

Tempting fate? Tight on time with no ticket! No surprise, then, that there was a queue to buy a ticket to get out. I stood impatiently behind a man in a navy overcoat and designer shoes.

My phone buzzed with a text. Catrin. She wanted to know what time I was setting off, and not to forget the makeup! That I didn't have yet!

I paid for the day-return ticket and strode swiftly on to the shopping concourse. The phone interrupted again. A call. The lab. I had to take it.

"Hello. Hal Rogers."

I looked around in a frenzy. Where was the makeup shop?

"Hello, Hal. This is Kirsty at the lab. I just wanted to double-check your Gauge Precision samples."

So many boutique shops and cafes on the ground floor and on the first floor above me.

"Oh? What do you need to know?"

I searched for the makeup store on the map. Top floor, above the old Bull Ring, as far away as possible.

"Some of the results are off. I mean, quite a way off."

"That's okay. Just send what you have." Got to be Barry's machine.

I jogged through the shoals of shoppers, taking stairs two at a time.

"Is this a bad time?"

"Er, no." I panted. "Just on an errand. Which results are you calling me about?"

Skimming along shining, stone-paved balconies with success in my grasp, I reached the tinted-glass-fronted shop.

"The metals suite in the sample you labelled machine seventy-six is nothing like the one in your sample machine seventy-five."

"So?" I panted, panic welling up as I read the sign on the locked door advising potential customers to use their outlet in Selfridges.

"Are you expecting the samples from these machines to be different, or could the samples have been taken from different factories?"

"What? Er, no. Er... Could you just email the results over and I'll take it from there? I can get back to you once I've seen your results, though?"

"Certainly, not a problem."

My time was running out. "I've got to go. Thanks for calling."

On a frenetic pinball course, I arrived at the department store's glittering, scented perfumery and makeup department, only to be lost in a sea of graphic design. I swivelled on my heel, conscious of being the only male in the area.

"May I help you, sir?" A sales assistant in the white, fitted tunic of a dental nurse appeared at my elbow.

"Er, MAC eyeshadow, for my sister," I blurted. As I spoke, the MAC counter defined itself clearly to my left. "Uh, it's okay. I can find it."

I asked the girl on the counter for the eye shadow and glitter I required.

"Would you like it gift-wrapped, sir?"

I thought of Rowan Atkinson's extended gift-wrapping performance in *Love Actually*.

"I'll take it as it is, thank you."

I ran back to the station. At last, I could reply to Catrin with honesty!

***

It was a relief to be back in the familiar driving seat of the pickup in the aftermath of the traumatic pink-glitter run. *Ha! What fun it would be to give a pink glitter delivery as an excuse for speeding, Officer!*

No more excitement; just deliver the goods. Don't spoil Catrin's big night now.

I wondered what the lab had found. Their email had not arrived by the time I set off.

On time, I parallel parked the big vehicle in the street outside the house I had called home many years ago. It was one of a row of red-brick terraced houses fronting onto the street. When I was growing up, I thought it looked the smartest street in Tai-Bach, with white painted bricks surrounding every front door and window.

Waiting at the curb by the red front door, I listened to the sounds of a once-familiar life: cars and lorries on the M4, a dog barking, children squealing as they played in the little park at the bottom of the road. Seagulls screaming, always seagulls.

I hugged Catrin on the doorstep. Her hair was damp and smelled of shampoo. I had forgotten how much I missed my family, especially sunny little Catrin. Port Talbot was only two hours or so from my flat, so there was no excuse not to visit more often. Always managed to find one though, didn't I?

"You know, I'm really glad you came." Catrin's muffled comment reached me.

I held the tracksuit-clad young lady at arms' length and smiled down at her. "I'm glad too. I missed you and would love to see where you work, the people you work with."

She grinned and poked me in the chest, "No you wouldn't. You hate these things. It'll be fine, you'll see."

"Could you be getting an award?" I asked.

Catrin shook her head but blushed. "I don't know. I doubt it, but..." She trailed off. I could sense the longing.

"But it's possible," I added for her, giving her another hug.

"I've still got to get ready. Do you want to come in? I'll be another hour."

I knew Mum would stop everything and fuss over things I'd got wrong before I even got through the door.

"No, I'm fine—I'll just get in the way," I said. "I've got a couple of emails from the lab to check for work. See you in a bit."

That wasn't just an excuse. I did need to find out what the call was about earlier in Birmingham—*ah, the shopping!*

"Your makeup!" I held out the prized package.

"Hal! You are brilliant! Did you find it alright?"

"Of course. No problem!" *Possibly a sparkly-pink white lie!*

She headed back inside, and smiling, in comfortable good humour, I leaned against the truck and scrolled through emails, searching for one from the lab. I felt keyed up, anxious. The cause of Barry's dermatitis would be in the analysis results. Whatever it was, it had to be in the sump of machine seventy-six but in no others. I knew the lab were pretty good with their turnaround; they had to have sent it by now, surely.

With eager anticipation, I opened the email with the subject *R20-14783 Gauge Precision*. With bated breath, I downloaded the attached PDF and scrolled to the tables of results.

Liquid bulk samples—the sumps. I scanned the table of results: columns for sumps, rows for metals. All the figures seemed very similar across the table, except for two results standing out in the thousands. The entries were for cobalt and aluminium, and they were in the column for machine seventy-six. *Result! Yes! Machine seventy-six sump results for cobalt and aluminium are more than one hundred times the concentrations for the other three machines! What's going on there? What should be in superalloys?*

I scrolled down to the table of results for air monitoring. These just gave micrograms of metals on the filter paper. I'd have to calculate the actual results by dividing the mass found with the volume of air that went through. A guestimate would be easy, though, since they all ran for about seven and a half hours at around two litres per minute. The volumes of air would have been pretty similar. *Ah-ha—Barry had breathed in more cobalt and aluminium than his neighbours!*

One thing to find an answer, but it only led to another question. What were cobalt and aluminium doing in Barry's machine? Where did they come from? I was tempted to start Googling turbine blades and cobalt.

The red door with its familiar repair scars opened and Gareth, in pressed trousers and shirtsleeves, came out of the house with a mug of tea. I straightened up, stretched, and met him on the pavement.

"Drive down okay?" Gareth handed me the red Kit-Kat mug. He shared my height and lean build but with short grey hair and spectacles.

"Yes, thanks." I took a long draught of the tea. "How are things with you and Mum?"

"We're fine. My brother Huw—I don't know if you remember him?"

"Of course, I remember Huw. He taught me climbing with ropes, and he came surfing with us loads of times."

Huw was Gareth's older brother, and he had been a real laugh, but tough on me, daring me to climb higher when I was a stroppy teenager.

"Mm, he's been diagnosed with silicosis." Gareth looked pensive.

"He's always been so fit!" I was dismayed that someone so active and well now had a life-threatening respiratory disease. "How is he?"

"Oh, he's fine in himself. Still goes walking, bouldering. Still the same old prankster."

"Are they sure that's what he's got?"

"They took X-rays when he took a long time getting over the flu last winter."

"Oh. Still, it's a very slow disease to progress." I said, trying to look on the bright side.

Silicosis was a progressive lung-scarring disease, like asbestosis, caused by breathing in fine quartz dust from mining, from concrete cutting, from sandblasting, even from making granite worktops for kitchens. At some point, Huw would be confined to a wheelchair with oxygen tubes up his nose. Hopefully, for his sake, many years in the future.

I placed the empty mug on the pickup's bonnet.

I pointed to the red front door. "Do you remember when Huw thought it would be fun to abseil out of the bedroom window and his foot went through the bottom panel of the door?"

"We patched it up and painted it before Mum came back from work." Gareth smiled at the memory. It had been a proper panic to hide the evidence and cut a new panel in time.

"Oh yes—and she didn't notice what we'd done for years!" I added.

Naturally, we'd had no chance to prime or undercoat the replacement panel, so it had remained a peeling, less glossy corner of the door for a very long time.

I vowed to myself to catch up with Huw before the end of the year. "I'll remind Huw of that next time I see him!"

Gareth laughed. He checked his watch. "The girls will be ready in ten minutes. Won't you come in?" As if sensing my hesitancy, he added, "Your mother will be upstairs with Catrin."

"I'll wait here if that's okay, Gareth. They won't be long now anyway." I handed back the mug. I wasn't sure how I felt about my mum, but the older I got, the harder I found conversation with her.

"Well, if you'll excuse me. Ties to bow and all that!" Gareth disappeared behind the door.

Very shortly, my family emerged from the house. Gareth, resplendent in a black suit and bow tie, held the door for my mother. Mum, dyed blonde hair pinned up, bright red lipstick and rouge on her round cheeks topping a large, gaily-flowered dress and navy jacket, marched straight up to me and presented herself for an embrace with accusation in her blue eyes.

"You are working too hard, Henry. You could have come in to read your emails. We see so little of you."

Why did she put me through this? Every time. So, maybe I did avoid going home—why did she have to go through this rigmarole of saying I worked too hard when she was really blaming me for choosing work over seeing her? All that achieved was to bury me in a rockfall, an avalanche of guilt.

"It's a nice day out here. A bit of fresh air." I shrugged.

My sister, all glittery makeup and long black eyelashes over excited blue eyes, tottered in an outrageous sparkly pink minimalist dress thing. Her normally straight hair was curled; it bounced as she walked. I wolf-whistled her and she grinned delightedly.

Formal suit and perfumed posh frocks scrambled up into the black leather seats for the short drive to the Sterling Ace Aerospace Visitor Centre. Mum fussed about invitations—and had I got a tie? (I had.) Catrin was busy on her phone. I hoped she had given up asking me if I had a girlfriend.

Mum started on her barbed conversation. "This car is very spacious."

"Thank you. Are you comfortable enough in the back there?"

"It's very high. Don't you think it's a bit high? Can you see the road alright, to drive?"

"Actually, Mum, being high makes seeing the road conditions easier."

"Why do you need to make seeing the road easier? Are you driving too much? Have you had your eyesight checked?"

"No, Mum, it's okay."

I heard Catrin's muffled snort of laughter.

Gareth wisely changed the subject. "How's work going?"

"Work's been good, thanks. Busy, lots of referrals. New dermatitis investigation a couple of weeks ago. They've taken action already, even though I haven't finished my report," I answered, still slightly side-tracked by the results that had just shown up in the lab's email.

I fielded the question back. "How's the schoolwork?"

"Never enough funding, but the kids are great." He sighed, then his tone brightened. "Using the outdoor facilities at the Forestry Commission has been a game-changer."

What Gareth lacked in personal ambition he made up for with his drive to improve the lives of youngsters in the locality. I wished I were more like him.

"Talking of outdoor stuff, are you still running the Scouts?" I enquired, keeping my eyes on the road.

I remembered enjoying Scouts until I was fifteen and too old. I liked the routines, the expectations, the camaraderie. And the camping, fires, archery, adventure stuff. There'd been no older groups available when I was at home, but Catrin was a Ranger until she left school at 18. She liked organising people, being a leader.

"Mmm. Didn't Catrin tell you she's running the Beavers on Tuesday evenings?"

"Doesn't surprise me. I bet they like her." I could imagine Catrin winning the confidence of little children with her easy smile. I called over my shoulder, "Hey, you didn't tell me this."

"If you looked at Facebook and Twitter occasionally, you'd know," Catrin retorted, still typing on her phone. "When was the last time you even posted on anything?"

I could not answer. Social media was one of those things I had convinced myself would not benefit me in any way. The idea of putting my thoughts down and being misunderstood concerned me sufficiently to deter me from finding out how to do it properly.

"You know, it's not that hard—even for an old man like you—once you get into the swing of it. It's not all about breakups, fancy food and lost dogs. Plenty of professional people post their technical work advice and blogs."

"I expect you're right," I replied unenthusiastically.

"Come on now—what was the last thing you did? Have you been climbing? Driving anywhere? Interesting factories? You could post a picture of the last place you went to." My social media mentor carried on her motivational speech.

"What's the point in that?" We stopped at traffic lights. "This left?" I asked tersely.

"Ooh, who's getting grumpy," teased my sister, who did not know when to stop. As if speaking to one of her Beavers, she said, "So, you go to a different factory, what, two or three times a week? And you post those photos. Many people who work in the same place every day would love to do that—wouldn't they, Dad? And the fact that you visit all different places for different jobs would show how successful you are." She took a breath, ending on a flourish. "And more people would ask for your services!"

"Okay. Today I will post a photo from Sterling," I conceded. "Just for you."

My sister made me feel older than my thirty-two years. I wished I felt as at ease when communicating with people as Catrin and my peers seemed to.

One more set of lights coming up. Mum spotted them.

"You need to slow down! The car in front has his brake lights on. Slow down!"

With teeth gritted, I crawled towards the red light, holding up traffic. The gap lengthened between my pickup and the little Fiat in front.

"Gareth, make him slow down!" My mum's continued panicky bullying engulfed my stepdad too.

"He knows what he's doing, Cariad."

The lights changed to green. Emergency over.

Run-down brick terraces peppered with corner convenience stores and bookmakers lined the approach to the final roundabout on the dual carriageway. Late afternoon sun shimmered on the graceful angles of the stainless steel, delta-wing planes mounted over the island. A sculpture for all to enjoy, it signalled the company's industrial largesse. Designed to impress in this impoverished area.

Turning between double-decker-height turquoise-and-gold signs for Sterling Ace Aerospace, the truck rumbled over a mile of private pale concrete road along the length of the factory towards the gatehouse.

I thought back to what Aunt Miranda had told me. She had worried me about Sterling Ace Aerospace, so I'd looked it up on Google. Their slick website advertised the bespoke design and build of jet engines for commercial and defence aircraft. It applauded itself as a world-leading company, boasting a large factory dominating the side of the M4, where it vied for recognition with the famed steelworks, a historical pillar of Port Talbot. The imposing, glass-fronted visitor centre, their pride in being the major local high-technology employer—it all fitted in with the high-profile, publicised awards evening. There were no cracks in their online presence. No hint of their troubles.

The concrete road was separated from the dark-green-panelled industrial unit of Sterling Ace on its left by two lines of security fencing. On the opposite side of the road, the car parks, low brick buildings, tall, grey, steel-clad production towers and squat storage cylinders told passers-by of operations taking place at the steelworks. Sterling's covertly uninformative green building continued onwards past the steelworks, with the other side of the road now flanked by low green marshland extending to the sea. Abruptly, the road turned left, away from the marsh, around the end of the factory building and left again towards the gatehouse.

At the first barrier, Catrin leaned out of the window to wave her pass at the sensor and the barrier lifted. Straight ahead, beyond a mesh security gate, the plant loomed. Blue-painted box-shaped air handling units and filters lined the wall, between closed roller-shutter doors. A high-security fence ran between the factory internal road and the outer area where we were.

Catrin proudly leaned over and pointed to the left of the building. "That's where I work. You see the fire doors? It's the second one."

Now I was actually here, I was really curious to see inside.

Signs and arrows beckoned us right towards the gleaming curved glass front of the two-storey visitor centre. A grassy airstrip behind wire netting peeped around the far edge of the building, a buffer between it and the rumbling motorway.

"That's Andy and his parents, and that's Sara and that's Ste." Catrin pointed out a succession of young people with middle-aged parents making their way across the car park on the marked pedestrian route.

"Hi, Ste!" she squealed excitedly out of the window while I navigated shining signs and polished visitors.

I knotted my tie and shrugged on the dark suit jacket, checking my reflection in the truck's window. I looked nothing like my curvy blonde and blue-eyed sister and mother. My lean frame, dark brown hair and brown eyes came from my father. In the spirit of cooperation, I took a selfie with Catrin.

The family sauntered across the supermarket-size car park towards the building, my mother happily linking arms with Catrin. I followed on, dreading the social hours ahead.

Chapter 5
High Pressure

Receptionists in light grey suits, pseudo flight attendants with scarves in official Sterling turquoise and gold greeted us. I noticed with amusement that Catrin had taken charge of our little group. She pointed out our names on the receptionist's screen with a smile and efficiently signed us in.

Inside the large, sunny, two-storey glass vestibule, canapés were laid out with trays of Prosecco and fruit juices. The soft, short-pile carpet was uniquely patterned in turquoise and gold, no expense spared. People were mingling, chatting, happy. Air conditioning counteracted solar heating, contributing to global warming instead. I sighed, feeling critical, already ill at ease. A heady cocktail of over one hundred perfumes and aftershaves assaulted my nose.

Catrin guided us to the food. "Hal, you'll like Ste. I'll ask him to show you our exhibits if you want." She looked round, evidently not seeing him. "Will you be okay for five minutes while I sort out Mum and Dad?"

"Sure, I'll be fine. Go ahead." I smiled at her. It was Catrin's day, after all.

Behind her, Mum took a glass of pale golden bubbles and giggled. My sister rolled her eyes at me in mock horror and bounced Mum and Gareth off to meet people she knew. I was stranded.

Displays around the walls were complemented with presentation screen showing a silent, looping video about the company. I knew Catrin was keen for me to see the factory where she worked, so I took the opportunity to watch the video for a while. The first few shots were of aircraft fitted with Sterling engines, then some very arty clips of engine parts, followed by shots of employees assembling engines. Being professionally nosy, I sucked in the details of where my sister spent her days. The factory, or at least the assembly part, was sparkling and light, all surfaces painted a very pale grey. I supposed it would have to be clean, like with my clients who made car seats— their factories had to be spotless, with good lighting for detailed work. It was a different universe from my normal Black Country fabrication workshops.

In the video, jet engines the size of Transit vans were suspended from yellow overhead cranes on tracks running the length of the factory. An engine was built in time-lapse. As the upended engine grew taller, the floor on which the employees stood rose as a platform around it. I thought that was a great idea. I had never seen a working platform that could do that before.

The employees in the film wore dark work trousers and grey polo shirts with a gold and turquoise Sterling motif. They were as spotless as their surroundings. I could see this would suit Catrin. Upmarket, classy engineering.

Watching people working in the video brought home my earlier concerns. None of these dedicated workers, especially Catrin, deserved the company to fail.

I looked around, unsure of what to do next. Catrin, Mum and Gareth were laughing with a large group by the window. I felt I should not intrude. I watched them a second longer and then, almost without thought, found myself outside.

The salty sea air was pungent so close to the marshes. After the chilled shared air inside, I delighted in the sun on my face and the breeze buffeting my hair. I took a deep breath of ozone and seaweed, feeling my shoulders relax as I breathed out. A seagull took off from the factory roof and headed out to sea. *Good luck with your fishing, mate.*

Idly, I wandered along the front of the car park, matching cars to their space reservations. There didn't seem to be a brand preferred by the company for their executives. An Evoque for the finance director—a woman maybe? White Tesla plugged into a charger for the managing director. A hulking black BMW. Instinctively, I stepped back from the aggressive beast crouched on lowered suspension. Raw elemental power threatened by the four exhausts, the subtly small blue and red warning badge.

I looked across at my reassuringly pragmatic truck. *Yes, that conveys competency, understanding, approachability.* Bemused by the BMW, I wondered what its owner saw in the black-robed muscle. *Power? Intimidation? Narcissism?* One more step brought the name on the parking space into view. Reserved for the CEO. *Well, well!*

I felt calmer, happier, energised by the brief solitude, fresh air and car inspection.

A shout came from the doorway I had left. I took in the slim, mixed-race young man with his mop of curly black hair, shaved sides to a narrow head, lively green eyes in a dark tan face and hesitant smile. He pointed to my truck.

"You're Katy's brother. You drive the grey Mitsubishi L200 Barbarian." It wasn't a question. His eyes glinted. "Two-point-two litre sixteen valve MIVEC intercooled turbo diesel."

"I'm Hal—and I'm guessing you're Ste? Stephen?" I grinned at him. "You certainly know your engines."

"How do you find it, the Barbarian, to drive?"

"Okay, I guess." I shrugged. "It's practical, does the job. I should use it off-road more to make it worthwhile."

"Why don't you get a van?"

"Oh, not you too!" I laughed. "I've got a mate who's always saying that."

Ste turned round to face the visitor centre. "Come on, there's something Katy wants you to see."

Across the room from the door, bodies parted, revealing a cut-away jet engine model the size of a small car. I was drawn in by curiosity.

Blades and chambers were exposed. A red button mounted on the casing invited a pressing finger. Intrigued, I obliged. A blue light came on in the front of the model. A sign lit up telling me this was the inlet. For four seconds the inlet shone, then the next section lit up with an orange light. This appeared to be a chamber filled with layer upon layer of fans on a central shaft.

"That's the compressor," Ste explained. "You can see there is less and less space for the air, so it gets compressed and heats up."

The space for the air became smaller, I saw, because the centres of the fans got wider with less space for the fan blades. The first fan looked like the one under the bonnet of the truck, but the last one looked more like a solid disc with lots of tiny blades sticking out.

Ste, with his strong local Welsh accent, spoke beside me as the red light in the next chamber came on. "Now that's the combustion chamber. Fuel—that's aviation kerosene—is burned continuously in the compressed air to increase its pressure, see?"

The red lamp faded, and an orange lamp came on further along the model.

"This is the real biggy that makes or breaks your jet engine: the high-pressure turbine fan." He paused while I looked. "And then the low-pressure turbine." My new companion pointed at three sets of curved blades with a brown finger. The high-pressure blades appeared to be stubbier, less aerofoil-like than the low-pressure blades.

Turning slightly, I said. "Thank you for explaining."

He pointed to a plate at the base of the model.

I read the plate aloud. "Design Project Year 1 Higher Level Aerospace Engineering Apprenticeship," with the previous year's date. "That would be Catrin's group—er, Katy's group—and yours?"

"Yeah, that's right." He smiled broadly. "We made this when we first come. We had to cast all these little fan blades and programme the CNCs to machine the fir-tree mounts and then TIG welded the shanks together."

It all sounded very impressive, although he had kind of lost me at fir-tree mounts. When I mentioned this, he amenably pointed out the stepped bases, which did indeed look like chunky metal Christmas trees.

He added, "They're not, like, real. You couldn't really use an engine like this."

"How do you mean?" I asked.

"We just cast solid pretend blades. Real jet engines have hollow blades and vanes."

"But won't that weaken them?" I was puzzled, trying to keep up.

"That's where the alloy comes in. No. they're not weakened." Ste smiled in anticipation of sharing a prize nugget of information. "Most of the blades are hollow so cooler air can blow through inside them to stop them melting. The air in the high-pressure chamber is about five hundred degrees higher than their melting point. Can you believe that?" He shook his head in wonder.

"You mean they should be melting in the engine? Sounds really hot," was my pretty useless reply.

Disappointment in his audience clouded my young teacher's face momentarily. "You're looking at an operating temperature of two thousand degrees centigrade. That's two thousand! The alloy melts at fourteen hundred."

I gave a low whistle of appreciation. Engineering like this defied belief. "So, if you didn't make holes in yours, and you did casting and milling, how are real turbine blades made?"

The young man drew me to exhibits of single, real blades on a shelf. These were like the ones at Gauge Precision, perhaps a little larger, but I could have sworn they were the same shapes.

"I've seen some of these in a precision-machining company I visit." I offered, pointing to the casting and one that I now recognised as having a fir-tree mount.

"If you look carefully," Ste said, "you can see pin-prick holes."

"Ah!" I exclaimed triumphantly. "Those lead to the hollows in the blade!"

"You got it, man!" the Welsh boy exclaimed, dimples showing either side of his smile. Typical of South Wales, he spoke like the boys I had been at school with fifteen years ago. I never seemed to have picked it up. "Do you know Katy's brilliant at programming the CNC grinders, and she's not a bad welder either? Just thought you'd like to know." His face lit up when speaking about my sister.

"Thanks for telling me." I looked at him "Are you getting on okay with the course?" I asked.

"It's interesting and gets a bit full-on. The uni sends us assignments. I've got three with deadlines coming up in the next couple of weeks, and we don't get extra time here to do the coursework." He picked up the high-pressure turbine blade and absently ran his finger over the holes along its edge.

"Must be hard," I said. "What do you do here?"

"We have to learn each section, so we work like anyone else on assembly. Electronics is probably the trickiest and hydraulics is the fiddliest. After the summer, we will be involved in R and D in the test rig unit. We, I mean Sterling, are looking at ceramic matrix composite for turbine blades. General Electric use them already, so we're getting behind." His fervour for research and development was tangible.

As I looked at the turbine blade in his hand, I had a creeping feeling that I'd missed something important.

"Good luck." I smiled at him. There was a lot more to our little Catrin's world than I'd previously realised.

My unease was soon forgotten as I was approached with a welcoming smile and a cloud of expensive aftershave by a crisply suited man. I guessed he was around ten years older than me. He held out a manicured hand.

"Richard Sterling, CEO." He introduced himself smoothly.

"Hal Rogers, Catrin Davies' brother." It felt churlish not to smile back as I shook his hand. His grip was surprisingly strong, but brief. A glimpse of steel.

Pectoral muscles and a six-pack were hinted at by his tailored shirt. A thick, pulsing vein in the strong column of his neck provided the M-decal power badge. My instinct was to step away.

"Is Stephen looking after you well?" he asked. "Did you understand his explanations? I find aerospace can be a little technical for most people." As he spoke practised lines, his battleship-grey eyes were scanning the visitors in the room.

"Absolutely fine, thank you," I responded, not sure whether the CEO had tried to disparage me with his last comment.

"Excellent. Do enjoy the evening." Richard Sterling walked off while he was talking, leaving me with no doubt I was just a visitor statistic. I felt shaken, like I'd had a near-miss with a bus on a crossing.

"So, that's your boss then?" I asked Ste.

"He's *the* boss, yes. But our boss is Stuart, over there talking with your family and Katy."

"What's he like? The big boss, I mean?"

"I suppose he's okay, but you don't get on the wrong side of him." He looked round and lowered his voice. "Stuart says he's holding the company back. He really doesn't like him. And he can't sack Stuart."

Miranda would lap this up. "Why not?"

"The directors, they won't let him." Ste gave an ostentatious cough and drew me over to some more exhibits where Catrin was holding forth.

After catching up with the family, I heard the receptionists call out that we were all to move into the theatre to our designated tables, toilets were on the left of the corridor before the theatre doors.

"We've got to look for table eighteen." Catrin dramatically swept her arm across the thirty or so round tables covered with cream linen.

"Seating plan?" I suggested, walking towards a notice attached to a flip chart-easel. "It's over there—third table from the fire exit."

We curved our way round, bumping into and apologising to others on a similar mission. The theatre was a large, wood-panelled room, squarish rather than long, with a lectern on a low raised platform at the end opposite the door. Twisting my neck round to look behind at where we had come in, I'd not seen the projector over the door as I'd expected, but a full projection room complete with busy technician.

Catrin pointed to the low platform. "It's got a hoist. We put full-size engines on there to show our overseas customers. It rises and rotates. It's amazing."

Sterling Ace Aerospace certainly knew how to show off. True masters of image.

Ten cream leather seats nestled under table eighteen, waiting for the inevitable confusion over who was going to take which seat. We sat with Ste and his parents and a well-groomed young woman from HR. Catrin introduced our party, and Ste introduced his mum and dad. Hellos and smiles around the table.

Lights dimmed; curtain went up; show started. That was the feeling—but there was no curtain, just a screen dropped to the side of the lectern before the showbiz-smart master of ceremonies took to the floor. With outstretched arms and a huge white smile on his tanned face, he shouted, "Are you all having a good time?"

The room was silent. A voice squeaked, "Yes!"

"Louder! I want to hear you're having a good time!"

I watched as people nervously eyed each other and then shouted out, "Yes!" and, "We're having a good time!"

"Welcome to the Sterling Ace Aerospace awards evening!" he boomed.

This masterful master of ceremonies was none other than the person I had sort of met earlier: Chief Executive Officer of Sterling Ace, Mr Richard Sterling.

With a dramatic flourish, he flung off his jacket, and paced in front of the screen, looking into the audience, giving each table the benefit of his direct attention. As he did so, he spoke quietly. The room fell into hushed attention.

"I was walking through the factory last week checking the state of play with one of our R and D guys." He paused. "R and D guys, are you here?" he shouted.

There was a cheer from the side of the room.

Richard Sterling continued his narration. "The last model they worked on was definitely sub-standard. Tatty. When I confronted our chief research engineer about this, he took me to the canteen kitchen and opened the fridge. I asked him why the model for the new development was kept in there." He paused for effect, before delivering the punchline. "They'd made a mint Aero engine!"

Despite my misgivings about the event, I laughed with the rest of the table, imagining a green bubbly engine with a chocolate coating.

Richard Sterling continued pacing while talking to the audience. "Last month, as you know, I was in the wonderful US of A giving a presentation on engine mounting to the great Boeing. Right in the middle of my talk, the projector failed. I had to wing it!"

Appreciative assents, laughs and groans greeted this. Everyone on our table appeared to be comfortably amused and smiling. Privately, I was disconcerted by how Richard Sterling was like a chameleon, changing to influence his audience. This wasn't the same man I'd met earlier, whose employees were careful not to get on the wrong side of.

Dazzling in the spotlight, he manipulated the audience to feel special for having been invited. The screen came to life showing colourful good news: sales graphs, health-and-safety graphs (no reportable accidents for over 1093 days) and quality achieved graphs (0.01% non-conformance). Each department's slide vied for the greatest applause. How could sales graphs be going up when Aunt Miranda had said that share prices were falling?

Ste's mother, a strikingly beautiful woman with smooth ebony skin, leaned forward. "Did you know that this man has barely any shares in his own company? A bit strange, don't you think?"

"Ma, you're not at work now," Ste hurriedly whispered.

The screen went blank, showed an enormous number three, and Richard Sterling, with building drama, intoned, "After three years of development and testing..."

Pause.

"I told you," Catrin whispered across to Ste. "It's the SFT 303."

"After three years, we have impressed," continued Richard Sterling. "We have wiped out the competition from Rolls Royce, Pratt and Whitney, General Electric, with our excellence. The SFT 303 has been chosen by Volantes NV to power the fastest commercial four-teen-seater jet plane in the world. The Viktor XIV."

A storm of clapping erupted from the employees and their guests. Images of a narrow, sleek plane came onto the screen. It had twin jet engines, one mounted on each side of the body, but didn't look that much different from any other small plane.

"Huh, bring back Concorde," my stepfather muttered.

"Still working on that one, Dad," laughed Catrin.

"Actually, we *are* working on that one," Ste added. "Did you know that the Dutch and Germans are making a delta-wing passenger plane with seats in the wings?" He looked around to see if we were listening. "There was an article in *The Engineer* magazine, and I asked Frank in R and D and he said we are looking at the engine spec for it. He thinks it'll happen sooner than we think."

Ste's mother smiled encouragement to her son as he spoke with fervour about the future of air travel.

"If Ste says it will happen, you can believe it will happen." Catrin was vehement in her support of him.

Back on the podium, Richard Sterling cleared his throat noisily, demanding attention. The chatter in the room subsided.

"We have been granted the engine certification from EASA, the European Union Aviation Safety Agency. On Friday the nineteenth of May, the Volantes Viktor XIV will be taking off from our airfield for its first commercial flight. On that flight will be the Volantes crew and engineers, two of our engineers plus—*plus*—invited guests: we have the Prime Minister, journalists from four main papers and, in this exalted company, the winning apprentice from this year's awards!"

A round of clapping broke out. We all joined in, but I noticed Ste's mother was clapping thoughtfully, with a preoccupied expression.

Richard Sterling quietened the audience. "And on that bombshell," he said, parodying a popular car programme, "back to the food. The buffets are open; please enjoy the feast that our wonderful catering company has provided."

The show, the lights, the panache, the dramatic timings all gave me a bad feeling. Maybe I was used to working factories, maybe it was South Wales bling culture, but I felt an unease and annoyance with it. Uncharitably, I thought that this was the kind of whitewash that held the local workforce to the company. The razzle-dazzle blinded those seeking the inner flaw, the paint job on a rusty old banger. The seeds of doubt had been cast.

Chapter 6
Jack of All Trades

We could have been in the buffet restaurant of a five-star all-inclusive. The food was exceptional. Fragrant, spiced, traditional, something for everyone. I had wondered why there was no "dietary request" form with the invitation—there was no need for special treatment, for dietary discrimination. Inclusion with no fuss pleased me. Inclusion with no fuss, like the cohort of apprentices, I reflected. Different sexes and nationalities supported together to become aerospace engineers. A definite tick in the box for Sterling Ace Aerospace.

So why were their shares dropping, if they were such a good company?

Companionably comparing plates like Sunday supplement restaurant critics, we tucked into the banquet. Gareth had a taste of everything on his plate, which I thought was fitting for an open-minded schoolteacher, although I did wonder how he stayed slim. Mum had tandoori chicken strips and chips. As a community midwife, she joked that she had to keep her strength up as the babies got heavier every year! Catrin, nowadays a health-conscious vegan, had stuffed peppers, falafel and salad that she was pushing round her plate. Her normally happy face was tense, troubled.

"May I?" enquired a woman, touching the back of one of the empty seats for consent. She stood politely erect, waiting for a reply.

We all nodded and smiled at her. With a welcoming "Go ahead", Gareth flapped his hand in assent.

An older man, the one who I had seen talking with Catrin, Mum and Gareth earlier, came over with two plates of food and joined the lady. Was this Stuart, their boss, who disagreed with Richard, the big boss?

I openly watched the new arrivals, as you do at any function—well, as I do anyway. Now they were closer, I judged they were in their early sixties, healthy but with a kind of knowing worldliness and intelligence in their eyes. With crinkling eyes, they had an aura of understanding and approachability, like a favourite aunt and uncle should. Not severe and serious like my adventurous journalist aunt, Miranda.

Black jacket hung over the back of the chair, the man reached a veined hand over to firmly shake each person's hand.

I rose for my turn. "Pleased to meet you. I'm Catrin's brother."

"Stuart Nicklin, engineering manager, for my sins." Then he added, chuckling, "Well, Catrin's brother, do you have a name?"

My sister butted in. "Catrin's brother will do nicely." She giggled. "You don't need a name, do you, Hal?"

With a smile, I sighed and threw my hands open, signalling defeat. "Hal Rogers."

Stuart Nicklin nodded sagely. He continued round the table and introduced his wife, Glenda. Catrin and Ste were relaxed but respectful of the new arrivals.

Polite conversation: how were we enjoying the event, good weather for Wales, practised pleasantries, nothing memorable. Waiters came round topping up glasses. Onto my soft bread roll, I piled ham and frondy fennel, bright green basil and crinkled parsley. Then, as an afterthought, I added a dollop of fruity salad with mayonnaise and took a bite. Crunchy texture, fruity acid, solid, sweet saltiness of ham and the nose-clearing zing of the herbs.

Half the table were looking at me, I realised, as my concentration shifted from my plate.

"Did you say something?" I asked to no one in particular. *Oh no, what have I done?*

"Henry!" warned my mother, looking pointedly at a cream splodge on my dark orange polyester tie.

I cringed, as mortified as a ten-year-old whose mother tucks in his shirt in front of everyone in the playground.

"Part of the pattern." I brushed off the incident. Hopefully. *Stupid thing to say.*

Catrin quietly offered her napkin, turning the light splodge into a less noticeable dark stain.

Conversations resumed around the table. The engineering manager was quietly discussing the event with the HR lady; his wife and my mother were animatedly grilling Ste's father for gory medical details from his job as a paramedic; Gareth and Ste's mother were attentively listening to both conversations and dropping in comments.

"She does that to me too," Catrin whispered. "God, she is so embarrassing. Like she doesn't even think we're grown up. I can't wait to get my own place."

"Is that why your friends call you Katy instead of Catrin—a work version of you?" I suggested.

"How...?" Catrin's black-outlined blue eyes were wide in surprise.

"Ste, earlier." I nodded towards the young man.

"Oh, no the Katy thing just happened like. None of us except Sara gets their full name." She pointed round the room. "We have Stephen—Ste, you know. We have Andrew and another Andrew so they're Andy S and Andy T, Mahmood Ras-something so we call him Maz, and over there is Sara."

"Is Sara not part of your group?" I asked.

"Oh no, nothing like that. She's just really cool and can have her full name."

Ste joined in, pointing a finger across me, "Kate, you fibber, you were mean to her."

Catrin frowned in disagreement. "No, I wasn't, it's something everyone says."

Sitting back in my seat, fascinated. "What does everyone say?"

"We called her Sas," Ste explained. "You know, like sassy."

"I only said it sounded too much like soz—what you say when you're sorry but not sorry," Catrin said.

"I never say that."

"That's cos sorry's not in your dictionary." The good-natured bickering continued.

"Children, play nicely!" I laughed.

"What about your name then?" Ste challenged me. "Didn't you want to be Henry? Henry Ford? Lots of kings called Henry."

"Off with her head!" joined in Catrin, gaily quoting the Queen of Hearts—or more likely making up a quote for Henry the Eighth. Catrin could get a bit theatrical.

"We did Henry the Fourth parts one and two and Henry the Fifth at school—you know, Shakespeare in English—and Prince Hal was who I wanted to be like in those days." I apologised as it sounded so naff. Explaining why I'd changed my name made me hot under the collar. I had been thrown into high school in an impoverished area of South Wales after my first eleven years being brought up in a wealthy upper-middle-class family in Staffordshire. Taunts, "Posh Henry" jibes, never fitting in, escaping to the hills for solitary walks in wind and rain, adrenalin shots of soul-calming rock climbing.

I continued my defence. "Yeah, well, he was good-looking, a rebellious teenager picking up bad language with the locals, rode horses. When he became king, he was popular and led men into battle, all that sort of thing." I shrugged.

Catrin nodded with a grin. "You were Prince Hal! Of course, you're good-looking. You should hear what the Beaver mums say about you when you were all at high school together.

"Never, that's rubbish," I protested. "The girls hated me at school."

"Megan Shrewley insists you were an enigmatic pin-up. Her exact words!" Catrin seemed to be enjoying embarrassing me.

"Enough of that! I'll tell everyone about the ladybird!"

Catrin wisely changed the subject. With arms folded, glaring at me, she said seriously, "Tell Ste about your work." With a glance at Ste, she added, "He likes factories."

"Hal goes into factories that machine parts for our engines," offered Ste. I noticed Stuart Nicklin's flicker of attention.

"Why would you do that? Do you service the CNCs?" he suggested, looking at me for a nod of agreement.

"I think he's the gauge tester; we're always having them round here," said Ste, before I could reply to the engineering manager.

"I know he tests the extraction systems or changes the filters or something," added Catrin.

"That's closer," I encouraged.

"Darren told me."

"Dustco Darren?"

Stuart cleared his throat. "Er, Darren said he knew Katy's brother. I saw no harm in introducing them. He's a good man."

"Well, well!" I was pleased my little worlds were joining up, like a jigsaw! My favourite people now knew each other.

Ste practically leapt up as a thought struck him. "The van. It was Darren who suggested it, wasn't it, Hal?"

I laughed. "Just leave me in peace with my pickup. I don't want you both ganging up on me."

"Whatever," Catrin said. "Hal, you were going to tell us what you do." She was not amused at the interruption.

"I'm an occupational hygienist. I go into factories and test for things that make people ill, such as fumes and dusts, noise and vibration. I check that the controls do the job, too." I waited for the inevitable tirade.

"Health and safety, you mean," sneered Ste.

"Like pointless rules and high-vis vests," added my sister.

"And masks."

"And lectures about stuff you already know?"

Health and safety, or maybe the associated enforced compliance, rarely brought out the best in people! I couldn't have been a health and safety manager. Philip Wheatley's careworn face hovered in my mind.

"I agree with what you're saying." I placated them. "But what I do is prevent employees from losing a healthy old age, and I use numbers and facts rather than opinion." I saw they were listening. "It's a different sort of health and safety."

"Like what sort of numbers?" demanded Ste, in verbal combat mode.

"There are legal exposure limits for fumes and dusts and noise and vibration. Most of them are averaged over an eight-hour shift, so I compare my results with those," I explained. "But more usually, I find out where emissions come from and try to get them reduced. Observations and photographic evidence are supported by measurements rather than the other way round."

Stuart nodded. "I see where you're coming from."

"That's backwards," Ste argued. "In all our uni investigations, we get numbers and then we explain the numbers, sometimes with photos like you said."

"Okay…" I tried to explain what I meant in terms of a hypothetical uni experiment on a car's fuel filter. All I got in return was blank looks.

Stuart Nicklin sat relaxed on his chair. With an amused twinkle in his eyes, he suggested, "Can I trouble you to give us a simple example of your work? I'm not sure that everyone understood your explanation."

"I don't know if I can. They all end up complicated. And I can't always compare against the limits either."

"Surely limits are limits? They must have legal status?" asked Stuart.

"Our law in the UK puts an overriding onus on reducing levels of anything harmful to as low as reasonably practicable. So that's despite the limits."

"You mean limits aren't limits? That's just rubbish." Ste sounded frustrated.

"Come on, Hal, you must be able to tell us something," prodded Catrin.

"There was a company that machined turbine blades…" I started slowly, realising this one was the opposite of what I was trying to convey. I now had crazy numbers from Gauge Precision and no idea how they got there.

"No, actually, I've thought of a better one." I changed my mind with a clearer picture in my head. "I went to a pressing factory where they pressed sheet steel to make car body panels. You know, doors, bits of sill and the like. Specks of dirt in the presses caused tiny bumps in the panels, which employees had to sand out using handheld pneumatic sanders. I measured hand–arm vibration from the sanders. I saw one sander with a broken support pad. Why do you think that was important?"

To my surprise, stepdad Gareth answered. "It would unbalance the machine and increase the sander's vibration." Mum patted his arm. *I didn't think she was listening.*

I nodded. "Yeah, that's right." I smiled, getting into my stride. I was quite enjoying explaining about my stuff, things I knew about. "Okay, the next thing I photographed was a convex panel that reverberated pretty loudly."

Ste took the challenge and gleefully beat Gareth to an answer. "The panel was vibrating in sync with the sander, so the amplitude of the vibration increased. The operator of the sander would have felt it. It needed a better jig to prevent flexing, or an anti-vibration mount to absorb the energy."

"Hey, well done."

Cockily, he jested, "Anyone can do your job!"

"'Fraid so. I'm a jack of all trades and master of none at all!" I agreed with a grin. Then, with a pantomime-quality menacing, dark chuckle, I added, "But I know a lot of trades—ha ha ha!" It was true. I used every aspect of the three sciences to make sense of industrial hazards, and as Catrin had pointed out on our way here, I went into a lot of different factories.

"Anyway, the highest results were for the damaged sander, an operator with poor technique and the unsupported panel. Like I said, I observe and then use the measurements to prove a point. When I compared the measurements with the exposure limits, they were way over. To be within the limits, most would have had to stop working after two hours, and just ten minutes with the broken sander."

"Interesting." Stuart nodded with a frown of concentration. "I presume you recommended training, checks on the sanders and support jigs?"

"Well, sort of. Those were the quick fixes, but what I recommended they should consider was to improve pressing and to identify blemishes earlier. Did you know one major luxury car manufacturer uses laser beams on its press line to monitor for imperfections? Three identical faults are allowed through before the presses are halted automatically. They have maybe one or two employees reworking panels, rather than five on each shift as my client had."

"Of course," Stuart agreed. He straightened his glasses. "Would they do that? Quite considerable outlay in the system you are suggesting."

"No, not yet. They have done the quick fixes, but they will be back to square one with exposure if they don't actually manage the working times and tool condition." I sighed.

"In your experience, what would make them opt for a process change? Anything?" Stuart's interested question was inevitable.

I found I was invigorated by explaining to Stuart Nicklin. His grasp was good and tempered with realism.

"It takes a special company to see the bigger picture and support capital expenditure. In this case, the reduced labour costs would probably pay for the laser checking equipment within two years. But from experience, changes only happen when insurance claims and the HSE get involved."

"Ah, yes." The engineering manager nodded.

"Tell us about the turbine blades factory, please Hal," interrupted Ste.

I told them, without naming the company, about the investigation at Gauge Precision and Barry's hands.

"What's the big deal about dermatitis?" Ste asked.

I started to explain. "It's inflammation of the skin. It could be just a bit of dry skin, like when you get wind chaps on your knuckles in cold weather, or chemical burns from acids, or it could be allergic contact dermatitis. That's where chemical groups or proteins are recognised by the body..."

"Henry, let me explain to the young man." My mother interrupted me with a tut. She turned to Ste. "Your body's playing *Doom*, or *Call of Duty*, at cell level. The attackers are recognised; you send your emergency squad out. You have all guns blazing to repel boarders, to kill or trap forever those that get through. The battlefield in your body is awash with inflammation, pus and scarring. In the case of this poor man, it's his hands, but it could easily be lungs, organ transplants, you name it."

I was surprised that Mum could say anything so sensible, never mind paint a graphic picture as relevant to Ste as that! I would never have thought of it.

"Well said, Mrs Davies!" acknowledged Ste's dad.

"Wow, Mum, that's brilliant!" Catrin sparkled.

I felt shame that I hadn't believed my mum capable of it. Maybe I should try conversing with her more.

Catrin, the machining problem firmly in her mind, wanted the rest of the story. "Something must have changed for Barry. What did you find with your tests?"

"The lab results have come back with much higher concentrations of cobalt and aluminium in the operator's machine sump and on his air sample filter than from the other machines."

"I'm sure you'd find cobalt and aluminium in most alloys for turbine blades," said Ste. "The man must be allergic to cobalt—like I can't wear nickel." He pointed to his silver ear studs.

"Yes, you're right about that," I said. "But why now and why that machine? What had changed? That's what I need to find out so no one else is harmed. Luckily, they have really good mist extraction on their machines, otherwise the operator would probably have serious breathing problems as well."

"Could he be allergic to the neat coolant?" offered Catrin, leaning forwards on one elbow. "One of the techies got red sores across his hands when they tried a different coolant in R and D."

"The coolant was the same." I shook my head.

"Were they grinding or milling or drilling? Maybe it was just swarf you measured," suggested Ste, looking at me.

"I thought of that as well, Ste. But it still doesn't explain why the cobalt concentration was so much higher than in other similar machines. I was wondering," I said thoughtfully, "if it could be possible for the blade material to be dissolving into the metalworking fluid."

"No, no, that can't happen," both the apprentices agreed, talking over each other.

"Every part and especially blades are tested all the time. Blades don't dissolve in metalworking fluid."

"It couldn't possibly happen. It would not have left the foundry."

Stuart Nicklin spoke. "That's an interesting hypothesis you have there. What makes you think a blade could dissolve?"

"Well," I said, "I know it's not blades at all, but when I was sampling for contaminants in metalworking fluid in a factory making valves for car engines, the coolant turned turquoise with dissolved copper and nickel. They had skin problems and asthma there," I added.

"That would not have been a true alloy. Aero-engine turbine blades are made from a single crystal of alloy where every metal atom is joined to others in a matrix. *Most* aero engines." A fleeting look of frustration crossed his face as he corrected himself and then carried on, "I think you will find that the automotive valves were made from a sintered alloy—more a mixture of metal particles pressed together."

"Maybe it was a property of a different sort of turbine blade?" I ventured, throwing out ideas as erratically as a road gritter in winter.

Ste voiced the pragmatic option. "Your results are wrong."

"Possible, but it doesn't explain the dermatitis flare-up."

"Who were they machining the blades for?" This time, the HR lady showed interest.

"Sorry, I don't know. I know they deal with three or four major engine manufacturers and export to Canada and the USA as well as the UK."

Was it my imagination, or did her frown ease?

A gong sounded, cutting off our conversation and heralding the pudding course.

Chapter 7
No Explanation but an Award

"Do you even know anything about what we do?" asked Catrin between bites of tarte Tatin.

"I know you've learned to programme CNC machines, you can weld, you—"

"That was last year. And it wasn't just making things—we had loads of maths and physics and engineering theory stuff. This year we are learning about the design of real aero engines like the ones we make here, and engines for rockets, which are totally different, and afterburners and fluid flow and shockwaves and trajectory analysis."

"Don't forget aircraft performance and stability and structures," added Ste, green eyes glinting under raised eyebrows.

"Do they teach you this here?" I asked.

"Most of it is online lectures from Teesside University," explained Catrin. "This year we went for two weeks intensive—"

"Urgh, very intensive," interrupted Ste.

"—lectures and practical at the University in Middlesbrough," continued Catrin, throwing an amused glance his way.

"That was brill though." Ste's eyes were alight.

"Yeah, gotta go again." Catrin sighed happily.

"We are going again, in October, stupid."

Did this pair never stop winding each other up? I would never cope with that, but Catrin and Ste never flinched. If anything, it seemed to bind them together.

"Do you remember that lecturer who kept telling us about brewing when we were supposed to be learning about fluid dynamics?"

"And he was in the Students' Union café with that jacket."

"Yeah, proper weirdo he was."

Stuart Nicklin took up the thread. "This is the first cohort to study with Teesside University. At Sterling, we have quite specific knowledge and skill-set requirements if the apprentices are to take the company forward."

His wife flashed a look, lips compressed, at the mention of taking the company forward.

Stuart smoothly continued, "Teesside had the facilities to provide the modules we were after." He paused, noting our interest. "We invest quite heavily in training. I feel it is key to our remarkable staff retention record." He looked at the HR lady, who was resolutely keeping out of the conversation. "That's what you have found, I suspect?"

"So, you are investing in apprentices as part of the future development of the company," I summarised. "What is the plan for the company, and what roles do you expect these apprentices to be playing, in say, five years' time?" I asked with interest.

Other conversations around the table had stopped, with all attention on Stuart Nicklin.

"As you found out earlier, we are producing engines for faster commercial flights. The faster engines run hotter and are more efficient with respect to fuel costs and global warming emissions." Stuart paused to gather his thoughts and, with a little shrug, carried on. "The latest engine, the SFT 303, is quite likely to be the last engine we produce using nickel superalloy."

Catrin gasped. "We've not even got it in production yet and you're saying it's the last one?"

Ste supported Stuart. "We've run out of cooling design and coating options for this blade to run any hotter."

"The next five years will be a race for the development of ceramic composite blades that can operate at temperatures five hundred degrees higher than even the SFT 303," Stuart said. "Carbon fibre is being looked at again by the main players, so we have work to do for Sterling to be a frontrunner in this race."

Murmurs of appreciation around the table.

The HR lady cleared her throat and brought the subject round to jobs in the future. "We will need people with an enthusiasm for aerospace, with technical knowledge and with big dreams for the future of air travel. We aim to nurture creative ideas and support thinking outside the box," she added with a nervous smile.

Parroting promotional blurb. I looked across at Ste's mother to gauge her reaction to this. Her face was impassive. She was not taken in by the company hype.

"We definitely need skills and new ideas in research and development, and we anticipate employing some of our apprentices to work on and actively manage the manufacture of new models, ironing out production issues. I expect some of our students will support airlines with training for new engine maintenance protocols. There is quite a considerable future for everyone at Sterling." The engineering manager finished his little pep talk with a self-deprecating smile.

Catrin seemed enraptured with the picture of her future.

To me, Stuart said dryly, "I hope that answers your question."

"Thank you," I replied politely.

I was quietly impressed by this man. Catrin and Sterling Ace were in good hands. So, what was going wrong with the company? How could such a good team be shedding its shareholders?

Taking advantage of the following lull in conversation, I stood up. "Anyone for coffee?"

I collected orders as Stuart rose from his chair.

"Could you use some help?" he asked.

The two of us wound our way to the short queue by the thermos flasks delivering hot drinks.

I struck up a conversation. "My aunt, she's a business journalist." I paused. Stuart Nicklin looked as though I had threatened him with a gun! He paled, his step faltering. Shocked at his reaction, quietly I carried on. "She said that Sterling's performance has not been so good over the last couple of years. It's losing shareholders."

Stuart Nicklin looked down. "Your journalist aunt is right. Our shares have been going down in value for the last two years." He paused, assessing me, before divulging, "Personally, I think they're looking to sell out to a new owner."

"What about the new engine, and Volantes?"

Leaning over the steaming thermos, Stuart Nicklin sighed. "We are not keeping up with the competition. Even the new engine is old technology. We are still using aligned-crystal turbine blades in the harshest part of the engine."

I counted the coffees and added one more cup to the line the engineering manager was filling. Keeping the coffee flowing seemed to keep the information trickling too.

"What should you be using?" A gentle nudge.

He looked up from the coffee cup, startled, for a second.

"Ah, er, single crystal or ceramic composite."

"So why is the new engine using aligned crystals?"

"Historical lack of investment, it's all we've got."

I could not help but feel puzzled, cheated by the pizazz of the evening.

"You mean this is all fake? Everything you are doing here?" I whispered as we took our loaded trays back to the table.

Stuart spoke gravely. "Not at all. The SFT 303, the awards, the journalists"—he nodded to cameras dotted around—"are keeping the confidence of our investors. Giving us breathing space for the apprentices to bring this company back into healthy competition."

Catrin, her future. Would the company survive long enough?

"So, really, you need the SFT 303 engine and your relationship with Volantes to get the company through this little dip you're in."

He nodded.

The moment we reached the table, lights dimmed, and the room descended into calm expectation.

"It's got to be Sara—she got highest marks in the tests," whispered Catrin to Ste.

"I think it will be Andy T, because none of his systems failed," the young man quietly replied.

"Could be you."

"Could be you."

The tense apprentices grinned. "Nah."

Stuart Nicklin, grabbing his jacket, took his leave of us and joined the Chief Executive on the podium.

Twenty minutes of increasing tension later, after awards were given out for sales, production, safety and too many other things to remember, came the moment our table had been waiting, anticipating, dreading.

"Our cohort of second-year higher and degree apprentices has been of the highest quality this year.

It has been extremely difficult to choose one out of the group. All of you"—Richard Sterling smiled benevolently at the tables holding the apprentices—"all, I repeat, all of you, deserve recognition for your high level of academic achievement and input."

He took a dramatic breath and squared his shoulders. "Your university lecturers, mentors here at Sterling, and I have unanimously singled out one apprentice for unfailing encouragement of their peers and strong leadership of the group in Middlesbrough."

Ste winked at my sister. Her knuckles were white, breath held.

"Miss Catrin Davies. Katy, come on up!"

A joyous explosion of cerise sequins, diamante sparkle and blonde curls erupted from our table to riotous cheers and thundering applause.

I stood, clapping harder than anyone. That Catrin was so popular made me swell with pride to be her brother.

Catrin stepped up to the immaculately dressed Chief Executive at the podium to shake his hand and collect a small plaque. He smiled charmingly down at her, and she flushed. Moving along, she shook the hand of the slightly dishevelled engineering manager and laughed at some joke, pretending to roll her sleeves up.

"The award for Overall Leading Apprentice of the Year also goes to Miss Catrin Davies."

Catrin held high the award that would put her on the flight of the Volantes Viktor XIV.

Breathless and glowing with happiness, Catrin returned to our table. With Sterling's catering-quality bubbles, I toasted my sister's future in this jet engine company in South Wales.

It would need all the help it could get.

Chapter 8
Inspection Jeopardy

Driving the familiar route home between Port Talbot and Cannock, my thoughts returned to the survey at Gauge Precision. I'd often get lost in detail; ideas often clarified when I was driving to and from factories, up and down the motorways of Britain. Hands on the wheel, M4 following the coast from Port Talbot, ticking off the signs for Bridgend (*the water board's lab survey*), Cardiff (*Christmas shopping with Catrin*), past the A470 valleys road to Merthyr Tydfil (*welding fume survey*), towards the A449 turning for the Midlands.

So where had the additional cobalt come from? I needed to work it out to stop it happening again. I did not want any more dermatitis blighting the employees, the factory, Philip. I had to admit to myself it was more than that, though. I wasn't just concerned about preventing further damage—I couldn't bear not understanding, not knowing!

I thought back to the machining process I had seen at Gauge. I had noted down that the machined parts were turbine blades for a jet engine. The model at Sterling had proved how many different blades there were in a jet engine—different sizes depending on where the fan was.

Indicating and off onto the A449 slip road. Down to the roundabout, first exit and up the hill. *But were the turbine blades all made of the same alloy? Do different engine builders use different alloys? Was this a normal production run, or were these specials from R and D using something unique? Is it possible for different batches of parts with the same product number to be cast from different alloys?*

Keeping in the left-hand lane, moving over for slip roads, steady sixty-five to seventy miles an hour. No camera flashes, no hurry to return home. Mind back at Gauge Precision. *Revs, heat, and coolant condition? I don't know enough about machining. Maybe, this CNC programme made machine seventy-six cut deeper and hotter than its neighbour? I'll have to ask. Then again, maybe Ste was right, and it is the lab results at fault after all. I'll ask them to double-check.* So many questions running through my head. So many things it could be.

Tired of spiralling thoughts, I settled into the drive back. Despite Darren and Ste saying I should get a van, the truck was probably the most suitable vehicle I had owned for a long time. Not brilliant on fuel consumption, not as fast or as fun as my Ford Focus RS had been, but it did everything I asked of it. I had driven many cars, and some I would never willingly drive again. Automatics with impossible lags, BMWs just tail happy the way I drove them, and a pain in the wet, ice and snow, which meant most of the time in the UK. The Ford Focus RS—*my little orange cannonball,* I smiled to remember—did not like seventy miles an hour; its engine sounded happiest when it was exceeding ninety miles an hour in fifth. Its all-wheel drive took it into corners from which I could drive or drift out as I chose. I missed the adrenaline of its soundtrack, of being there in the moment or crashing.

Back on the road, my dependable truck continued eating up the miles north, uncomplaining, cooperative at seventy, keeping my last three points intact. On the A40 through the tunnel and traffic lights. The short tunnel lit in orange neon, quiet, no endorphin shot from pulsing and crackling exhausts to open the windows for today. Imposing, old, brick building of a school on the left, the gently swaying greenery of willows over the River Wye on the right. Out of Monmouth and up the snaking, wooded dual carriageway past signs to Goodrich Castle and up to Ross on Wye. Roundabout and onto the two-lane M50.

Raised stretches of this little motorway floated monotonously over featureless floodplains. The truck cab was warm; tyres hummed on the road surface. Eyes heavy. More floodplains. Mirror. Car coming up to overtake; *I am doing fifty-five*. Open the window. Squinting to force eyes open. Radio on; talk to the radio. Noisy vibrations under the car; heart jolts. Swerve back off the edge strip. Motorway ending at the M5. Left onto M5 and immediately left into Strensham Services. Follow the curved road into the car park. Turn off the engine. A minute of silence, eyes closed.

Sleepiness was a familiar foe. Normally when setting off early for full-day surveys, I would bring coffee to avoid falling asleep at the wheel, but today, leaving my parents' after a late night and a strenuous morning, I had none. Yesterday's awards dinner had finished early, around 9 p.m., and we had taken the opportunity to join the other apprentices and their families for a drink or three in Swansea.

What felt like half an hour after I had gone to bed, Catrin had knocked on my bedroom (now the spare bedroom) door with a "Surf's up on the Gower. You'll enjoy it. Your wetsuit's still in the garage, so you can't say no!" So, we went surfing at silly o'clock on Saturday morning. Llangennith sand dunes saw us donning rash vests, and black mid-weight full-length wetsuits under a promising blue sky patterned by wheeling gulls. We paddled out on shortboards, watching waves grow, judging height, turning, racing to match the wave speed, crouching, balancing, standing, exhilarating, tiring, laughing, sandy, freezing... We had given up mid-morning and returned to my mum's hearty fried breakfast.

Fully awake after a ten-minute power nap, I downed a coffee to make sure I made it safely to the end of my journey. Through Cannock, traffic crawling with supermarket shoppers, and out towards Stafford and Cannock Chase. Short private road and into the weedy gravelled forecourt of a large Victorian house. One-bedroomed flat on the first floor.

Home on my own, the black haze settled back familiarly. Reports to write. Reports carefully explaining why this or that factory was slowly harming its employees. That was all I could do—it was up to my clients to actually take action. Occupational hygiene was my life; I had gone into this work to make a difference, but did it really? The mess of Barry's hands—I should have prevented that, but I didn't know how.

The flat was rented. Like everything in my life, it was transient. I would move on when the time was right. Occasional dates had loved the gracious main room with its tall windows, original fireplace and classic antique tables. It had been furnished by the landlord. I thought it a bit pretentious, if I were honest, but had no inclination to put my stamp on it. I was single: no children, no pets, no dependents, no ties. The women I took out to dinner these days mostly had children, animals, dependents, ties. I was their momentary escape.

After being with family, my solitary existence suddenly felt empty. Catrin's bubbling happiness contrasted like technicolour against my mono-chrome life. I hadn't been truly happy since Carla. Evading close relationships had left me with an equable, undemanding but barren existence.

I was a coward when it came to emotion. The risk of loving another being had been excruciatingly stripped from me by a freak climbing accident in Patagonia the year after I left university.

We'd both been students in the same building. I had noticed her in the stairwell. I had long hair; she ignored me. Then, with the climbing club in North Wales, Carla, beautiful, blonde chemical engineering student, had laughed and thrown water over me when I set fire to my blue Adidas top. She said it had been silly to dry it over a camping stove. For two years we climbed, we studied, we loved. Together forever. Two years and two months was too short. Torres Del Pine was meant to be our big adventure before settling down.

I wiped an errant tear.

Carla came back in a coffin. I never settled down.

***

Monday morning saw me in jeans and a T-shirt, sitting at the dining table, laptop out and notebook with certain key scribbles highlighted. I needed an update on how things were at Gauge Precision so I could complete my report. I had six other reports to do, but like a tennis ball on a string, the curious sump analysis results kept flying back at me, knocking out my concentration.

Mechanically, I entered measurement data into tables but failed to make meaningful commentary. My head was filled with Gauge. Like being stuck at a level in a computer game, no matter what else I tried to think about, my mind kept defaulting back to Gauge Precision.

I emailed the analysis laboratory to ask if they would check the results of the Gauge samples for transposition errors. If they had the decimal point wrong, that would make a big difference. But there was still the skin reaction. That fitted in with the original analysis results. The strange results had to be right.

Probably procrastinating, but justifying it to myself as necessary, I searched the internet for information on turbine blades and cobalt. With increasing fervour, clicking links, articles started coming in, query following query. Google threw up an article on turbine blade failure as a cause for military plane crashes. I clicked. I read. I was hooked.

Unsurprisingly, planes crash when turbine blades break. The article said that turbine blades mostly fail due to something called creep crepitation. If the blade casting is made from lots of tiny crystals and it's put under stress, creep crepitation occurs, with little cracks joining up and spreading between the crystals. Stress is caused by high pressure and high temperature. That put the most highly stressed blades in the high-pressure turbine section of the jet engine. On Friday afternoon, by the model, Ste had said that the high-pressure turbine would make or break the engine.

Feeling I was getting somewhere at last, I continued the search and found a report in *Archives of Metallurgy and Materials*. I read that the inner surface of the mould in which the metal is poured at the foundry has cobalt aluminate added to make the grain smaller and the blade (or any other casting) harder.

I stretched and sighed, then printed out the articles linking cobalt aluminate to nickel alloy castings. It came from the coating in the foundry. However, this did not explain why sump levels of cobalt were higher in Barry's machine only. That must be to do with the individual parts that were machined, I reasoned. So, what were they?

Reviewing the notes and photographs from the Gauge survey, I looked for pointers to the identity of the parts being machined. In the photos enlarged on the laptop screen, the blades and stubs were short. Thinking back to the jet engine model at Sterling and my conversation with Ste, that meant that the parts could only be from the high-pressure turbine: the blades with the toughest job in the engine. Maybe an extra-strong solution was used to make those blades extra hard? Even as I thought it, I cringed at the naivety and how wrong it sounded. Like adding salt to food, a little makes an improvement, too much wrecks it.

Key-tapping furiously, I refined my search terms, using "cobalt aluminate" and "high-pressure turbine blades". What I learned increased my misgivings: cobalt aluminate weakens nickel alloys operating at high temperature. The close packing of minuscule grains in the casting made cracks creep faster than without the treatment. Cobalt aluminate should not be used with high-pressure turbine blades.

So logically, if there was cobalt in the sump, they could not have been machining high-pressure turbine blades. Feeling like hitting my head on the oak table in frustration at the lack of a sensible explanation, I was sure they were doing the impossible: machining cobalt-coated high-pressure turbine blades.

Seeing as the only explanation I had was impossible, I decided to dig deeper back at Gauge Precision. There was so much more information about the machining operation that I needed to know and had not noted during the survey three weeks ago.

I called Philip Wheatley at Gauge to ask if I could come over to check a few details. Not asking why, his immediate response was an effusive, "Come over, come over any time. Can you make it before two? Can you spare ten minutes? Only, we've got the HSE woman coming in about the dermatitis, and I'd rather you spoke with her."

The lunchtime news programme that I'd had on in the background caught my attention with historic aerial footage of Port Talbot and the Sterling engine plant.

"Sorry, did you say the HSE were coming in?" I asked.

"—share price stopped falling as a new export contract is expected."

"When did you find out?" I asked. Then, "Which her? This Rosa—I mean, Isobel Fleming —woman?"

"Yes, yes, her! Her office telephoned an hour ago, asking if I would be in this afternoon. She's going to shut us down! I know it! You've got to talk to her!"

The business correspondent on the news reported speculation about a takeover of Sterling by one of the global engine companies and suggested that this new contract may be sufficient to delay it. Had Catrin heard this?

Poor Philip, he did sound in a state. As his consultant occupational hygienist, I, too, took some responsibility for ensuring his company were compliant.

The Health and Safety Executive, always known as the HSE, is the government body with a remit to ensure people are not made ill, injured or killed by work. Unstoppable, this arm of the law needed no search warrant. Inquisition by the merciless Colonel Rosa Klebb! No wonder Philip was anxious!

I spoke calmly and reasonably. "I'll come over now. I'll speak to her with you. We have followed all the guidance as best we can. It'll be fine."

On the news, the mention of Volantes NV in Belgium slammed into my attention. Angry protestors were shouting outside the gates of the aeroplane makers. The scene barely lasted a couple of seconds before similar scenes were shown from America: a smoke-belching power station, an electronics giant, culminating in rioting protestors smashing the gates down outside a shale oil drilling rig. The newsreader explained these were scenes of environmental protestors targeting the parent company, Beech Tree Investments.

Would this affect Sterling once the protestors knew about the Volantes contract?

***

Dressed in practical working clothes of pressed black cargo trousers, work boots and a professional white shirt with my company's logo and clasping my A4 hardback notebook, I approached the tinted glass reception door of Gauge Precision Engineering. Reflected back at me was an entirely ordinary white man—slim, six-foot, with short brown hair and dark brown eyes. Tidy and professional. Hopefully professional enough to convince the inspector we were doing all we should.

I caught the receptionist's eye and the door buzzed, the lock releasing with an audible click. Pushing the door open, I stepped through and smiled at the receptionist, and she responded, "It's Hal Rogers, don't tell me, er, IDT?"

"Close, IDP: Industrial Disease Prevention. Pretty good memory you've got, er, Shona," I replied, reading her name badge.

"Are you here to see Philip? Would you mind signing in and I'll let him know you are here?" Instead of calling, Shona used her keyboard, and soon the professional smile was back. "Please take a seat; he will be with you shortly."

Philip, bony and grey as Gandalf on a bad day, appeared. "Hal, good to see you again," he said, extending his skeletal hand. His sharp, pale eyes creased into a good-natured welcome.

"Good of you to see me, Philip," I replied, shaking his hand, genuinely pleased to see him but shocked at how he had aged in the last two weeks.

"Would you like a drink?" he asked.

"I'm happy to wait until the visitor arrives," I replied, anxious to get answers to my cobalt questions.

Philip was lucky to have had warning of this visit. If the inspector found that official guidance had not been followed, then that would normally be proof that the employer had failed to comply with regulations and had committed an offence under criminal law. Depending on the professional advice and how it was handled, industrial dermatitis might be evidence of a criminal failing.

"What do think she will want to see?" Philip asked.

"A hierarchy of controls in action."

"Do we have this hierarchy?"

"Yep, course we do!"

"The HSE, this Isobel Fleming inspector person, will want to see that you have taken action to keep everyone safe from harm from metalworking fluid."

"But... but no one can do that. I don't have the budget for PPE for everyone." Philip protested as I was speaking.

"PPE just protects one person at a time. Don't worry, that's not what they're after." I paused for inspiration. "What if you had to have cyanide in the metalworking fluid?"

"But you wouldn't. Everyone would be dead."

"Exactly, you use a really low toxicity metalworking fluid. But what I'm getting at is, what controls would you have to be able to use cyanide in the machines? Would you be able to run the open lathes, for example?"

"Ah." Philip sighed in understanding. "We enclose the machines, we extract from them to make sure they don't leak, we make sure the mist has cleared before the operators open the doors and that protects the operators and everyone else."

"Easy, yes? And you know your controls work because you manage the fluid, test the extraction and check the health of the employees."

"The only PPE we need then are gloves, which we provide." Philip sounded positive.

I folded my arms, thinking about the one big issue with no controls. "There is one thing I'm worried about. Going back to the cyanide scenario, what is the one thing that would spread cyanide through the air and cover employees' skin and clothing with spray?"

Philip thought for a moment. "The airlines."

"Mm."

Changing the subject, I got around to the information I needed. "I'm afraid I have a few questions I need answers to. Would we have time to look at these before the HSE inspector comes, do you think?"

"We should have time. Fire away." Philip seemed glad of the diversion.

"I need to know exactly what was machined on Barry's machine in the last three weeks, not just part numbers but the serial numbers, what parts they were and for which company, and any tests the lab did. Then I want the record of tests made on the metalworking fluid up until my visit."

Philip nodded. "Production first and find out what products went through, then maintenance to pull up fluid test records, then the lab upstairs and you can ask them about the tests you want."

I followed in his wake. Finishing at the locked lab door, we knocked, and a white-coated, bearded metallurgist came out to speak. I explained that I needed to know what testing they'd done on the parts to see if there was anything that would explain the cobalt levels we had found in one machine sump three weeks ago. He smiled at my simplicity. Even to me, it sounded impossible.

"Get me a bit more information, and we'll see what we can do," he offered. "We do tests for hardness, weld structure and surface quality. We keep the alloy specs from the originating foundries. We don't look at the chemistry here. You might be better off asking the foundry."

"Anything you can do," I said gratefully. "I'll let you know the batch serial numbers I'm interested in."

That was it. I had cast my bread on the water, and now we'd wait to find out what would appear. We headed back to reception.

"Is that what you wanted?" asked Philip as we made our way down the carpeted office stairs.

"To be honest, I don't know what I want, so I'm trying everything," I replied. "I will let you know when they have emailed me the data, and if it makes sense."

We found ourselves back in reception. It was time for the inspector.

Glass-fronted meeting rooms led off from the reception area. Philip opened the door of the second room, moving the slide to "in use". The small room was painted white, with grey skirting boards merging to a grey carpet, and four grey armed chairs on castors around a light wood meeting table with a pillar of sockets in the centre. More workmanlike than the visitor centre at Sterling but sufficient to reassure potential customers, I thought. Colour in the room came from huge, close-up, arty photographs of parts being produced, sprays of coolant mist and sparks creating drama and beauty. The HSE would not be bothered, but I considered it fitting that the visual art inherent in production processes was displayed: a tribute to the engineering science that made it happen.

I took a seat, opening my book and absentmindedly underlining today's date. "Philip?" I asked. "Did the Inspector want anything in particular?"

"I think she's just coming to see what she can find to pin on us. That's what the last one did when the forklift hit the wall," said Philip bitterly, fidgeting with his pen. "We got an improvement notice and a fine for not testing the hoist over the degreasing tank, and he said we didn't have good enough proof that we had trained the lad on using the hoist. The hoist had just been installed and didn't need testing, and he never even looked at the forklift trucks, but there you go, no arguing with them." He shook his head, then earnestly looked me straight in the eye. "You will talk to her, take her round and show her anything she wants to see." He paused. "I think that would be best." He nodded as though it were settled.

I did not argue with my customer.

Through our open door, I watched as a slim, dark-haired young woman in an ill-fitting grey skirt-suit and low-heeled black shoes pushed ineffectively at the locked doors to reception. She looked round and jabbed the intercom button and the door was released. Briefcase in hand, head high, she marched in, energy fizzing around her. The colonel in disguise! I was transfixed, my mouth dry.

Philip rushed out to greet her, putting on his smoothest manner. "You must be Miss Fleming? Can I get you a drink?"

The woman's head, shoulders and energy dropped a minuscule notch in her professional recovery as she replied, "Mr Wheatley, how do you do?" shaking his hand. "Coffee please, black, no sugar."

Philip brought the inspector into the meeting room and introduced me as their occupational hygienist. We duly shook hands; hers was a firm, dry grip that lasted no longer than necessary. Clean, short nails—I approved. We settled down around the table with small talk about the state of the roads and the weather as Shona came in with a tray of teas and coffees and a plate of chocolate biscuits. Biscuits signalled this was an important visitor.

Miss Fleming opened her official pad and said in a clipped business-like tone, "Right, Mr Wheatley, I'd like you to run through the actions you have taken since your employee was diagnosed with allergic contact dermatitis."

She waited, her face impassive, giving no clues as to what she wanted covered. Philip, although prepared for this question, was reformulating his answer. I could see he was wrestling with doubts by his very stillness.

Miss Fleming softened the tone of her voice, coaxing. "Mr Wheatley?" She maintained eye contact while relaxing her body language.

In unconscious response to her lowering of energy, Philip sighed, brought his elbows to the table and leaned on them. I was amazed at how this had worked.

Philip eventually replied. "Initially I brought in Hal, Mr Rogers..."

A kilowatt flash of her curiosity startled me, then it was gone, her focus returned to Philip.

"...to identify the cause."

"And did you find the cause, Mr Rogers?" It was there, just a fractionally raised eyebrow. I felt the pressure of her expectation, an order I could not obey.

Shamefully, I replied, "I'm sorry, no. Er, not yet." How could I tell her that cobalt was involved, and maybe endotoxin, but I wasn't sure exactly, especially as the cobalt should not have been there according to everything I had found so far? She didn't need to know all that.

Miss Fleming sighed sharply, arms now loosely folded in her lap—were my words not worth writing down?—and batted the inquisition my way. "I presume you had a plan for this investigation for which you have no conclusion?" She tilted her head and looked at me probingly, continuing the offensive. "Are you familiar with the hazards of metalworking fluid?"

Ouch, that hurt!

Taking up the gauntlet, I smiled. "Barry, the employee, was machining parts on machine seventy-six. I covered the bases of inhalation exposure as well as direct skin contact. I considered that he may have reacted to a change in neat metalworking fluid, tramp oils from the machine, possibly different metals from the machined part, and of course, endotoxin from bacterial contamination. I took samples of metalworking fluid mist, samples of sump fluid and microbiological samples for bacteria. There was no difference in the neat fluid used, the parts machined or the machine cycle."

"What information did the sump and air samples give you?"

"Well, there were higher concentrations of cobalt and aluminium in the sump of machine seventy-six and in the air sample for Barry than anywhere else. At the time of my visit, the bacterial count in the sump was very high, ten to the power of six or thereabout."

"Fine, thank you." The dark head looked down as her elegant fingers danced through bullet-pointed notes with a fountain pen. She looked up, giving me the full benefit of incredible hazel eyes. *Hal, get a grip!* "No conclusion? I presume you must have discussed your findings with Mr Wheatley."

"We only just got the lab results on Friday afternoon. I am currently following up different avenues to find the source of the cobalt." I felt like a schoolboy blaming the dog for eating his homework.

The tightening of the inspector's lips told me she was dissatisfied with my reply. *She must have meant the general conclusion about Barry's dermatitis. Stop focusing in on the cobalt, Hal.*

"Sorry, I see what you mean, Miss Fleming. Yeah, Philip and I did discuss the issue, and we decided that we would presume that the sump fluid was causing the skin reaction. I advised that Barry should be sent home on sick leave and that the machine sump should be cleaned and disinfected."

The ball was neatly back in Philip's court.

The inspector nodded briefly and turned to him. "Was Mr Roger's advice followed?"

"Barry was sent home on sick leave at the end of the shift. The machine was shut down and we had the sump contents pumped out and sent for disposal." Philip rubbed the back of his neck, showing his discomfort.

The inspector softened her gaze, gently running her delicate pink thumbnail along the fountain pen's clip.

Pressure released, Philip continued, "Disinfectant was run through the machine over two days and then it was refilled and put back into service." Sensibly, he refrained from adding that to replace coolant in a machine was extremely costly in downtime, disposal charges and the cost of replacement fluid.

She could not fault that answer.

"Thank you, Mr Wheatley. Now, on to the dermatitis. I have a report from your occupational health provider that the gentleman was referred to a dermatologist for allergy testing. Do you have those results?"

Without thinking, I gave her the answer. "He was found to be allergic to nickel and cobalt."

The inspector frowned at the interruption and made a couple of notes.

"Mr Wheatley, what happened to the condition of the gentleman's hands once he had been off work?"

What a horrible question. By answering this truthfully, it would leave no doubt that Barry's condition was the fault of Gauge Precision—in other words, me and Philip.

Philip spread his hands in submission. "The skin condition cleared."

Was that a triumphant smile touching the inspector's lips? She nodded, smile swiftly erased. "I take it that he is still off work, Mr Wheatley?"

"Why? Should he be? He's back at work."

I frowned. Philip was playing a game; consciously or not, he was asking for disbelief from the inspector. Every one of the thirty or more CNC milling, drilling, eroding and grinding machines emitted mist containing nickel. There was no way an allergic operator's damaged skin would remain unaffected, no matter where they worked on the shop floor.

Cautious disbelief flashed in her hazel eyes and a shapely eyebrow raised. Miss Fleming made a slight show of writing down Philip's words. She was waiting, playing the unspoken game, each side wanting to be the first to correct the other's erroneous statement.

Smiling to myself, I broke the stalemate. "He has been relocated to the toolroom unit down the road. He's still machining but the materials are mild and hardened steel, no nickel or cobalt superalloys."

The inspector replaced her frown with a very human rueful smile, as though she had caught herself jumping to conclusions.

She started a fresh page in her notepad. "Controls of mist and your fluid management." She looked at me expectantly.

"Gauge have the oil supplier contracted to do tests every week. I can show you the charts on the machines."

Miss Fleming nodded and noted. "How are issues reported by the contractor?"

"They fix it themselves and make a note on the chart on the machine. I believe they email a summary report to maintenance every month," added Philip helpfully.

What if endotoxin from the bacteria had somehow exacerbated the operator's allergy? Maybe increased levels of cobalt were incidental. But the cobalt should not have been there. Back on the merry-go-round, stuck on the same game level.

The inspector's questioning of Philip Wheatley slowed to an end. She was asking about servicing frequency of the machine extraction.

She had a pleasant, if stern, face. Not stern perhaps, just focused, but betraying no emotion. I put her age down to early thirties, from the lines appearing at the corners of her luminous, hazel-brown eyes. Her voice was low, musical. She had kissable lips, I decided. Not overblown pouty monstrosities nor a tight line, just lips, normal lips.

The normal lips opened. "Do you have somewhere I can change, Mr Wheatley?"

Chapter 9

Identity Unveiled

How could black industrial overalls and work boots do that? The inspector had left the office as just another grey-suited civil servant. Miss Fleming now swung round the doorway in full command mode, figure accentuated in black cotton, movements fluid and sure, eyes of fire. Involuntarily I took a deep breath as my heart constricted. *Bloody hell, Hal, concentrate on work!*

Philip seemed unaffected. Affably, he decanted responsibility onto me. "Hal will escort you round, Miss Fleming. He's best placed to answer any questions you have."

"Thank you, Mr Wheatley. Now, Mr Rogers, are you ready?"

That was a million-dollar question! I was taking a government HSE Inspector round a factory, for heaven's sakes, so why the chest-tightening thrill of approaching a tight bend at one hundred miles an hour?

"Sure." I smiled confidently.

I gave her a whistle-stop tour of the production process. Personally, I found it easier to understand processes if I was shown them in production order rather than simply walking through the factory. I gave her the same tour as a courtesy.

The factory processes were laid out in a ragged U loop. At the front of the factory unit, roller-shutter doors opened to the ends of the "U": goods-in and despatch. Vans from the foundries offloaded deep plastic trays of castings into one side of this area. The other side was where machined castings were packaged and sent onwards to the next process supplier, such as for heat treatment or coating. Since the last HSE visit, the area had been fenced off from pedestrians.

"Just the one forklift truck?"

"Yes. Would you like to check it?" This was an inspector after all.

"Of course."

I knew she would! I suppose I wouldn't have taken my word for it if I were her, either.

We carried on around the factory. The first half of the building had five-axis CNC milling machines that cut the shapes that the parts needed. Machine seventy-six, which Barry had operated, was one of these. Parts could be on these machines for hours at a time. The operator would open the machine door and check the progress every so often. Machined parts would then go to the rear of the factory to the EDM machines, where a multitude of fine holes were made with a fine electrode, and intricate shapes etched.

I stood and watched as the vision in black took out a torch to highlight fume emanating from the open EDM erosion tanks. There were six of them on each side of a walkway at chest height. They were about one metre long, half a metre wide and half a metre deep. Neon-pink dielectric liquid swirled and bubbled under the submerged electrode. In the past, I had seen fume from the bubbles sometimes drift away from the extraction hoods when the operators had not positioned them close enough. There was no excuse for poor design of extraction.

I was quietly impressed at how the inspector was going about her work. This lady obviously knew her way round a machine shop; she pinpointed the hazards and the key emission points. She was thorough. I began to believe that if she did find a fault, it would be a fair cop, something we genuinely had missed. Worryingly, if she found something, it meant I would have missed it. That thought, that my work was not good enough, was enough to bring me out in a cold sweat.

A slim, tanned finger beckoned me over. Her straight shoulders raised momentarily in a frustrated sigh. I was glad she felt the same as I did, at least about mis-sold fume extraction.

"You see the fume?" Her voice was level. "How would you describe that degree of control?"

I straightened up, as though being caught out doing something wrong.

"It's the design. The original extraction company that made these units designed them to remove oil mist from enclosed CNC machines. Their sales engineers convinced Gauge that they would work on open tanks."

"Do you think they work?"

Why was the Inspector drawing this out?

"No, the control is rubbish. They do remove some fume though. I have measured exposures to the metals in the fume, and they have been low. None of the employees have any breathing problems. Trouble is, they cost quite a bit to install and the finance department here at Gauge have not agreed on any capital to replace them. Not while the air monitoring results are low, anyway."

Miss Fleming was nodding her understanding as I spoke. I stopped my tirade of frustrations with a sigh.

"I see," she said. "What would you say about the risk of harm from emissions from the EDM tanks?"

This was like the diploma exam for the Faculty of Occupational Hygiene at the BOHS. Miss Fleming raised her eyebrows encouragingly as I explained what I thought and the plans for improvement.

The company had to use the EDM tanks for the extremely fine shaping of intricate parts. Back in the Sterling visitor centre, when I'd been looking at the model jet engine, Ste had told me that the blades were hollow for cooling. Other CNC-enclosed EDM machines would make the holes we'd seen that would allow cold air into and out of the hollows in the casting.

I thought I'd share my new little snippet of jet engine information with Miss Fleming. "Did you know that the blades have holes drilled in them so cold air can get inside and cool them, otherwise they'd melt in flight?"

Miss Fleming looked momentarily confused. Politely giving my story the benefit of the doubt, she said, "Sorry?"

"High-pressure turbine blades, they operate at two thousand degrees, but their melting point is fourteen hundred! They are hollow and have to be air-cooled. Amazing, isn't it?"

She regarded me with consideration, her head tilted, a small smile transforming her face. How I wanted to smooth an errant wisp of hair from her cheek. *Hal, just get a grip.*

She gave a little chuckle. "I'll think of that next time I see a plane."

She stood close to me as we peered at the tiny holes in the EDM-drilled parts. All my senses were on red alert. I could feel her body heat. She smelled of soap.

Then back down the factory, following the process to CNC grinders, on to very fine secondary machining, and back to the despatch side of the starting area. On the outer edges of the production floor were sectioned-off bays where parts could be tested, welded or hand-finished as needed. The infamous degreasing tank was here too, with a fully-trained operator. No more improvement notices for Philip here this time!

Most of the factory floor was taken up by CNC machines. The main hazard from machining was inhalation of coolant mist, so any oil outside the machines was a bad sign. If bacteria contaminated the coolant, then the mist was even more hazardous, with endotoxin causing asthma and life-threatening allergic lung conditions. Oily mist and coolant condition were what our Inspector would be looking for.

She made notes as she stopped to talk to operators and nod at proffered checklists.

"Find anything amiss?" I asked my slim black shadow.

"Mr Rogers, my job is to keep people safe, not to catch out anyone, as your tone suggests," she rebuked. "If you could show me machine seventy-six, where the injured employee worked?"

We followed the yellow-painted walkway around large van-size black boxes of CNC milling machines. Was she really not here to catch anyone out? I became highly aware of signs that normally I took for granted: the slightly sweet, metallic smell of coolant in the air, the staccato fire of coolant spray hitting the windows of the CNC machines, the hum of pumps and motors, air movement from extraction systems, the oily sheen on machine casings, brown staining on the two-storey-high white-panelled walls and roof. This was one of the cleanest machine shops I had worked in, but at that moment, I doubted that Gauge Precision and I had done enough.

The glass door of a CNC machine slid open. The operator leaned in, holding a slim, pistol-shaped gun attached to a red plastic airline. I waited for the ear-splitting hiss and whistle that would accompany him blowing coolant off the parts in the machine. I waited for the spray of mist that would rise around the operator, giving him the retirement presents of deafness and lung disease. I waited for the inspector to criticise me for allowing this bad practice to continue.

She stood to attention, the operator's guardian angel on high alert. I cringed. I had spent years trying to get the company to wash parts, vacuum parts, drain parts, but to no avail. The holes in blades were safety-critical and had to remain clear at every stage of production. All machining was super precise, and the jigs that held parts during cutting had to be totally free of anything that could cause even a nanometre of misalignment. Only airline blowing cleared them reliably.

SSSHHHsssssssshhhhh went the airline, with a hiss no louder than a leaking tyre valve. I breathed a sigh of surprised relief. Miss Fleming looked curiously at the airgun. *New guns!* I saw now that they had bought new guns that reduced the air pressure and diffused the air coming out of the end. No longer ear-splitting, and the mist created was minimal. I could have punched the air.

The inspector continued inspecting. She inspected the service and test stickers on the mist-extraction systems; she inspected the coolant management graphs on the sides of the machines; she lifted sump lids to inspect for brown tramp oil on the milky grey coolant; she checked for odours around the sump filters and watched operators in company-logo black polo shirts working, for compliance with door-opening delays.

I noticed that the part being machined on machine seventy-six looked very much like the part machined three weeks ago. It was a short, stubby blade. While the inspector's attention was focused on the sump at the rear of the machine, I took the opportunity to ask the operator about the part.

"It's an aero-engine turbine blade," the stocky, ruddy-faced man proffered, but unfortunately, he did not know what sort of turbine blade.

"See, that's the part number." He helpfully pointed to a thirteen-digit number on his worksheet. "We do machining for General Electric and Rolls Royce," he added proudly.

I watched him testing the dimensions of the part he had just taken off the machine. He used an automated laser scanner for the outside dimensions and then inserted specific-sized rods into the holes. He was painstakingly thorough.

Noticing me watching, he explained, "It's what they call safety-critical, you see? I stamp this to say that I have checked it, and if it breaks and causes a crash and they find it in the wreckage, they'll know it's me who let this one through. Every safety-critical part on a plane has been tested by someone like me who's put their name on it. God forbid any part of mine causes a crash."

"Would a broken blade cause a modern plane to crash?" I asked. "I thought that engines had to withstand bird strikes and breakages."

"Oh yeah, you wouldn't believe it. Most engine failure and air crashes happen at take-off, but there was a famous crash where broken blades from the engine cut the hydraulics line—and you can't fly a plane with no hydraulics, see. All goners. Mind, there was another that cut the lines to the tail in a DC10 where they had no steering. Half the passengers survived that time." The operator shuddered, vividly re-enacting these crashes in his head.

"And that's why you take such good care," I said. "Well done and thank you for telling me."

Abruptly, I felt like my heart had stopped. As I thanked him, the familiar digits, *SFT303* suddenly stood out in the thirteen-digit part number. Why had I not spotted this before? I had even written it down, for heaven's sakes!

"Can you tell which company this one is for?" I asked with bated breath.

"These are for Sterling Aerospace. We've been doing these for the last month or so."

"How long have you been working on this machine? Have you had any problems with your hands or anything?"

"You mean like Barry?" He turned his hands over. "No, nothing like that. Barry's hands were really bad like. Skin just split across all his knuckles, even on his fingers and thumbs, and he had scabs and sores so he couldn't move his fingers or pick things up. He was in a right state. I came on here after they changed the coolant. They didn't want no one else getting like Barry."

"Hmm," I replied.

"To be fair," the operator continued, "they did sort it out pretty quick and Barry's back at work down the road."

Miss Fleming had been listening to the exchange. She asked a few more questions about skin rashes and breathing problems in the workforce and asked the operator to show her the coolant management chart.

We moved on, studying a few other machines. Without sharing her thoughts, we returned to Philip in the meeting room.

"Thank you, Mr Rogers," she addressed me. "Thank you for your time. It has been very interesting meeting you. If you would send me your survey report when it is finished." She placed her business card on the table.

Mouth dry, I shook her proffered hand, holding on for a fraction longer than needed. I desperately craved her professional approval. What I really wanted at that moment, more than anything, was to stand by the EDM tank with her again.

I let go of her slim, warm hand, feeling momentarily, stupidly bereft.

After Miss Fleming had left, Philip sat crumpled, tired and grey in one of the meeting room chairs.

"Well, how do you think it went?" he asked, his pale eyes searching my face for clues. "I have to report to the MD tomorrow, and he will want to know if it's going to cost him."

Leaning back in my chair, I stretched and sighed. I really did not know what our inspector, Miss Fleming, had decided. I guessed that if we were in for an improvement notice, or worse still a prohibition notice, she would have told Philip and written some sort of statement for us to sign. We discussed this and decided that if she thought we had an issue to resolve, it would be in a letter, which wouldn't have the stigma or legal implications of a notice.

"Anyway." I frowned at Philip. "You didn't tell me that the airguns had changed. I was bricking it when I saw one picked up while she was with me."

"Ah, I thought you'd like them. From Sweden. They are very good, aren't they?" The older man smiled ingenuously.

I made my way back home with thoughts of turbine blades, dermatitis, air crashes and the desirable factory inspector in a glorious technicolour jumble.

Chapter 10
Investments and Invitations

Catrin was not actually a blood relative of Miranda, but that did not matter. I called my aunt that evening to give her the good news about my half-sister's awards.

"She is going on the inaugural flight, a week on Friday."

"Well, Henry, that is good news. You must be very proud."

I was proud. It mattered to me that Miranda thought it was a big deal. However, there was another reason why I'd called my journalist aunt.

"There's something you may be able to help me with," I started. I explained about the trail leading me to suspect cobalt-doctored turbine blades made for Sterling. "Do you know any reason why anyone would want to damage something of Sterling's? The company is run by a Richard Sterling, if that helps."

"Hm, Richard Sterling has been quite active recently. Active as in buying shares. Curiously, he holds very few shares in his family's company. However, he has a holding company, Nemesis Trading, and has been buying shares in Beech Tree Investments."

"What, the ones that were on the news the other day?"

"I dare say they could be. In what connection were they on the news?"

"There were environmental protestors blockading all their companies. Did you know they own Volantes?"

"They are an offshore investment company with a very wide portfolio of European and American businesses. They could own Volantes. Belgian, isn't it?"

"Mm. They're taking Sterling's new engine for their new aeroplane."

"You know more than I do, Henry." Miranda laughed.

I could feel tension developing across my forehead. The intricacies of business deals were beyond my comprehension. They were what excited both my aunt and my father.

"So, let me get this straight. Uh, Richard Sterling has shares in a company that own a company that is doing business with Sterling Ace, but he doesn't have shares in Sterling Ace himself?"

"You do realise it probably means that Richard Sterling may have enemies wanting to discredit the way he is running Sterling Ace, for a start," Miranda said. "He may have enemies resenting his purchase of shares in Beech Tree Investments."

"But why would anyone go to the trouble of sabotaging their engines?"

"From what you say you saw, it could be to get at Beech Tree Investments through Volantes, not Sterling at all. Have you thought of that?"

"Oh, but why?"

"We are looking at millions of pounds of share value, possibly tens of millions."

I raised my eyebrows and whistled. "Have you met Richard Sterling?"

"Hmm, once. He's a very clever man. Self-made millionaire by the time he was twenty-three, trading in the city at twenty-four, then laid low for a while and most recently appeared running Sterling Ace. He gets what he wants through connivance and manipulation, an autocrat. Personally, I can't stand the arrogant fellow."

"Oh? I met him." I said, remembering the welcome-but-it's-actually-a-brush-off in the Visitor Centre. "And yes, he did seem arrogant."

"Not a nice man to get involved with."

"No." I agreed.

"Right then, Henry. If you find out any more, let me know, and I'll do the same. Just promise me you'll be careful!"

I said goodbye to my business-minded aunt, while the connections between Sterling Ace, Volantes, Beech Tree, and now Richard Sterling, made a slippery spaghetti tangle in my brain.

***

Friday morning a week before Catrin's flight, and my paperwork day. Morning sunshine, birds soaring, life and growth took centre stage over the damp, chilled recesses of early-morning shadow below.

At 7:30, during breakfast, Catrin called me on my mobile. I was sitting at the old oak dining table with toast and a mug of tea.

"Catrin, what's up? Are you okay?" was my initial reaction to being called out of the blue. That, and a feeling that something bad had happened.

"Hal, you'll never guess, the Viktor XIV is coming to our airstrip on Monday!" Catrin sounded extraordinarily happy.

"That's good," I said cautiously. "I thought your CEO said it was flying on Friday?"

"It is, dummy. They have to get it here, don't they? Anyway, there's two things I wanted to tell you."

"Go on then." I imagined her happy face. "You're pregnant?"

"God no, don't be such an ass! This is important! First, I've put your name down for you plus a guest for Friday, so you should be getting your invitation by post or email, and next, it's about the Volantes engineers coming with the plane on Monday." The pitch of her voice had risen in excitement.

"I'm all ears." I took a bite of toast and leant back in my chair, smiling. It was hard not to share her enthusiasm despite my lingering doubts, the engine warning light on the dashboard of my consciousness. Was it triggered by the intricate knot of businesses involved? The cobalt puzzle?

"They are going to stay in Swansea and every day they are going to be working with us at Sterling."

"What do you mean by working with us?" I asked. *Am I missing something here?*

"They are going to be looking at all the processes in designing and building our engines, and they are looking at the work we are doing in research and development."

"So, you mean us as Sterling, not you personally." I accidentally put the dampers on her enthusiasm, trying to figure it out. I sipped the scalding tea.

"No, Hal, you just don't get it! Me and Ste, we're their facilitators; we're going to be looking after them."

"Wow, that's awesome that they've chosen you and Ste!"

"I'm going on the flight on Friday, so I guess that's why, and Stuart put Ste's name forward because he... Well, I don't know why. But Ste just knows so much about new aircraft you would not believe—he's in about six different aircraft design groups on LinkedIn and Facebook." Catrin rabbited away, unable to contain her exuberance.

She undersold herself. She hadn't been chosen because of the flight itself—she'd been chosen for the same reason she'd won the award that got her on that flight. She would be perfect for organising and assisting foreign engineers. I wasn't going to tell her that, though! But what a boost for her career.

I teased her. "So, what are you going to wear next week?"

"Oh no..." Catrin sounded crestfallen. She soon rallied. "I'll ask HR if I can have a new polo shirt, maybe tie my hair up in a turquoise-and-gold scarf."

"Very dramatic. I was only teasing—I'm sure no one will mind what you wear; it's you that counts."

As I was saying this, it occurred to me that putting the onus on "who you are" was pretty unhelpful. At least clothing was something she could actively control and have confidence in, like the makeup for the awards dinner.

"Actually, now you mention it, a bright new polo shirt would set the right tone," I amended.

"I knew you'd see it my way."

I gave a sigh of relief that I hadn't given her more cause for stress.

Catrin reminded me of another of her little victories. "You posted photos on Facebook! See, it didn't hurt."

"No, you were right," I conceded, sighing.

And then, as driven to change people and as subtle, this sword-wielding knight of the Crusades said, "You can bring a guest on Friday. You need a girlfriend, Hal."

I took another bite of toast. "That's enough, Catrin, go back to work," I laughed through my crumbs.

We said goodbyes and rang off.

I shared her happiness, all the time feeling a tingle of dread down my spine.

***

My mind, like a dog with a bone, kept returning to the Gauge Precision turbine blade machining fluid puzzle, turning it that way and this to see if it would break open.

What had caused the skin condition to flare up? Was it excess cobalt or was it triggered by endotoxin, or both combined? The metalworking fluid management report from maintenance had identified very high levels of bacteria two days before my survey. High levels of bacteria produced high levels of endotoxin in the sump, and therefore it would be in the mist released from the machine and generated by airline blowing.

The analysis laboratory had confirmed that the reported concentrations for my samples were right. There were definitely high levels of cobalt in the metalworking fluid. That meant that the excess cobalt had to have come from the parts they were machining at that time. I needed the identity of that part.

In the weeks prior to the survey, when Barry's skin condition started, they'd milled the high-pressure turbine blades for Sterling Ace, but the same blades from other batches had been going through the factory at the same time. I knew sump levels of metals were low in the other machines with the same part. That left only the batch being different, which should be impossible. I was still waiting for the individual serial numbers of parts that had been machined on CNC seventy-six before the coolant change.

The email from the quality assurance lab at Gauge apologised for finding no useful information. I emailed them back thanking them and asking for the quality data from the originating foundry for all the batches that had gone through that week.

Maybe I was overthinking, maybe I was simply wasting time. If cobalt aluminate had been used, then the blades would be harder. Maybe if the casting was harder, then the metalworking fluid got hotter during initial machining, and that made it warmer for the bacteria? But cobalt aluminate should not have been there.

But it was. Everything pointed to the impossibility of cobalt aluminate being present in high-pressure aerospace turbine blades. I even knew the engine. It was the SFT 303. Should I warn Catrin? What about Stuart, the engineering manager? What would I tell them? What could they do even if they believed me? I emailed Catrin for Stuart Nicklin's email address.

While I dilly-dallied, my report for Gauge Precision was not getting written. It was my contracted duty to identify the chemical causing ill health, show the employer how it was emitted, how the employee become exposed and what to do about it. Providing them with this information was law under the Control of Substances Hazardous to Health Regulations 2005 as amended.

Because the first word in the regulations' title was *Control*, I always made a point of recommending actions that would reduce emissions first. I thought through the controls for exposure to metalworking fluid mist. I was sure Gauge Precision had tried everything possible, but I had to make certain. This report was going to Isobel Fleming after all!

Health and safety managers seemed to like putting people in masks. Philip Wheatley and I preferred to contain the problem, not the person.

There was nothing here to stop me writing the report. I didn't want her reading about dermatitis and coming back with complaints about something else.

My stumbling point was I did not believe the problem I'd uncovered. It hinged on parts being tampered with before they got to Gauge Precision. How likely was that in real life?

I wrote the report of my investigation, giving the results as tables, with high levels in red, bar charts to show the exceptional height of results over normal, photographs of the machine enclosure and the extraction system, and made my conclusion and recommendations. I concluded that it was a one-off event triggered by endotoxin and increased levels of cobalt in the sump. The actions taken by the company were suitable. I recommended more frequent testing of sump fluid and suggested precautions to be taken by the affected employee should he return to work with nickel alloys.

I emailed the report to Miss Isobel Fleming of the HSE. I imagined her reading it. Would she agree? Would she find something I had overlooked? What was she wearing today? *Maybe I should call her.*

I could not concentrate. I went into the tiny kitchen for a drink and instead stared out of the window at the large, mature trees, every shade of green from the lime of unfurling oak to dark leylandii, with a foil of pink copper beech and maroon cherry. The textures varied across the view, a gently swaying, impossible painting. Carla, windswept, tanned, vividly real in the Romsdal Mountains, wild camping above Åndalsnes, encouraging me to look, to really see the view. So much beauty in the world and I could not capture it. I could not share it. I had no one to share with.

Kicking myself out of self-pity, I realised that if I really wanted, I could take a photo and post it on Facebook or Instagram. Remind people of the undemanding pleasure of nature. Yeah, maybe another day.

Activity, exercise, fresh air would clear my head. I grabbed my wallet, pulled the heavy, weathered front door closed and crunched down the gravel drive to the main road and the newsagents. Carton of milk and a paper, then back up the hill in light drizzle, smelling the scent of damp earth over oily wet roads and the sweet chemical smell of a two-stroke as a blue moped strained past. Front page of the paper headlined local election predictions masquerading as journalistic outrage. In the bottom right-hand corner was a photograph of lesser royals on an airfield with the headline, "Global Warming Betrayal".

Back in the cool, tiled hall of the house, I collected my post and climbed the wide stairs to my flat. I dumped the paper and post on the dining table and took the milk through to the kitchen. Kettle on, no melancholy tree thoughts, strong coffee with a splash of milk, and back to the table.

The A4 envelope from the post tray lay benignly under the damp newspaper, a catalyst that, once exposed, would herald the final challenge of this cobalt Jumanji game.

With mild interest, I scanned the paper, following the environmental story to page two as instructed. A duke and duchess who had been very public about global warming awareness had apparently been seen using a private plane, when according to their doctrine they should have used bicycles or the train. Further instruction in bold type told me to turn to page fifteen for more stories on global warming. I flipped over the pages and was confronted by a half-page photograph of protesters outside one of Sterling's big aero-engine rivals. There was a sea of all nationalities in everyday casual clothing, a woman on someone's shoulders shouting into a megaphone, banners with messages held aloft. "Planet Before Profit". Many people like me: my age, normal-looking, no extreme cult statements. The only middle-aged representatives in the throng were a couple of older men with grey ponytails, rubbing shoulders with students.

These protestors were targeting aero engines. The TV rebels were at Volantes. Sterling Ace ticked both sets of boxes. It could not be long before both groups ended up in Port Talbot.

I had never protested. I agreed with reducing global warming, but work and life just got in the way of making changes. I bought only what I needed and had been brought up to re-use and repair. Global warming was a problem just too big to get my head around. Maybe if I confronted it, I would be terrified at what I would find, and being terrified would help no one.

I strived to make a difference, to lead a useful life. My Aunt Miranda had saved a village in Africa by the time she was my age. She had identified foul water as the source of deaths and had raised funds for a well and water treatment. Aunt Miranda made things happen. In comparison, my tiny contribution seemed worthless.

Finally, I got around to the A4 envelope. I expected a brochure from the feel of it. More than a brochure, it turned out to be a glossy booklet about the Sterling Ace Aerospace company, with an embossed personal invitation for me plus a guest (as forewarned), to celebrate the first commercial flight of the Volantes Viktor XIV from their runway in Port Talbot. The invitation was for 11 a.m. with take-off at 12 noon on Friday the nineteenth of May. RSVP to their admin email address.

I put it on the mantelpiece next to Miss Fleming's card.

Isobel Fleming. My guest. Could I? Should I?

I went to pick up the phone.

Chapter 11

Unintended Invitation to Dinner

It took several indecisive false starts, but I finally worked up the courage. I was afraid she would and also would not answer, in equal measure. My fingers were clammy.

I remembered the enchanting inspector vividly: her poise, her confidence, her beautiful eyes.

Isobel Fleming answered her mobile. "Isobel Fleming HSE, can I help you?"

My chest tightened, heat rising. Brain in emergency fog mode, I tried, "Is that Ms Fleming?"

"Er, yes. Speaking."

Obviously, duh!

"Who is this? Is there something you want to speak with me about?" Her voice was terse.

Oh no, this conversation was not as easy as I thought it would be. I got up from the table and wandered to the tall bay window. *Get a grip, Hal!*

"Hi, it's Hal Rogers from Gauge Precision."

"Hello, Mr Rogers. Yes?" Polite, no warmth.

"I showed you round about a week ago."

"I remember. Thank you."

I tried to compose my invitation, but the silence just lengthened. I circled back to the table, unable to stay still.

She broke the silence. "Sorry, did you want to check on anything? I emailed a letter to Philip Wheatley. I presumed he would have forwarded it to you."

On my screen, there was an unopened email from Philip. It must have come when I was reading about global warming. Why had I called her without being prepared?

Mouth open, subconscious desire took the upper hand over the rational mush of my brain, and I said it. "Are you free for dinner tomorrow night?"

No, no, Hal! It was supposed to be the flight on Friday! What have you done?

"I expect you are far too busy, you have family, you don't eat dinners." Inanely I gabbled on, making excuses for her.

I heard a peal of laughter down the phone.

"In order, my answers are yes, yes but it doesn't matter, yes but the cat doesn't mind, and I do eat dinner. That covers it."

"That's great." *Where? When? Think—think, Hal!*

I couldn't guarantee any good restaurants at short notice. I would cook!

"Dinner at eight at my place in Cannock. Do you like Italian food? Are you okay with fish?"

"You realise I don't know you. You could be a mad axeman." She laughed. I sensed a wavering under the positive tone.

"I know you don't know me, but I promise it's just dinner. Two colleagues having dinner. You will be safe," I added.

"Okay," she decided. I admired her for being so intrepid. "I'll be round at eight; Italian would be lovely."

I gave her my address. Not wanting to intrude, I didn't ask where she would be coming from.

I felt overjoyed and nervous, my heart pounding, palms damp, slightly shaky.

I knew exactly what to cook. Starters would be bruschetta al pomodoro (garlic tomatoes on ciabatta), the main course oven-baked fish and Serrano ham with olive, capers, tomato sauce and salad leaves. No pudding, but coffee and chocolates to end. I couldn't wait! Isobel Fleming would be here in just over twenty-four hours!

Hunger drove me away from emails, quotes, and other outstanding reports. There was no room in the kitchen for a table, or even for stools, so I made a toasted sandwich and ate standing up. I collected the crumbs fallen onto the chopping board and the stainless-steel countertop. The contrast between the dull board and the shining metal struck a chord.

Contrast between shiny and not shiny, or not so dull and dull! Excitedly, I went back to the laptop to search for photos I had taken at Gauge. It was hard to tell, but the parts coming off some CNC machines were a deeper, duller grey than others. The blades themselves were not machined, only the ends of the fittings were, so the colour of the blades must have come from the foundry. Maybe different alloys made castings of different colours—or maybe, I thought, it was this cobalt aluminate layer. The cobalt aluminate that should not be there.

A good excuse to call my sister. I disturbed her at work in what I judged was a break.

"Hiya, Hal." Catrin was always chirpy.

I walked into the kitchen, soaking up the warmth of the sunshine. "Hiya yourself. How's things?"

"Oh, you'd never guess, but Ste's been quoting Mum all round R and D—you know, the allergic contact dermatitis thing about *Doom* and game warfare?"

"Uh oh, does Mum know?"

"Well, yes! Tony—you don't know him—well, his wife's had a baby and he met Mum when she came to do the six-week checks."

"I'm not following."

"Ste had told Tony what Mum had said, and then when he met her, Tony told Mum that Ste had told him. Anyway, Mum's famous now as the health visitor that knows about *Call of Duty* and dermatitis."

"Good grief," I said.

Catrin's voice rose an octave. "Isn't that exciting? We've got a famous mum!"

I laughed, imagining her excitedly waving her arms.

After a couple minutes' more chat during which I made my way back to the dining table, I told Catrin I was curious to know about an engine blade that had possibly caused an issue at Gauge. I read out the thirteen-digit part number from my notebook. Catrin recognised it and confirmed that it was for the engines destined for the Volantes Viktor XIV planes.

"We've sent six more engines over to Volantes in Belgium and now we've got overtime on the engine line. It's so frantic here, Hal! Was this to do with the man's hands you were telling us about at the dinner?"

"Mm, the results all point to the addition of cobalt aluminate. I'm thinking it was a coating applied to the high-pressure turbine blades. There's no other explanation. If that's the case, then there's a problem. Do you know anything about coating applied at the foundry?"

"Er, no, sorry Hal. Cobalt aluminate coating, you say? Are you sure you don't mean the thermal barrier ceramic coating? The blades have that." Then she muttered quickly, "Richard the boss is listening, not allowed to talk about our engines, hang on a minute."

A muffled exchange, then Catrin was back.

"All sorted. Can't wait to see you on Friday. Byeee, Hal!"

I Googled "thermal barrier ceramic layer". The article said that it was applied to the high-temperature parts in the jet engine, to insulate the blade by 70 to 150 degrees C against an air stream of 2000 degrees.

It confirmed what Ste had said, that the melting point of the parts was around 1400 degrees. That left a lot of questions but did at least clear up one: the TBC as it was known, was applied after initial machining, and it was not cobalt based. If, as I suspected, the cobalt aluminate layer had been applied to the casting, it would not be seen by employees at Sterling at all, as it would be hidden by the thermal barrier ceramic coating. I definitely needed to know what happened to the casting at the foundry.

I plucked up the courage and opened the email from Philip dot Wheatley at Gauge. Subject "HSE Visit". According to Philip, our inspector was satisfied with the actions taken and would be closing the case. Not even a fee for intervention! Isobel Fleming had conveyed her approval of having Hal Rogers as their occupational hygiene consultant. The specialist inspectors saw very many reports, and she had reported that apparently mine were the clearest, most thorough, and with the most practical recommendations!

Greatly cheered, I emailed a reply to Philip and asked if he had any contact details for the foundry that sent the Sterling turbine blades.

After that, I decided I had put it off for long enough. I emailed Stuart Nicklin at Sterling. I wrote that there was a coating of cobalt aluminate on some of the high-pressure turbine blades of the SFT 303. Cobalt aluminate that should not be there, that would break the turbine blade when it was running, that would crash the plane it was on.

I read it through. Put like that, it sounded far-fetched. Implausible. I erased it and just requested him to call me.

Anxiously, I waited for his call, not really sure what I was going to say. Time passed. I responded to more emails, ordered sample media, and kept the consultancy business running over the rest of the afternoon.

Just as I was thinking of packing up, a distraction jumped at me, third new email down. Sender Brian Robertson at Nicast Limited. Subject "Questions about Cobalt". I quickly tapped onto the email to open it, wondering if this was going to unravel my knotty problem.

"I have been given your contact details by a colleague. You have questions about casting aerospace alloys, I believe. Would a short tour of the foundry facility be helpful? I am available between 10 a.m. and 11 a.m. on Thursday to escort you and answer any questions. I look forward to hearing from you. Kindest Regards, Dr Brian Robertson, Chartered Chemist, Senior Metallurgist."

I smiled. Philip Wheatley had been pretty efficient at finding me a contact at the foundry.

I responded to the metallurgist with an equally low-key polite acceptance and set about clearing my calendar for Thursday morning.

It was getting on for seven o'clock when Stuart Nicklin called. Friday afternoon had passed, and I'd thought he wasn't going to call. When the phone rang, displaying his name, all thoughts of how I wanted to explain the problem went out of my head.

"Hello, Stuart. Thank you for getting back to me."

"Hal? What can I do for you?"

The man on the phone sounded reserved, polite, but crucially, intrigued.

"I don't know if you remember—at the awards dinner I mentioned cobalt coming from a turbine blade?" I paused, allowing him time to get in gear.

"You've been asking Catrin about cobalt aluminate coatings. She asked me too."

I nodded, despite being unseen. "Oh... Er, that's good then."

Stuart continued, sounding puzzled. "I'm afraid I don't understand why there shouldn't be a layer of cobalt aluminate. As far as I recall, aluminium is included as a sacrificial metal in these superalloys."

I realised I was hitting a problem here. Stuart was a top engineer, but he would be unaware of the crystal chemistry going on with cobalt aluminate. Production engineers knew everything about mechanical processes, not the nitty-gritty of what was going through them.

I spoke firmly. "Stuart, I have reason to believe that blades have been tampered with by giving them this coating. The coating will cause rapid creep crepitation in the blade itself once it gets to working temperature. This could shatter the turbine blade in flight."

"Right." Stuart paused briefly. Then he was back, speaking decisively. "If I were to check the turbine blades here, what would I be looking for?"

"Well, er, that's the thing. The blades will have a thermal barrier ceramic coating by now, so there will be nothing to see."

"Sorry, Hal—you're saying our blades may have been tampered with and the only way to find out is to remove the coating and destroy the blades?"

"Er, yes. But if a blade breaks in flight, then that could bring down the plane."

"Hal, I see what you're saying. Find me some concrete proof, then I'll arrange for tests on batches. I'm not saying I don't believe you, but I need proof to justify action."

I said nothing. He continued, "We cannot scrap millions of pounds worth of blades with no evidence. I am sure you understand that."

"It's not all the blades; we narrowed the coating down to one batch," I added helpfully.

"Great. Email the numbers over and I'll see to it they are quarantined."

"I don't have that information from Gauge Precision yet, I'm sorry."

"Hal, you are not making this easy." He sounded exasperated. "Okay, as soon as you get the serial numbers, email them over and I'll get the blades out of production."

I reckoned that was all that could be done for now.

What a waste of time! What had I been thinking? I'd known that call wouldn't go well the moment I answered it. I could argue a case on paper but verbally, I was always hopelessly ineffective. My cheeks burned.

And no physical proof. Just two odd results and a pile of conjecture.

***

The next morning, I bustled about the kitchen making sure I had everything and took a whole sea bass out of the freezer. I could not stop smiling. I hoped she would turn up. We could talk about the Sterling invitation. I could ask her if she had visited Italy. I wondered what car she drove. I didn't know her well enough to guess with any accuracy. To me, she seemed clever, practical, confident, in charge. I settled on a practical Ford Fiesta, or maybe a VW Golf.

I was munching scrambled eggs on toast for late breakfast when it occurred to me that I had been so engrossed in finding out about blades and coatings and possible tampering that I had given the 'why' of the scenario no thought at all. Aunt Miranda would have been hot on this angle first.

Was it coincidental that the parts that may have caused the issue were from the engine plant I had visited last week and would be seeing again this week?

Could the turbine blades be specifically targeting the new engine that was being produced for the high-speed Belgian Volantes plane? Or was it possible that someone was trying to destroy Richard Sterling?

So, what had Aunt Miranda said about Richard Sterling? Knowing nothing about finance, shares and holding companies, I opted for finding out more about who he was as a person: his childhood, education, employment. He was part of the wealthy Sterling family. I guessed he must have had a very privileged early life.

Sterling's LinkedIn profile held nothing beyond his current position as CEO of Sterling Ace Aerospace. I now knew he was forty-seven, fifteen years older than me. *So, I was nine and taken in by Aunt Miranda and Prue, when he was a rising star trading in the city.* A chill shuddered down my spine.

I did what all good investigators did and showered Google with search terms. Google didn't seem to realise I was trying to investigate something important. If I had wanted to know how many Richard Sterlings there were in the world, I would have asked! I tried a few more attempts, getting nowhere. This wasn't procrastination; this was just a waste of time.

If he had enemies, then it would be because he was someone with influence. I looked him up on the Companies House website to see if he had influential fingers in other people's pies. And there he was! He had been a director of one of the other engine manufacturers for four months, around two and a half years ago. Now, that resignation smacked of a disagreement somewhere. He was also a director of Nemesis Trading, just as Aunt Miranda had said.

Playing with what I could find on this website, I tried my own company and found myself on there, with my date of birth and my accountant's address.

Well, well! I looked up Sterling Ace Aerospace and found a multitude of Sterlings, including Andrew, Charles and Edward. Well, that answered a question I hadn't thought to ask!

I clicked back to Nemesis Trading and onto the "Filing History" tab. Three years previously, Nemesis Trading had bought seventy percent of Nicast Foundry Limited, the foundry that had sent the SFT 303 blades to Gauge Precision. I rubbed my forehead, wondering what all this meant. Could Richard Sterling have tried to get more business for Nicast through the board of the big engine manufacturer? Was he snubbed? Was there another foundry out there feeling threatened by Nicast or Richard Sterling? More questions for Aunt Miranda rather than Google.

My head was buzzing with a swarm of snippets of information, but I gave Google one last shot. I typed "Sterling success Wikipedia". The online encyclopaedia told me that page did not exist. No surprise there, but on the sidebar under "Results from Sister Projects" it came up trumps.

'A Biography of Power – Socioeconomic Implications for Success.' It was an article from *Industrial Psychology Today*. The first words grabbed me: *"Sterling Ace Aerospace hit gold by bringing their black sheep back into the fold."* I scanned the article, skimming over a copy about the facing of personal hardship being necessary for building resilience into a company mindset. Then I too, struck gold—or was the metaphor oil?

"Richard Sterling is the son of gifted engineer John Sterling, a relation of the wealthy industrial Sterling family. Richard's childhood was troubled. His mother left when he was thirteen. He was excluded from several Watford state schools before leaving with no qualifications, aged sixteen. At eighteen, he started work for his

father. In the intervening years, Richard collected cautions for burglary, car theft and possession of class A drugs. He spent three months in prison. Around the time that Richard joined his father's business, the small engineering company suffered a devastating fire. No cause was established. John Sterling appealed to the Sterling family for help, but none was forthcoming. Over the following few months, John Sterling threw his son out, lost the business and turned to alcohol."

So, I was wrong, then. Richard Sterling did not have a wealthy upbringing. He was on the outskirts of the Sterling empire and had not been a happy child. While I'd sought refuge of solitude in Wales, he used destruction. While I'd dreamed of acceptance by the bullies in school, Richard was dealing drugs with them. He'd ended up out on the street with no home and no income, no family. So how did he become CEO?

Hooked by the account, I forgot to look for enemies he may have made through his journey. Richard Sterling had defied all prophecies and used the welfare state to fund himself a place in a hostel, education and a computer. He studied business finance. While others in the hostel played through the night on PlayStations, he was running a cyber auction house, ultimately being bought out by eBay to become one of Britain's self-made millionaires under twenty-five. At the turn of the century, dot-com millionaires were the new gold rush. Richard Sterling took his millions to mop up in the city.

Photographs in the article showed the fully-formed version of the man I had met. White teeth, expensive suits, clinking glasses with celebrities of the day. The article suggested his rise to success was the natural outcome of a rough childhood. So, he had learned charm and manipulation; by the time he was my age, he was rich. What happened to that inner anger? Why had he become the CEO of the company that hadn't helped his father all those years ago?

I looked up from the phone, feeling slightly out of it, reliving the manic rollercoaster of Richard Sterling's early life. I flicked the kettle back on, my hands in the kitchen in Cannock, my time-warped mind in 1990s Watford.

With a jump, I surfaced back to the present. *Isobel Fleming's coming for dinner tonight!*

***

Table laid for two, open bottle of wine, fan-oven humming, ciabatta topping and sauce for fish made, I was ready. It was a beautiful evening; the sun had slipped from the departing rainclouds, bathing the world in gold.

Ten minutes to eight. Was she going to turn up? I washed the salad. Five minutes to eight. I couldn't really expect her to turn up to that shambolic invitation. Could I? Eight o'clock on the dot, willing her to appear on the drive. Five past eight. I knew I had made a fool of myself; the lovely evening I had imagined would not turn out. The weedy gravel was an empty disappointment, subdued further by a cloud passing the sun. I turned away from the window, surprised at how strongly I had wanted to see Isobel Fleming again.

Into the bedroom, ironed pink shirt off and comfy black T-shirt in hand... And it happened! The doorbell rang! I raced down the stairs two at a time, pulling the T-shirt over my head and calling out, "Coming!" in case she went away. I opened the door to a dream of a woman. Black hair with russet highlights framed her beautiful oval face. Her skin was lightly tanned, eyebrows sleek, firm, black lines, eyes hazel with long, soft, dark lashes. Her nose was straight, slightly raised at the bridge, her mouth a smile of perfect white teeth behind pale-pink-glossed lips. She looked like a Mediterranean film star.

The film star held out a bottle. "May I come in?" she asked my gawping statue.

I snapped to attention. "Yes, yes, do come in. Wow! I am so pleased you came—I mean, pleased to see you."

"Thank you for inviting me," she answered politely but with an amused curve of those beautiful lips. Subtle scent followed her in. Citrusy, floral, light, expensive.

I gestured up the stairs to the open door of my flat. "After you."

Belatedly, I realised I should have taken the bottle. Should I have given her a welcome peck on the cheek? Is that what people did? She was an HSE Inspector. She had power, standing, yet here she was seeing me. At my flat.

I closed the front door and turned to watch her figure mounting the stairs. She was wearing a long-sleeved, loose, embroidered white blouse tucked into slim-fit cream jeans. Her bottom swayed with each step, the muscles in the calves tightening. She had perfect, sculpted, muscled legs. The perfect woman.

"Smells delicious," she called as she entered the flat.

As the chef for the evening, I could smell only her fragrance. Delicious indeed.

Feeling on cloud nine, I eased myself into the role of perfect host. I took the bottle, at last. We shook hands, mutually assessing each other.

"Hal," I offered with a play-it-cool shrug.

"Isobel. Issy."

"Pleased to meet you, Issy. Again." I quipped.

She raised an eyebrow. Hazel eyes told of amusement, doubt, confusion. Was I not living up to the image she held?

"Wine?" I suggested, picking up the open bottle.

"That would be lovely, Hal, thank you." Hearing my name on her lips brought a flush to my cheeks.

The delicate atmosphere was as easy to shatter as the panes of Victorian float glass in my bay window. I asked how her drive over had been while I busied myself in the kitchen, giving her space to sort out her thoughts. I left the flat keys conspicuously on the table, hoping to reassure her that I was not a mad axeman intent on mad axeman-y things. She surprised me by coming forward.

"Can I help?" She stood in the doorway to the kitchen, looking with curiosity at my hanging utensils (no axes) and array of herbs growing on the windowsill.

I was just about to take the ciabatta out of the oven, ready to put the tomato and garlic topping on. Her white shirt and my cooked tomatoes seemed like a recipe for losing friends, so I indicated the pot of basil.

"Would you mind tearing up some basil leaves to scatter over the toast once I've spooned this on, please?"

We worked in companionable silence as the bruschetta was assembled on the stainless-steel workbench. I felt at peace. At that moment, the kitchen was home, and I would not change a thing.

I popped the tomato-topped, basil-sprinkled toast back in the oven for five minutes and added the foil-wrapped fish. We stood close together, not touching, staring out of the window. Watching the low sun catch the tips of the trees.

"Have you lived here long?" Issy sighed. "It is a beautiful building."

"Mm. This is my third year here," I answered, still looking straight ahead. I felt that if I looked at her, she would take a step away. "It's only rented. I'll probably move on, buy a place of my own when I'm ready. What about you, do you rent?"

"Sort of. My parents have a barn conversion near Stone and I'm using that."

"You live with your parents?" I glanced at her, hearing the incredulity tingeing my words.

"Ha, nothing like that." She laughed, taking that step back. "They are both professors in London and I'm taking up their escape cottage."

"That sounds very brainy—what do they teach?" I asked. Was it possible to be overawed by people you had never met?

"Dad—he's my step-father, really—teaches doctors how to manage acute trauma in battle zones. He's a doctor but he spent a long time in war zones, like Syria." Isobel's eyes gleamed, her face wonderfully animated as she spoke about him.

"He treats soldiers, like in Camp Bastion?" I suggested.

"No, it's far more than that. He volunteers for the International Red Cross in the hospitals in the towns. Civilians get caught up in fighting; sometimes schools, hospitals, churches are the targets. Women and children lose limbs, and all they're trying to do is to live, to get food, to wash clothes. He has delivered babies, sometimes conceived by soldiers of both sides raping women." Isobel was impassioned.

I was struck dumb by the horrors her few words had painted. I could think of no comment that did not sound crass.

"And your mother, you said she was a professor also?"

Isobel's eyes softened. I was even more aware of the long, dark lashes, sweeping down towards faint freckles on smooth cheeks. "Yes, she teaches political economics at the LSE."

"Incredible parents," I said politely. "I have a step-father, too. My father died when I was nine. Gareth is a teacher in a junior school. He taught me climbing and surfing." *And listening.* "My mum is a community midwife. They live in South Wales."

It seemed our backgrounds could not be more different; nothing in common except that we were both proud of our parents. That had to be a good thing, surely? Interesting, at least?

"Not too far away then. Do you see your parents much?" Isobel's question brought back the perennial guilt.

"Not as much as I should, I suppose." The guilt came tumbling out. "It's Mum. She keeps commenting, criticising me, without saying what she means, and it makes me annoyed and then guilty because I am annoyed, and then more annoyed because I feel guilty, and so on. So, I don't go. She was the same last weekend."

Isobel looked at me, her head on one side. Quietly, she said, "If your mother doesn't say what she means, how do you know it's a criticism?"

"I didn't come into the house straight away, and anyway I had emails on my phone to look at, and I couldn't face the mum thing. So, when Mum came out of the house, she said I was working too hard when she meant I should have come into the house to see her."

Isobel laughed. "Oh, dear! Your poor mother! Are you sure she meant that? Could it be you, criticising yourself?"

Maybe this lovely woman was right. "Don't be so sensible!"

I took our efforts out of the oven and turned the temperature down for the fish. Issy laid out two plates and I served up.

"Teamwork, huh!" I grinned at Issy, taking the plates to the table.

"To teamwork," she laughed, lifting her glass.

We toasted teamwork. We laughed together over toasting toast-teamwork. It was silly. Fun.

Toast eaten and fish safe in the oven, we popped outside to see her car. I'd guessed wrong.

Outside, the air was cool after the heat of the kitchen. On the gravel, a racy little soft-topped sports car greeted us in the fading light. This Fiat 124 Abarth, based on a Mazda MX5, was white with black wheels and a matte black bonnet. Black scorpions on the red and gold badges denoted it was something special. I noted the Bilstein dampers and Brembo brakes. It would be fun to drive, but not in the same league as my orange RS.

"What do you think?" Isobel asked, looking from me to the car with a smug smile. She knew I loved it.

"Can you drive it?" I blurted. *What, Hal? Why did you say that, you nugget?*

"Of course. Why wouldn't I?" Isobel was affronted, eyes flashing, heat in her cheeks.

"Extra power, rear-wheel drive, could be tricky, that's all," I replied mildly. *Why am I such a chauvinist?* "It's a beautiful machine, and I am dead envious." I laughed.

"Top speed one hundred and forty-five miles an hour, and I have done that," she said, proudly indicating her expertise. "Nought to sixty in six-point-eight seconds."

"Okay, how many points left on your licence?" I teased.

"All of them; I know when to push the revs. How about your licence?"

"Three left."

"Why does that not surprise me?" Issy remarked, tossing her fabulous mane.

"How do you mean?" I asked, a little hurt.

She took the sting out of her words. "You're a man of action. You do things as the moment takes you and then think about it after. Like inviting me here for dinner tonight."

It would be alright to be a man of action, and it certainly put a nicer slant on simply being unprepared. I gave an amused chuckle.

We went back indoors. The evening progressed in friendly harmony. We discussed life, the universe, cars. Issy was the most amazing person to talk to; she was amusing, intelligent and had an informed opinion on every subject we touched.

The fish course was fantastic, the coffees cautious. I badly wanted to kiss her, but there was never a suitable moment. Was Isobel engineering out opportunities? Maybe she didn't like me in a romantic way. Maybe she feared being alone with a barely known man in his domain. She had drunk only one glass of wine. Was that for driving, or was she retaining her wits in case I came on to her?

"Aeroplanes one of your hobbies, Hal?" Issy asked.

I looked up in surprise.

"You have a pile of research papers." She pointed out my work pile, topped with the aerospace information I had printed from Google.

Lowering my stratospheric eyebrows, I decided to share. "I believe there is an issue with some turbine blades that were at Gauge. I don't know what it is. Everyone says there can't be a problem, but I have a really bad gut feeling about it. I think it's important. I don't know about aeroplanes, so I'm finding out as much as I can."

"Okay, want to run it by me? I don't know about planes either, but if you explain to me what you know, maybe it would clarify it?"

"I'll bore you," I warned with a smile.

Issy sat looking at me, listening with elbows on the table, her pointed chin on one slim hand as I haltingly explained how each piece of information linked to the next. Her frown deepened.

Issy summarised: "One particular batch of turbine blades, but no others, for reasons unknown, were probably treated with cobalt aluminate at the foundry. This will weaken them at high temperatures. They are destined for the very high temperature fans of aero engines where they will surely break. Breakage in an engine may bring the plane down."

"Yes, that's as far as I've got." I nodded.

"Why would someone go to all that trouble?" Head tilted, Issy looked at me with a sceptical raised eyebrow. "Surely a bomb would be simpler and more effective?"

"Mm, you'd think so, wouldn't you?"

"Could it be personal?"

"Well, funny you should say that. I was thinking along those lines myself. Richard Sterling—he's the CEO of Sterling Ace Aerospace—also owns part of the foundry that sent out these blades. My aunt, who's a business journalist, thinks that someone may have a grudge against him."

"There could be someone out there trying to destroy this man's engines by using his own foundry to cast faulty parts?"

"Could be. Talk of adding insult to injury!"

"Do you have any evidence?" asked Issy the HSE Inspector.

"Well, no," I said, frustrated.

"Try the foundry then," suggested Issy. "But keep me informed, if you would. You should contact Sterling Ace with your concerns."

"I have, but there's nothing they can check until Gauge get me the serial numbers for the batch." Total inadequacy swamped my words.

This beautiful, intelligent woman came up with a suggestion. "Do they use an XRF gun to segregate scrap?"

"What's that?"

"It's a small handheld device that you point at a metal, and it comes up with the rough composition. It's used by companies when they need to identify and separate their scrap."

"Really?" I was excited, certain Sterling would have one. Perhaps, because it used X-rays, it would see through the coating as well. "You are brilliant!" I gave her a huge smile. "I'll tell Catrin tomorrow and Stuart on Monday."

She just shrugged. Job done. Not one to bask in glory. My heart flip-flopped as I caught her eye.

Coffees finished, the sun had gone down an hour ago and the dusk had deepened into night.

Issy got up to leave. "Thank you for a lovely evening, Hal."

"Thank you for coming, Issy. I think you were brave to come here."

"Foolhardy, you mean!" She laughed.

"But it turned out well, didn't it?"

"Uh-huh. We should have dinner again sometime, maybe my place?" Issy offered the loose invitation.

"Love to." I smiled. "Oh, that reminds me." I grabbed the Sterling invitation from the mantelpiece. "This Friday, would you like to be my guest at an inaugural flight in Port Talbot? We don't go up; we just watch the plane take off."

"Sounds interesting. How do we get down there?"

"I could take you down in the truck; you can leave your car here."

"How about we meet halfway between yours and mine? I know a pub car park we can use, just off the Chase," Issy suggested, writing down the pub's initials and time on the back of her business card, which was also on the mantelpiece. "Meet at eight a.m.?"

I turned the brass handle of the front door. This was it, last chance. Issy held out her hand and I chickened out, lightly kissing her fingers instead. Ever gallant. A fraud. Not the impassioned kiss of a true action man!

Amusement and fleeting relief flitted across her face.

With a last smile, she left, calling out, "See you Friday," as she unlocked her car.

The 124 Abarth roared into life and crunched down the gravel. I watched it go, hoping the little white car would turn round. It disappeared into the night.

Issy could not have known how her words about finding the answer at the foundry would be so painfully prophetic.

Chapter 12
Serious Doubts

Sunday, full of enthusiasm for the XRF gun, I called Catrin. Outside the flat's bay window, sun poured down the gravel drive. It was a beautiful day.

"Hiya, Hal!"

"How are you doing?" I asked the cheerful voice.

"Sandy!"

Surfing, I diagnosed. "Gower?"

"Where else! Dad, me and Ste have been down to Llangennith. Good surf, and I did a bottom turn!"

I pictured her, blonde, windswept, expertly flipping her board on the wave. Ste had to be smitten. "Well done you."

"Nearly as good as you, now." She laughed, happily.

"So, you had a good time then."

"Uh-huh." Catrin waited for me to say why I had rung.

"I've got an idea about the turbine blades..."

"Oh, not the cobalt again! Hal, it's the weekend." Catrin sounded exasperated.

I felt a touch guilty, but carried on regardless. "I think there is a way to test the turbine blades."

Catrin allowed me to continue, saying, "Go on then. Which is?"

"It's an X-ray fluorescence gun. You point it at the part, and its screen comes up with the metals in the part."

"I don't think we've got one of those. At least, I've never seen one. I'll ask tomorrow if you like."

"Issy, she said it's used for sorting scrap."

My sister pounced. "Issy? A woman? You've called me at the weekend about something a woman told you? You must have seen her yesterday! Hal, what's this Issy like?"

"Er, she's just someone I know from work." A clever, exciting, beautiful someone.

"Come on, she's more than that! I can tell!" Catrin was in full swing.

"Her name is Isobel Fleming, and she's a factory inspector."

"Ooooh! Are you going out with her?" Excitement shot Catrin's voice higher.

I would love that to be true, but it was too soon. "No."

"I know—you could invite her down here on Friday. I could meet her!"

"Er, I have." I smiled as I heard her squeal. "Are you all set for the Belgian engineers coming tomorrow?"

"Yes, ready as I'll ever be! I've got a presentation for them tomorrow and a brilliant schedule with Ste. Trouble is the management are going nuts about it. They've even got decorators in today, sprucing up the factory offices."

"Are you okay with that pressure?"

"No worries!"

We chatted, I sent my love to Mum and Gareth, then rang off.

Was Catrin right? Was I really concentrating too much on the cobalt-in-the-sump enigma? From all I had read, it meant jet engines and aeroplanes would be at risk once the blades were in use. Maybe I'd caught this sense of doom, death, destruction from the CNC operators at Gauge with their safety-critical parts.

I mulled over it for the rest of Sunday. Even the thought of introducing Catrin to Issy barely lifted my gloom.

***

Misty, morose Monday morning, and I found out that Catrin was as good as her word and had asked Ste and Stuart about the XRF gun. Whilst I was trying to write reports, an email from Stuart Nicklin pinged in. Politely, he thanked me for the information about the XRF gun. He then assured me that he would get Ste onto it as soon as the Belgian visit was over. He had copied Ste into the email. What more could I do?

At lunchtime, my phone rang, the mobile number unrecognised. I lay down my sandwich.

"Good morning. Hal Rogers IDP."

"Hal, it's Ste at Sterling."

That surprised me. We hadn't communicated since the awards evening.

"Oh! Hi, Ste. How are you?"

"Good thanks. How serious is this cobalt aluminate coating?"

"It's not supposed to be on high-pressure turbine blades because it encourages creep crepitation at high temperature and pressure. It'll make the blade shatter." How many times had I tried to convince myself of this since yesterday?

"Stuart's been discussing this with me and Richard Sterling. They both agree that even if you're right, and Richard Sterling is sceptical, you're worrying over nothing."

"Why have they said that?" I felt a brick wall being built between me and my sister's workplace.

"It's highly unlikely you'll get two or more in an engine. They said creep crepitation takes thousands of flying hours to develop. And these days, especially with the SFT 303 casing, if a blade did break in an engine, it would just be ejected out in the exhaust."

I recalled the accounts of crashes on Google and from the CNC operators at Gauge. "But..."

"Look, Hal—Stuart and Richard want this hushed up until next week. We need this visit and the flight on Friday to go smoothly. There are a lot of orders; the whole future of the company is riding on it."

It seemed that Ste had been told to warn me off. "But..."

"Richard says even if there is an issue, it's not an immediate threat. We can find it and resolve it after the flight."

"But the cobalt really is there. And it should not be. A coating in the foundry is the only explanation, and these parts are safety-critical."

"Hal, look, I'm on your side. I believe you, but what can I say to Stuart and Richard when they think your results were wrong in any case?"

My head could not think straight. "I don't know."

"Could the sump fluid samples have been mixed up? Could you have mixed them up when you labelled them?"

Did Ste think this was helping? I had my own doubts, never mind his new ones. I thought back to the investigation. I had been talking to the machine operators the whole time I had been taking samples. I thought I had labelled them as I went along, but what if I had mixed them up without noticing? My face burned; my fingers tingled.

"Can you get another sample?"

"Er, no. The sump was cleaned out the day after I took the sample. The contents were sent for disposal."

"Did you identify which individual blades were machined?"

"Gauge are still trying to find this information."

"Hal, everyone here is going crazy trying to impress the Volantes engineers. I really want to help you solve this, though."

Did he really? He was sounding like a management puppet.

"Ste, thanks for being so honest. If you have the chance, maybe you could find out if Sterling has an XRF gun?"

"I have. The waste management company have a five-thousand-pound Bruker. I haven't told Stuart yet, but I don't think it will do what you want."

"Oh, why not?"

"The high-pressure blades have no bare-cast surfaces. The blades have a coating of ceramic and the shanks have had all their original surface machined away."

I couldn't think of what to say. Hearing Ste reporting all this, suddenly made the whole cobalt thing seem like a pointless fiasco. Maybe I had muddled up the samples and the results were wrong. Maybe Barry's dermatitis came from just the bacterial endotoxin in the machine. Maybe there was no issue.

"Okay, thanks for calling, Ste." I threw the sandwich in the bin.

"Hey, man, look, I'm with you. If you can find any proof, I'll be right there, pressuring Stuart to act straight away."

"Good to hear." I smiled wanly and hung up.

I sighed and looked unseeing out of the window, into the distance. I'd never had to convince anyone on such flimsy grounds before. In my mind, the evidence had been solid as rock, but now it was crumbling. I was no longer sure I wasn't adding two and two and getting five. Would there really be an engine, an aeroplane at stake? Had the blades been coated in cobalt aluminate at all? There was no proof other than a sump sample and an air sample. And the contents of the sump had been gone for a month now.

Issy knew the story behind Barry's hands. She had believed me the other evening. I needed to talk to her. I needed to hear her tell me I was on the right lines. Would I disappoint her with my doubts? I chewed my lip indecisively.

I didn't risk calling Issy. I would still see what I could find at the foundry on Thursday. I slept on the problem.

***

Next morning, spring showers splashed into short-lived puddles on the gravel outside the flat. My shirt clung to my shoulders as I lifted the last toolbox of kit into the back of the pickup. Setting off for the Birmingham spice factory, I wondered whether I should cancel the visit to the Nicast foundry. It would just be a waste of time for both me and the Dr Robertson person who had offered to show me round. I should focus on my clients and their real needs, not a puzzle that no one was concerned about!

Then, of course, Friday, and the prospect of sharing a journey and a whole day with Isobel Fleming. Just the rest of the week to get through. Hmm—*just*.

The whole of Tuesday had been booked for my client's spice factory, measuring inhalation exposures to spice dusts and chapatti flour. A tantalising aromatic smell from the factory reached out across the main arterial dual carriageway on my approach. The spices tickled my memory, recalling pictures of the Indian and Pakistani first-generation immigrant workforce with limited English on the factory floor. Management were second or third generation, with smart suits and superb English. They always gave me a warm welcome.

I was looking forward to my visit. I wanted to protect these people who communicated with me by smiles and gestures in this scented factory. It was up to me to prevent them from becoming ill through work.

The reason I measured dust from the spices and flour was that exposure to these dusts is in the top three causes of industrial asthma. The company knew they had a legal and moral duty to reduce exposures to levels as low as is reasonably practicable. Every year I was impressed by the changes they made. This year was the twenty-five-kilogram flour bagging operation's turn.

Short, rotund Ramon, the Health and Safety Manager, greeted me with a wide beam across his chubby face. I would try my best for him.

"Good to see you, Hal. How have you been?" He spoke with perfectly enunciated English overlying his Pakistani accent.

"Fine thanks, Ramon," I answered, shaking hands. "How are you and your boys?"

"Ah, they are growing, growing up too fast. I cannot keep up," the stout little man replied, shaking his head comically. I wasn't sure if he meant keeping up with technology, knowledge or simply height.

"And your sister?" I asked, remembering that she had been ill. Last time I saw him, he was planning to go back to Pakistan to see her.

"My sister is better, thank you. But she is in terrible danger in Pakistan."

"Oh?"

He sat at his ornate, inlaid desk and steepled his fingertips together, a frown across his brow. "You remember she is a teacher? In Pakistan, they do not trust teachers. The teachers are flogged and killed. My sister escaped with my elderly mother to friends in Jordan."

"Is she safe in Jordan?" I asked, remembering the horrors in the Middle East that Isobel had described.

"She is safe for now, but she cannot stay there forever. I worry." He sighed. "It is hard when my family are far away and there are terrible things happening in my country."

What if it were Catrin? What had Isobel's father seen in the war-torn cities?

"I am sorry." I gave him a twisted smile of sympathy. I did not know what to say. If it were my sister, I would be panicking with worry and on the next flight out to rescue her myself.

He gave a sharp sigh and sat up in his chair, eyes bright and smile back in place, changing the subject. "You are here to see our new machine."

"Yes, looking forward to seeing what you have done." I smiled back. "What do you think of it?"

"There will be no problem now. It is enclosed. The flour comes from the flour mill through tubes."

I was curious, thoughts of the foundry overlaid by flour. My last memory of the valve-packer bagging flour was of a huge cloud of the stuff, of snowman operators protected with filtered-air hoods, footprints on the floor.

The company had made huge improvements. The whole process had changed to an automated and enclosed form-fill-and-seal packer, with extraction systems removing loose dust from the enclosure. Bags came out of the enclosure filled, sealed and flattened ready for stacking.

I was gratified to see that the new dust extraction system had been installed by Darren's company, Dustco. I recommended his company when I could because their extraction systems were well designed and simple to maintain. They did the job. This one was no exception. The extraction filter unit had a pressure gauge fitted to the side panel, and a register of daily checks was held on with a magnet. Isobel Fleming the Inspector would have been pleased to see that, I thought with a nod.

This year there were just two operators, no masks needed, and their blue overalls were clean. I was extremely pleased.

With air samplers fitted to the employees and a few other samplers strategically dotted about, I stayed to observe the process. I photographed every improvement that reduced dust emission, such as the M-class vacuum cleaner which had replaced the broom. The dust exposure results were going to look great on a bar chart alongside last year's.

Driving back to the flat with my flour dust samples, my phone rang on the hands-free. Dustco Darren came up. I connected.

"Alright, Darren?"

"A'right, mate? Got a minute?" Darren's voice filled the cab with cheer.

I grinned. "What can I do for you? I'm just coming back from the spice company. Good job you did on the flour bagger, by the way."

"Cheers!" Darren sounded surprised that I'd commended him. "Look, one of the dust extractors at Gauge Precision is playing up. You couldn't see your way to bringing your test kit over, could you?"

"When? I've only got tomorrow free this week."

Reports would have to wait. "That'll do, see you 'round nine?"

"Yep, yeah, that's fine. So, how are you?" I pulled off the road into a supermarket car park.

"She wants me to come back. She keeps calling, begging. I don't know what to do."

I remembered his misery, the bruises, the poisonous messages on social media. I killed the engine.

"No, don't do it. You can't go back. She'll put you through hell again, especially if she's still drinking."

"She isn't drinking. She says she misses me, the fun we had. We did have some stonking times, Hal."

I sighed. "Seriously Darren, she won't change. Don't go back to her."

"Well, we'll see."

He was going to go back to his ex-wife. I knew it. I would have a chat with him tomorrow at Gauge.

"Better go. I'll see you tomorrow. And don't do anything stupid."

We said our goodbyes and hung up. I started the truck up.

Oh, Darren, that woman's done you nothing but harm. Silly, frustrating man.

***

"Smoke" billowed around the manual grinding booth at Gauge. I waved my hand to get the acid mist out of my face. I coughed as it caught in my throat.

"You're right—it's definitely not drawing," I spluttered.

Darren, pleased as punch with himself today, laughed at my discomfort. I had puffed sulphuric acid mist from a Drager air current detector tube around the extraction hood to show where the air was moving. I hadn't expected it not to be moving at all.

"But look." Darren reached up with a piece of paper and showed a blast of air coming from the exhaust of the extraction filter unit.

"How's the filter pressure?"

"Normal, I'd say. Maybe a bit high."

"And the fan pressure?"

Darren connected the pressure gauge to the spigot in the fan chamber. "Low. But it's not running backwards, if that's what you think." Darren had the local exhaust ventilation testing P601 qualification but rarely measured pressures in a system other than across the filter, which he had always done anyway. "Do you think there's a blockage?"

"Nope. Well, there might be," I amended.

There was air going through the extraction unit, but it wasn't coming from this hood in front of us. Also, low suction pressure meant that the fan was having an easy time of it. It wasn't sucking against a blockage. That didn't mean there couldn't be a blockage from this hood as well. The main problem had to be a leak, a hole, a disconnected duct.

"Make yer mind up! Is there a blockage or not? Get your pointy thing out and take some measurements." Darren was in a jovial mood today. He knew that we used a pitot static tube, and here he was calling it a pointy thing. Silly man. I knew what he'd done—he'd got back with his ex. He was always like this when she was around.

"Come with me." I called Darren round the back of the extractor and crouched under the benches, following the main duct. At the first junction, I spotted it: the duct's seam had split wide open. Now air was entering the duct from under the bench rather than from the hood above it. There was almost no resistance for the air to enter from here.

"There you go!" I said triumphantly.

"Here, take this tape and wrap it round."

"I don't think so—that's your job. I'm off to have a word with the lab."

I stood up, brushing the sparkling grinding dust from my overalls. I had to know for certain. "You went out with her again last night, didn't you?"

"It's none of your business!"

"Of course it's my business. She's bad for you."

"She's changed. She doesn't drink now."

I sighed. He'd said that before. "Whatever. Meet you back at the canteen. I've got things to do, people to see."

I walked away from the manual grinding benches, past the blue CNC grinder where I had remembered Barry working, past big, black CNC machine seventy-six and on to the offices and the lab. I was going to pick up the quality test sheets for the turbine blades that the Nicast foundry had sent with the castings. I knocked on the door. The bearded technician I had previously met with Philip ushered me in. There were white machines on the benches, but hardly any chemicals. It was more like a high-tech office than a school chemistry lab.

"We didn't email them over because there is nothing to see," he explained. "Scanning would have been pointless."

I looked at the two-inch-thick pile. Reading between the lines, scanning would have been a real pain of a job.

I seriously hoped I could spot a discrepancy that these scientists hadn't. I still had no proof to fit my theory of doctored blades, sabotaged engines.

The pile of reports covered all the HP-774SFT303X9 castings ever received by Gauge. I turned over the pages of the top report. They gave the serial number of the part and the composition of the alloy, plus images from X-rays of the inner shape of the casting and electron micrographs of the grain of the parts. The sheets were stamped with the date the part was shipped to Gauge.

Trying not to panic over the enormity of the task, I placed all the sheets less than a month old in one pile and then concentrated on the remainder.

To my untrained eye, they looked identical, as the technician had warned. On paper at least, there were no odd batches leaving the foundry.

I thanked the technician and left him to his work.

One vital piece of information I did find was the serial numbers of the batches of blades that went through when Barry's hands started to react. The ones from his machine were there, but their numbers were mixed with others that had been milled on neighbouring machines. I was getting closer but was not there yet.

I spotted Philip at his desk and he called over, "Good morning, Hal. What brings you here?"

"Just checking out one of the dust extractors with Darren from Dustco. I thought I would pick up the original turbine blade quality reports from the lab."

"They didn't send them?"

"No, I think it was an impossible ask, now I've seen them. I haven't got the batch numbers either."

He set down the reports he'd been looking at. "I'll have a word. They should have at least let you know." He straightened the papers on his desk. "Coffee?"

I was pleased to see that he looked back to his normal self. He no longer looked gaunt and defeated.

"Why not?" I smiled. "I told Darren I'd meet him in the canteen. Okay to go there?"

"As good as any. Let's get those batch serial numbers first." At least Philip wasn't questioning my continued pursuit of an answer. "Did you find anything useful in the quality reports?"

"Er, no. They all look the same."

"What do you plan to do next?"

"I'm visiting Nicast tomorrow. I'm being shown round."

Philip nodded, not surprised. But then, he wouldn't be—he'd arranged for Dr Robertson at Nicast to email me.

We approached the production manager's desk, and Philip said, "Morning, Graham. Could you get one of your young ladies to run off a list of all the parts machined on seventy-six last month? I'll be much obliged if she could give it to my friend here before he leaves."

We continued towards the canteen.

"The occupational health doctor is very pleased with how well Barry's hands have healed," Philip told me.

"That's good news. Did they say anything about asthma?"

"By the time Barry saw the doctor, his symptoms had gone. It's been put down to a virus."

I felt uneasy at this. All my training pointed to asthma because of exposure to endotoxin and nickel and cobalt. But if he was fine now, fair enough. I just did not want him going back into the production area.

"So, he's staying in the toolroom, then?"

"It depends whether we get short-staffed in production. The odd day won't matter."

"I don't think that's wise, Philip."

"He knows what to look out for. He'll be fine."

Barry may well recognise reddening of his fingers, a tight chest at night, but would he be pressurised into working in production to keep his job? Many employees knowingly risk their health to keep working. I sighed, defeated.

***

That evening, I emailed the list of suspect serial numbers to Catrin and Ste. I still wanted to talk to Issy, but driving to and from Gauge had helped sort out my thoughts. I was right about there being excess cobalt and aluminium in the sump of machine seventy-six, and that meant blades had been weakened by a cobalt aluminate coating in the foundry. Maybe the aerospace engineers were right and this would not in itself cause catastrophe. So why tamper with blades? Aunt Miranda said there were millions of pounds at stake. Maybe the tampering people had found a way to make this creep crepitation happen faster than the usual thousand hours flying time. I wanted answers from that foundry.

Chapter 13
Nicast Foundry Tour

Thursday morning found me excited to be driving into the historic engineering heart of the West Midlands, searching for the answer to a metal anomaly. I cut through streets of preserved brick façades with broken windows, silhouettes of rusting girders for roofs. The traditional integrity of the region was fast ebbing away. Industrial vultures and carrion crows, skip merchants and scrap dealers proliferated within the stripped carcasses of deceased factories.

New life replaced the old, with sites cleared and steel-clad industrial units providing an environment for new technology; businesses making robots, batteries, electronic doors, UPVC window frames. Modern production not inclined to work with the old.

Monuments to industry on the Black Country Route roundabouts were the only nod to tradition: bronze pit pony, steel cogs, stainless steel welding tip with a helix of wire for shielding gas. Who would understand these? Or care?

The Nicast foundry, backing onto a restored canal on the outskirts of Dudley, had developed from, but uncomfortably retained, its heavy engineering iron foundry roots of the late Victorian times. It was essentially a wide red brick building, not dissimilar to a Victorian railway station from the outside, with four roof bays running front to back. The apex of the right-hand end roof was raised by around a metre. Daylight could be seen under the raised portion. I surmised that the louvres under it acted as a vent, removing hot fume and noxious gases from the furnaces. A single tall brick chimney rose from the building, retained for posterity and now supporting a telecommunications dish.

The most obvious sign that the traditional iron foundry had developed into a state-of-the-art aerospace alloy casting foundry was the glittering, modern brick-and-glass extension to the front of the building. It was also reflected in the lack of parking, I thought, as I reversed round cars and barriers to get the length of the pickup into the remaining space allocated to visitors.

Parked up, I sent Philip a text with belated thanks for contacting the metallurgist here.

Reception was a lemon London Brick porch over the front of the original red-brick main entrance, to the side of the glass extension. It housed two low seats, an array of CCTV screens, and a cheerful girl behind a high worktop. It seemed that I was expected. I pinned the visitor badge onto my shirt and sat, as instructed, on one of the seats to watch a health and safety induction video. The video lasted about ten minutes. I signed to confirm that I had watched it, was wearing safety boots and safety glasses and did not have a pacemaker. A standard disclaimer. No pen. No surprise—I was wary of this company already.

I turned as the swing doors into the main building opened and a slight man walked in. He was about ten years older than me, with grey hair morphing into a ginger ponytail, and wore jeans and a white lab coat. He assessed me through wire-framed prescription safety glasses. He looked round in case another visitor should pop up, then, evidently deciding I must be Hal Rogers, approached with a wide but slightly apologetic smile.

"Come on through," he said, belatedly shaking my hand. "I'm Brian."

"Thank you for seeing me, Brian."

"I was told you have questions to ask pertaining to the casting process. Am I right?"

"I just wanted to know how it would be possible for a casting to lose high levels of cobalt in a CNC machine during the initial milling jobs."

"That would not be possible," the chemist assured me, his Adam's apple bobbing up and down disconcertingly in a scraggy neck. "The alloy castings we produce cannot dissolve in metalworking fluid. I am happy to show you proof, but I fear you are wasting your time."

There it was again, I thought in dismay. Someone telling me my only explanation was not possible.

"The chemistry of superalloys is quite complex, but I believe you are talking about the cobalt aluminate used to harden the low-temperature structures." The chemist's blue eyes, enlarged by the glasses, were intent.

"It's not used on all parts?" I queried, wanting confirmation that it should not be used on high-temperature blades.

"No, only low-temperature blades and vanes. We use it mostly on blades used for gas turbines in power generation."

"Oh," I said, wondering how I was going to steer this to the suspect Sterling blades. I would have to watch what I said. As Issy had suggested, if this was a plot against Richard Sterling, then the mastermind could be working here, in this foundry, right now.

Brian was watching me, wearing an anticipatory smile. "What do you know about investment casting?"

"Very little," I replied. "I know it is called lost-wax and plaster is used, but I couldn't tell you how."

This answer pleased my lab-man. Checking a bright-blue, plastic watch face, as wide as his bony wrist, he smiled. I couldn't help but notice the lines from his eyes joined the lines coming up from his mouth on his weathered face. He looked like the old-timer surfers with longboards back at the Gower.

"We shall start at the beginning, if you think that would be helpful." He stuck his hands in his lab coat pockets, taking the weight on one leg, and waited for my reply before moving off.

"That would be great," I said.

I couldn't wait to see how turbine blades were cast. I would keep an eye out for anyone with the opportunity to doctor the blades, if that was what had happened.

We marched through the office areas and out onto the concrete floor, edging a warm, brightly lit area of tanks, yellow-painted raised iron walkways and warnings of robots. Following a green-painted path, we eventually passed into a fresher, low-ceilinged room containing black benches. On each bench, bright green three-dimensional wax structures were tended by men and women in maroon company polo shirts.

"You see these wax parts?"

They looked exactly like wax copies of the parts I had seen at Gauge Precision.

"They are pressed around a ceramic core in one of four presses." Brian pointed to machines between the benches. Next to the machines were trays of plaster comb shapes. "The wax technicians fix them onto a tree. The whole tree will eventually become the casting, including the connectors, or sprue. The core will become the cooling holes in the casting."

"Like parts on an Airfix kit," I ventured, thinking of the plastic models I'd made in the mists of time.

"Sprue connectors are similar, as they enable multiple parts to be made from a single casting. Please don't confuse plastic injection moulding with casting," Brian reprimanded.

"The technicians are supremely skilful wax artists; they spot and correct any irregularities and imperfections," my host continued. "The room must be kept at a specific temperature and humidity to maintain the wax in optimal condition. The wax formers are attached to these plates that are hung from the overhead conveyor." I watched as one operator hung the green trees upside down from the orange conveyor. It passed through a wall recess into the tank area we had walked past.

Following the route of the wax tree from a distance, we backtracked through the white-painted door and into the humid tank room. We stayed on the green path while the wax trees passed into an area where signs warned "Danger: robot moves without warning", with a pictogram of a person being flung off their feet by a robot arm.

"There is no access into the rainer area because of the robot, but I can show you how the shell, er, mould is made." Brian puffed his chest out as he spoke, suggesting confidence in his knowledge. "This is the shell process. The larger tanks in front of us contain colloidal silica solution. The solution acts as a glue for the powdered refractory silicates in the rainer. The smaller tank contains the cobalt aluminate that you were asking about. Some parts are dipped in this first and sent round the track to dry before being dipped into colloidal silica."

Brian Robertson beckoned me up steps to a yellow-painted steel walkway along the front of the tanks. The larger tanks, which were around three metres high and three metres across, held a white translucent liquid. The smaller tank, about half the size, was filled with an opaque liquid the colour of cornflowers. I watched the process as upside-down trays on the conveyor approached a large orange robot arm that was attached to the floor behind the tanks.

The robot extended its arm and hooked a tray of small, inverted wax trees from the conveyor, holding them upside down. The robot swung them towards me and lowered them into the central colloidal silica tank. The arm lifted. The solution drained off. It rotated the tray, lifting the trees up by forty-five degrees, and the remains of the solution trickled out. The robot turned the tray sideways-on and swivelled on its base to face the so-called "rainer" unit.

Forgetting why I was there for a moment, I was transfixed. I loved watching robots. This one was simple, although quite big in robot terms. It was great. Before making decisions, it seemed to pause to think about what it was doing. Too easy to anthropomorphise, I chided myself. I had watched robots on a production line before that looked as though they talked to each other, pausing for the second robot to ask the other for permission. Strangely enough, one of the Scout leaders in Port Talbot was a programmer for industrial robots. He always introduced himself as an electrician as no one (except me, he said) understood what he did.

The rainer looked not unlike a five-metre-high, round spacecraft. The front of it split and two sides opened as wings. Powder rained down in the middle of it. Hence its name, ha! The robot held the trees in the stream of dust, rotating them slowly to get an even covering. Dust billowed all around, then as quickly as it had started, the dust stream stopped, the robot withdrew and the spacecraft closed up.

The robot returned the tray to the conveyor and waited to take another, to dip and coat all over again.

The next tray's wax tree did not look like a tree; it was two long blades joined at the top. The robot dipped this one in the cornflower-blue cobalt aluminate solution. So the robot was in control of what was dipped in the cobalt aluminate.

"So, why does it dip some in the blue tank and not others?" I asked.

He thought before he answered but seemed happy to carry on in teaching mode. "We use it when we require hardness. When the nickel alloy is in contact with it, the cobalt atoms are drawn into the middle of what we call a face-centred cubic grain structure within the crystals of alloy that makes the part. This gives a very fine grain structure, which gives the metal great hardness. However, it has been found that with increased stress, crepitation occurs at high temperatures—that's hairline cracks—and they travel more freely from grain to grain in a finer-grained alloy than in a coarser-grained alloy."

"Which aero-engine blades would be coated in cobalt aluminate, then?"

Brian frowned, giving weight to his answer. "You don't want to get cobalt anywhere near aero turbine blades; you'd get random grains all over the place. Only gas turbines—never aero."

The white-coated man did not seem to be a criminal mastermind, or indeed a villain of any kind. He was knowledgeable and enjoyed imparting that knowledge. He seemed proud of the process. I couldn't see him disrupting it on purpose. Well, not unless he had a very good reason.

I looked for the operator of the robot. Someone in this department would be able to get the robot to dip aerospace parts in the forbidden cobalt aluminate. There was no one to be seen.

The coated trees remained on the overhead conveyor, passing rows of fans that dried and hardened the layer of ceramic. Brian continued his explanation of the process. The wax formers would be recoated with colloidal silica solution and powder many times to achieve the desired thickness of plaster. I made a mental note when he said that the thickness of the plaster determined the cooling rate of the casting and its ultimate strength. At the far end of the room, out of our sight, the wax-filled ceramic moulds would be cut off the trays by an operator with an angle grinder. They would then get loaded onto a roller conveyor that would carry them to a kiln where the wax would melt and run out through the cups on which they had been built. Lost wax process—ah! I smiled in satisfaction. The name of the process made sense now.

Brian talked very earnestly, like a walking encyclopaedia. I may as well have tried to interrupt and question the platform announcer at New Street Station. I felt jubilant in a macabre way. I was right; blades could be doctored to fail. Brian had only confirmed the basic theory behind the cobalt aluminate. I needed to know if the blades had been dipped wrongly, either by accident or on purpose. I tried a different tack.

"I have heard that turbine blades for aircraft are single crystal. Do you cast single-crystal blades here?" I asked, remembering Stuart Nicklin's words from the awards dinner.

Brian grimaced. "I have been telling the board for years that we need to go in that direction." He looked frustrated. "We're losing customers because we're not casting single-crystal alloys."

"What's stopping you?" I asked.

"Cost, and they don't understand the limitations of the castings we produce," sighed Brian.

"Why does it cost more to make a blade from one crystal than lots of crystals?" I persisted. "It's the same amount of metal, surely."

"You see these moulds? To make the single crystal, crystallisation and cooling has to start in a curled tube attached to the mould. The alloy starts crystallising in the pigtail—er, the tube—with multiple crystals, but only one will come out at the end of the curl. This is the one that the entire casting is made from. The cooling process must be done very slowly and causes a lot of failures and waste, so that is one cost. The other is the alloy used. It uses a very rare metal element called rhenium. Global engine manufacturers secure three-quarters of the world's production. It is very expensive, and for a smaller player like us, we could not guarantee availability."

"Oh." I nodded my understanding. That sounded a bit final.

I tried again. "Going back to the cobalt aluminate dip, could the blades get mixed up by accident?"

The chemist's face paled momentarily before the confident tour guide reappeared. "No—that is not possible. Every part carries its own barcode starting from the wax room we have just been in. The robot here reads the code and follows its programme. We check the shell coatings as well. They are essential for the strength of the casting."

Why are my theories always not possible?

The rainer opened again and rained its powder onto the robot arm. Brian stirred beside me.

"Did you know that hotter engines are more efficient at burning fuel, and that faster aircraft are effectively more efficient than slower aircraft?" Brian animatedly furnished facts and figures. "The

Airbuses with the Trent 500 engine create one thousand six hundred and forty tonnes of carbon dioxide per average European flight, whereas the Airbus 330 with the Trent 700 engine creates one thousand and ten tonnes of carbon dioxide per flight."

Evidently on a roll, Brian continued to share his knowledge. "Aeroplanes emit two and a half percent of the carbon dioxide emitted globally into the atmosphere. Contrails—those water vapour trails—reflect long-wave radiation—uh, heat—back to the earth, so air travel is responsible for three and a half percent of global warming activities."

"What's the answer then?" I asked. "Fewer flights?"

"Airbus are developing a hydrogen-powered engine, but it will not see production for at least five years. By then, we will have catastrophic warming." Brian looked pale and terrified at the thought.

"What do you think we should do?" I asked, cynically gratifying him with a question on what appeared to be his favourite topic.

"Society, especially in the wealthier countries, should be aware that everything they do has a cost. We as a society need to live more frugally, not use what we don't need, re-use more, mend more, take fewer trips, including flights." He nodded sagely.

I could see that he lived by this principle. He had the flexible, athletically lean, almost scrawny physique of a cyclist, clothed with frayed-neck sweatshirt and faded jeans.

To confirm my theory, I asked, "Do you cycle to work?"

"Yeah, I do most days."

"What have you got?"

"It's an aluminium Cannondale frame with carbon fibre forks and Obermayer carbon wheels."

"That would be pretty light then. A racer?"

He shrugged modestly. "Just a road bike. Bits and pieces were given to me. The frame was sold off by the police. I found the wheels in a skip."

"You made it? Yourself?" This had to be seen.

My escort flushed with pleasure and nodded.

"May I see it, when we've finished here?"

"Ah, er, I came in the VW pickup today."

"Oh." I couldn't help but feel a bit disappointed. The modern VW pickup trucks were bigger than my L200 and all pickups were notoriously fuel inefficient.

Making a gear change from global warming, we marched into the wrap area. This was part of the original building, with a sharply apexed roof, brick walls and a painted concrete floor. Fluorescent lamps hung over benches where employees in white disposable overalls, gloves and masks with red elastics wrapped the ceramic moulds in a white fibreglass-type material: refractory ceramic fibre, or RCF. The operators looked well-protected at first sight, but I was quietly appalled.

I tapped my guide on the shoulder to get his attention. He stopped and looked round.

"Brian, did you know inhalation of RCF causes lung scarring and lung cancer? Under the COSHH regulations, exposures to anything causing irreversible health effects are supposed to be reduced to levels as low as is reasonably practicable. Giving out masks is not my idea of as low as is reasonably practicable."

He frowned. "What's wrong with masks?"

"Masks, and especially disposable masks, are only effective if they fit the wearer's face with no gaps. I wore a disposable mask on a job when I was measuring dust levels in a coal-fired power station. The mask dug into my cheekbones. You know that brain-freeze kind of pain? I was desperate to loosen it. See over there? That's why they don't have theirs on properly."

"How do you know they're not secure? Oh, I see." My new recruit pointed out masks with only one elastic round the head, and one worn just over the man's chin!

"You got it, Brian." I nodded.

"What should be here?"

"I would expect to see the benches housed in extracted open-fronted booths, or at least with extraction behind or under the bench."

If the company were as conscientious as they led me to believe about casting, why weren't they when it came to health and safety? I could imagine Issy taking notes with that disapproving look and then issuing an improvement notice. The directors would be ultimately to blame for breaches of health and safety law—and it was "the board" Brian blamed for failure to cast single crystal. I supposed it made sense.

I mentioned this to Brian and was rewarded with folded arms and a nod.

Whilst we were watching, a single alarm sounded and the employees put down their work, removed their masks and overalls and walked past us. Break time, I surmised.

"Break time," Brian confirmed, "so there won't be anything to see for twenty minutes. I can take you into the foundry to see the furnaces if you like. I cannot take you in when they are working. Or would you like a drink from the machine?"

No contest. We followed the darkened walkways (the lights to either side were on movement sensors), pausing to hit the forklift-crossing alarm across an open area in the next bay, and reached the foundry. I had been lucky enough to visit the steelworks in Port Talbot and had measured noise and fume levels in a

smaller hot rolling works here in Dudley. I was expecting heat, flames, noise, a golden river of molten metal,
a snake of fiery red steel, but no, none of these. It was
dim; warm but not hot. The air smelled of dusty, hot
metal, like a car after a run on the motorway, and was
filled with humming pumps and rushing air.

There were eight dark-green cylindrical ovens,
each about six metres high and at least five metres
wide with a smaller furnace in front. Rusty metal tins
of packed empty moulds waited to go into the ovens
to pre-heat. Similar tins holding filled moulds were
on cooling roller conveyors running the length of the
bay. My guide kept me to the centre of the central pas-
sage, which was wide enough for tin-carrying forklift
trucks to turn.

Brian warned, "Do not touch anything. Everything
here is hot, even if it's not glowing. Even oven number three, which was switched off yesterday, will
not be cool enough for maintenance to access until
tomorrow."

I noticed the red numbers at the side of each
oven, flickering from 900 to 1140. That had to be the
temperature!

"Okay, I'll be careful. How does the barcode system work here?" I asked, interested.

"The code is on the mould paperwork. When the
mould is placed in the oven, the code is entered and
the programme tells the oven the temperature and
duration for the pre-heat. It alerts the operator when
it should be released from the oven. The operator
tops up the furnace reservoir with ingots and clean
scrap of the alloy. He uses a forklift to take the mould
from the oven and place it in the fill position under
the furnace. When it fills, the door closes, and the
molten metal is automatically poured into the mould.
The rate of fill, temperature and final amount are controlled by computer." Brian swept his arm back. "Did

you see the racking in the bay we crossed? That holds cooling castings for up to twenty-four hours."

I realised automation made it possible to cast into tampered moulds once they got to the foundry. There were no sensors checking on them. Also, if the shell robot had been overridden, what if these casting systems could be too?

"Come with me."

We retraced our steps past the flashing orange lights and siren of the forklift truck crossing. Almost back at the packing area, we veered right and came to an area by a steel roller-shutter door. The door was half-open, letting in daylight. Overhead lights came on as we approached, showing a curiously open section of rubber matting in front of a wall full of extraction vents. There was a small skip full of plaster to one side of the mat and a trolley with neatly laid out castings on the other, along with a mallet and dust mask.

This was the knockout area, where the ceramic mould was broken off the metal casting by no more technical means than hammering. It released a lot of dust, including crystalline silica, another lung-damaging carcinogen. The area had rudimentary extraction, but I doubted its effectiveness at controlling dust over the mat. Others must have doubted too, hence the mask.

There was an enclosed circular saw in the corner of the area. Brian explained that it was used to separate parts from sprue.

A roller-shutter door with a red plastic roller and window led into what "Keep Out" signs stated was the acid wash area. My guide explained that the ceramic core was dissolved out of the casting using acid in an enclosed wash machine and then the whole thing was manually rinsed by jet washing.

Brian repeated his point. "The casting is washed in acid. That's how I know your metalworking fluid would have had no effect."

I had no answer to that. "Is it possible for the acid to remove some of the coating but not all of it? Or, er, what if the coating was an extra-strength solution?"

"You need to be a chemist to understand," he said with a patronising twist to his smile. "What you are suggesting cannot possibly happen. Our procedures are fail-safe."

I looked down into the skip and was interested to see the chunks of mould, some creamy white and others retaining a blue lining. Seeing me looking, Brian identified each one. "This cream one is from an aero part, and this blue one is showing the cobalt aluminate coating, so it is from all other parts."

The knockout operator should know whether he was knocking off the right colour shell. Maybe he was in on this as well. Shame he was at break, or I could have seen his reactions.

I opened my notebook. "Would you happen to know if this part does or doesn't have a coating?" I asked, showing him the thirteen-digit code.

"That's a Sterling engine, but sorry, I can't tell you more than that. Maybe if I checked the records in the lab. I could email you the answer, if that's what you need." He smoothed over the issue.

I pointed to a metal stillage half-filled with castings, all loosely placed in there; they were not in careful rows as on the trolleys. "Is that scrap?" I asked.

"Scrap defective parts. We collect them. They are waiting to be sliced on the saw so that they can't be used."

"Do you remelt them?"

"Generally, we send them up to a specialist foundry in Sheffield. If the parts are chemically clean, we feed them back in here."

My host was checking his blue watch, inching towards a fire door. He kept looking around. His enlarged eyes held a hunted expression.

"Have you seen enough?" he asked. "I'm, er, needed back in the lab, but if you have any questions, ask away." He took me out through the fire door, and I found we were in the car park, not far from reception.

"Would it be possible to see how you test the castings, please?" I asked.

"I am sorry, we never allow visitors into the labs. I can explain, if that would be good enough?" Brian was fidgeting in his eagerness to get away.

"Please do," I replied.

"Briefly, we use X-ray tomography to inspect the internal structures of every casting, and structured-light three-dimensional imaging of the outside of each casting. The resolution of these techniques is so fine that we can identify crystal structure. The image data is analysed by computer and compared to a standard. No faulty castings can possibly get through the screening. Now, is that all?"

Again, he was turning to go, hinting for me to leave.

Too many thoughts in my head; I needed time to work through them. "That's fine, Brian, thanks for your time today. Can I email you with any questions?"

"Sure, no problem."

We shook hands outside the reception foyer, and he backtracked the way we had come, towards the car park. Beyond the factory door we had come out of, I saw him open a vehicle cab door. Ha, I should have known! My version of this ragged little environmentally-aware chemist was restored by a rusty beige split-screen classic VW of the camper variety. His had a cab and flatbed, probably of 1950s origin. Its engine might not be particularly green, but by using it, another one had not been made (in theory) and no doubt mileage was limited.

With a smile on my face, I wandered over to the old vehicle. "May I?" I said, gesticulating that I would like to look around it.

Brian looked up from the sandwiches he'd started unwrapping. "No problem. Do you know about VWs?"

"Not as much as I would like," I replied invitingly. "I guess it is from the 1950s and it is very early, with a split screen." I pointed to the flap at the rear. "Does it have the original engine?"

"She was made in 1958. I have replaced her engine with a 1700cc Type 4 engine, which is acceptable, and she now has a little more power."

We looked in the engine compartment at the rear.

"Do you take her to rallies?" I asked.

"I do the Stafford winter one and Three Counties. Are you familiar with autojumbles?"

Brian happily shared an anecdote about parts sourced from autojumbles, while devouring a thick cheese sandwich. He checked the blue watch again.

"Cheers, thanks for showing me, Brian." I made to go.

Brian gave a sketchy wave as he walked round the corner towards the rear of the foundry on the canal. *Good bloke, Brian.*

But what to do. Standing outside reception, I checked my phone. A text reply from Philip Wheatley from Gauge. He had not contacted Nicast at all. Oh, so what had that last hour been about?

I began to feel hunted, watched, like Brian must have in the knockout area. I tried to see into the office windows, to catch anyone watching me. Brian was a lure, and I'd come at the appointed time. I felt the truck's keys in my pocket. I looked at the traffic freely moving on the other side of the barrier. My heart was racing. I did not feel brave. I had to sign out.

Still wearing my visitor badge, I popped inside to see the receptionist.

Brian was withholding something, despite showing me the whole process in detail. He wanted me to think that there were no suspicious blades.

Proof, everyone needed proof. This was my chance!

I did not sign out. With a slight quaver in my voice, I asked whether I could get a coffee in the canteen while, I fabricated, Brian went to fetch some paperwork. The girl opened the door and helpfully pointed to a half-glazed door in the far right-hand corner of the open-plan office.

"You can use the canteen—that's the door to it from the offices—but you must not go into the factory without Dr Robertson."

That was fine by me; I needed time to work out what I knew, what someone thought I knew and what they did not want me to find out. If I was going to find secrets, I needed a plan.

I ignored Aunt Miranda's advice to take care.

Chapter 14
Search for Proof

Heart thumping, a purposeful walk zigzagging between banks of desks got me unchallenged by their occupants and into the canteen. Pale-grey, scratched Formica tables with attached red plastic seats squatted over scuffed blue linoleum; dirty boots had turned the floor deep grey by the factory door and vending machines. A works canteen, not a place for visitors.

Two men, dressed in the blue overalls of maintenance engineers, stopped discussing football and looked up from a table as I came in. "Alright, mate?"

"Yeah, fine thanks." I stuck to my story. "Just getting a coffee while Dr Robertson runs off some information."

"Brian, that dozy git with the long hair? Did he get you talking about global warming or VW vans?" one laughed.

"Both."

"He bloody knows a lot," the other commented.

"He's a nut," the first concluded. He waved towards the vending machines. "Help yourself, every drink tastes the same."

Smiling, I thanked them for their expert advice and pressed the safest option of hot chocolate.

Obtrusive or unobtrusive? Should I sit at a corner table out of the way, or would that cause suspicion? I sat at a central table with my notebook out in front of me. Taking a sip of the scalding mushroom-coloured liquid, I tasted sweetness, but any chocolatey notes were too subtle to identify. The engineers were probably right about the other drinks!

What did I know? I ran through the facts as I knew them:

There had been cobalt in the metalworking fluid from machining a specific batch of Sterling turbine blades.

The main source of cobalt was a cobalt aluminate coating from the mould.

The parts were the right size for high-pressure turbine blades.

No aero blades, and especially high-pressure turbine blades, should be treated with cobalt aluminate.

The parts were for the SFT 303 engine.

The engine was used in the Volantes Viktor XIV.

Automation and quality checks meant that blade wax formers could not be dipped into cobalt aluminate accidentally.

I added:

Someone knew I was questioning the quality of that batch of blades.

Someone had asked Brian Robertson to convince me that there was no problem.

Brian Robertson could be motivated to ground aeroplanes to reduce global warming.

Who knew?

Feeling sick, I thought of Issy. She knew I suspected the batch. Is that why she'd come for dinner? With dread, I recalled her interest in the research reports I had left out. She had suggested that someone was using Nicast to get at Richard Sterling. Did she know the people here? I felt a flush of shame that I had believed her, believed she was on my side.

Then I remembered another detail: the invitation from Brian had been emailed before Issy came over. She couldn't be involved. I sighed with relief. It didn't last long.

With a physical pain at the back of my head, I realised that she had agreed to come over and then a short while later I had the invitation from Brian. Time enough for her to book Brian in case she found out that I knew too much. She had asked if I had evidence. She knew I had none. The torment of distrust was immense.

There had to be someone else. There had to be. I could not allow it to be Issy.

Philip knew. Did I trust Philip? Why would he risk machining the parts? I put him to one side.

I tried my phone and found I had internet service. Desperate for an alternative scenario, I remembered the global warming opposition to Beech Tree Investments. They owned Volantes. Maybe I had this all wrong. Maybe it was nothing to do with Richard Sterling but a planned offensive against the new Volantes planes. With renewed hope, I looked for an alternative villain. I Googled the newspaper photograph from the global warming protest. I studied it enlarged to blocks of pixels to try to make out whether the greying ponytail belonged to Brian. It was too fuzzy to be sure. I searched the edges of the picture and there, to the side, was the rare split-screen VW pickup.

I had looked. I had found. My head felt clear. I was on a mission.

With renewed energy to solve this, I decided I must make some assumptions to see if that gave me a plan.

The parts are faulty.

They were coated on purpose, to weaken them.

Brian had the motivation and know-how to coat them and cover it up.

What else did I know?

All failed parts are scrapped.

Scrapped parts are cut up so they cannot be used.

Parts would not have left the foundry for further machining at Gauge if they did not have supporting paperwork linked to their individual barcodes.

Ordering my thoughts as I swirled little bubbles round the edge of my cup, I could not believe where the facts were leading me. Swirling became too much for the bubbles. They broke away, and a brown splat of hot chocolate crash-landed on my list of facts.

I needed to know more about scrapped parts. My aunt had said there were tens of millions of pounds at stake. Brian was being used. A terrible suspicion formed that I was uncovering preparations made by a truly criminal mind.

I had stayed here too long already. Someone would notice. The original engineers had gone but had been replaced by three office people having a quiet discussion away from the land of desks.

Making a show of checking my watch, compressing my lips as though irritated to be leaving to attend a meeting, I swiftly snapped the notebook shut, threw away the empty plastic cup and marched out of the canteen through the forbidden door into the factory. With the same bearing which I hoped would translate as "Don't stop me; I'm late for a meeting", I marched round the wrap benches, with all their RCF-cloaked mould shells and lined tins, past the forklift truck crossing point and round to the knock-out area. I nodded to the masked operator hammering away and pushed the bar of the fire exit. For my plan to work, I had banked on employees propping fire doors open. I was not disappointed to find a distorted casting beside the door. I nudged it with my boot to prop the door ajar. As long as the knockout operator didn't close it in the next few minutes, I could get back in under the radar.

My phone vibrated. A text from Catrin. The news by then was not a surprise, but it was still the worst possible nightmare that I had been shying away from. Its implications hit me for six. The batch I suspected, every serial number—all the blades were in the starboard engine fitted to one targeted Volantes plane: the one now in Wales. My heart pounded a primeval war dance. I swallowed hard as bile rose in my throat. This was it! Action time!

If I could find proof in the foundry, I would get the plane grounded. I needed Issy's professional clout. I needed Issy to be on the side of the angels, not sending a plane load of passengers to them.

My sister. I must warn her to keep off the plane on Friday—tomorrow, so soon.

Quickly I texted a reply. *"Engine not safe. Blades break at full speed. Tell Stuart. DO NOT GO ON IT. Love you loads XXX"*

I had to get proof now. There were just under twenty-four hours left in which to stop that plane.

I needed to poke around the foundry for evidence and ask questions without raising suspicion. My plan was to act out a survey. Routinely, I carried a noise meter and extraction testing equipment in the back of the pickup. The employees were bound to recognise extraction-testing engineers who frequently returned for statutory examinations, but noise surveys were infrequent. An unknown surveyor would be less likely to be commented on. I just needed to avoid the only person likely to know I was not bona fide: the health and safety manager. I would have to hope that he, like many, was tied to a desk and did not roam around the factory floor.

I was on borrowed time for as long as Brian stayed in his lab and did not see my pickup in the car park, though anyone who was working with him would see me. I had to risk it. I had to find proof, to get the plane grounded. I felt shaky, overdosing on adrenalin.

Notebook, noise meter with bulbous foam wind-guard over the microphone, and tripod in hand, I skirted round the outside of reception and let myself into the knockout area. *Right, Hal, Act One starts here. Don't look suspicious.*

"Karaoke? You want me to sing?" joked the knock-out operator, seeing the noise meter microphone.

"I've just come to see how loud you are with all that hammering, but you can sing if you want. What's your best song?" I replied. "Is it alright if I hold this over your shoulder while you do your hammering?"

"Ha ha, funny. Yeah, yeah go ahead, I've bin telling them that this ain't the right way to do this since I come." The man jabbed a thick finger at the mat.

"How do you mean?" I asked, interested, and trying to keep him in conversation so I could slip my questions in later.

"I worked in Germany a few years back. Different company, mind, but the same castings, blades and that. Bigger blades than here, some as tall as me," he reminisced.

"You were saying about the process," I encouraged.

"Yeah, them Germans used a machine. It pressed it and then vibrated it, and the ceramic fell off. I just had to get the bits out the corners. None of this hammering."

"Wasn't the machine dusty?" I asked. Normal occupational hygiene issues diluted the frenzy in my head. I felt clearer, ready for anything if it would get the plane grounded.

"No, no, you don't get what I mean. The press and the vibrator was inside the machine an' I closed the doors."

From what he described, an enclosed vibrating press did seem to be the better alternative.

"I suppose," I said thoughtfully, steering the conversation round, "that the press is less likely to damage the casting than hammering. Do you have to scrap many parts?"

"'Ammering with these don't damage owt," he replied indignantly, waving his copper-ended mallet. "It's what I find inside what I scrap."

"What sort of things?" I persevered.

He described faults where the ceramic mould had been incomplete or there had been air trapped in the casting or odd colours had appeared on the casting.

"We had one lot, hundreds of little blades, that they said had to be scrapped because they should have had the blue on and didn't. A month ago. Not a waste—the scrap all goes away for refining and then comes back to us. Waste o' my time, though."

The hairs on the back of my neck stood up like antennae.

"Are you sure it wasn't the other way round, that they were blue and shouldn't have been?" I asked.

"I know what I saw, and them shells definitely wasn't blue. Aren't you supposed to be doing a noise survey, not yacking?"

That was it!! I know how they did it!!

"Hmm, sorry, just interested. Carry on hammering, I'll wait here while you finish that piece."

I watched my informant expertly tap on weak areas so great clods of shell fell from the casting. He seemed like a normal worker. Surely, he wouldn't have carried on working if he was in cahoots with Brian on this sabotage.

But scrapping uncoated parts that should be uncoated anyway... That meant the order would have come from the shell department. I needed to speak with someone there, as soon as possible.

"Thank you," I called, picking up the noise meter. I wrote down the sound level of 91 dB(A).

"Is it high?"

Oh no—I'd better explain this to him.

"Yes, you need to keep your earplugs in. It's about ninety."

"What's the limit? That's ninety, ain't it?"

"Ah, no they changed it to eighty-five, averaged over a day, because people were still going deaf."

"That's new."

"Er, not really, 2005. And there's another limit of eighty, where you have to be concerned about noise, in case you are susceptible to hearing loss in your family, or if you're already a bit deaf."

"Too late for me."

"It's never too late to protect what you've got." I couldn't help preaching. I did not have time to explain nicely. "But I think your idea of the press is the way to go for noise and dust. I will mention it to the health and safety manager."

I left him sweeping up debris (more hazardous dust) and, despairing of the place, took my noise meter back round the wrap area. I strode past the canteen door and hastened along the green-painted walkway into the air-conditioned shell bay. When I arrived, the bay was quiet, with just the humming pump noise from the tanks. It smelled slightly antiseptic, but that may have been from cleaning. There seemed to be no one around. I made a show of placing the tripod in different locations around the three tanks. I did not dare cause suspicion by entering the areas labelled "Strictly no access", where the operators worked.

I realised I could be seen through the long, glazed wall from the car park. It was lunchtime and office staff were hurrying out. Sincerely hoping that Brian and the health and safety manager were not among them, I carried on acting out the noise survey while I wondered what to do to attract the attention of the technician. I was anxious that the longer I stayed, the higher the risk was of being found out.

"What do you think you are doing here?" an officious voice called behind me.

I stopped breathing for a second, fingers tingling in alarm.

I turned quickly, seeing a thickset man in a maroon polo shirt, not an office suit.

He continued, "You can't come in without an escort. No one has warned me to expect surveyors today."

I suspected that this must be a supervisor for the shell plant, and he wanted to be in control of what was happening in his area. He had evidently missed my visit with Dr Robertson.

"Pleased to meet you. I am Hal Rogers." I offered my hand to the red-faced man. "I was called in today to look at the problem areas. You have concerns with noise?" I asked politely. "I can take a look at anything you are worried about and measure the noise levels from it. For you," I added for good measure.

Thawing, he gruffly replied, "Well, you won't find much out here—you want to be at the back." He swept an arm, blue with an intricate tattoo sleeve, towards the rear of the area.

"No," I agreed, risking a conspiratorial smile. "No noise and no people in front here." With my most helpful manner, I said, "Would you have a few minutes spare to show me what you would like measured?"

"You should have come earlier; shift finishes at two and we've done all the noisy work." He stood squarely in front of me with his arms folded, about my height but heavily muscled.

"Okay." I tried again. "Can you show me the noisy process, and maybe I can come back on the next shift to measure it?" I said, having absolutely no intention of staying that long.

"Follow me. You can't go down there without a hard hat, so I don't know what you thought you were going to measure."

I followed the confrontational supervisor up a short flight of steel-grating stairs to what was evidently the control room. There were lists of part numbers clipped together, most with pink highlighter running through. He turned the list over so I could not see it and pointed to the screen above. In nine squares were CCTV feeds showing areas of the building. All as still as photographs at that point.

He pointed to a bank of fans and to the area where parts were taken off the trays. "The blowers are noisy, and we stand by them to check the shells. And we cut the trays off with an angle grinder."

"Yes, that's definitely loud," I agreed. "I will come back later."

I needed to go. Every extra minute was getting me nowhere and risking me being found. They could only throw me off-site, surely.

I decided to risk the question that needed an answer. "I was talking to the knockout operator earlier, and he mentioned scrapping a load of castings that hadn't been coated in the cobalt aluminate solution. A month ago. What happened there?"

Thankfully, the supervisor's residual anger overrode his caution. "Bloody night shift we put on bloody ballsed up the effing cobalt aluminate solution and made it double strength and coated aero blades! I ask you! A whole batch of blades wrecked before I came in the morning! And who do they blame? Bloody warning from HR, the effing cheek. Don't know what those poncy bloody managers are effing paid for."

"How do you mean? Er, too blue?" I asked in a pause.

"Yeah, not only too blue, but those blades also weren't supposed to be coated at all. It would've made the blades too weak when the engine was running. Safety-critical, and whose name would have been on the bloody things if I hadn't scrapped them and a plane full of holidaymakers from Ibiza had gone tits up? Effing my name, I tell you. Not them effing bloody managers."

I gave him my heartfelt thanks that he had been so aware and had saved the lives of a plane full of holidaymakers. He calmed down, so I took that as my cue to leave.

If I understood it right, what I had learned was dynamite, and it was going to blow a plane out of the sky. A plane with a Sterling engine. A plane with my sister.

Someone out there, the person who had arranged Brian's tour, a criminal mind, did not want me to know.

Heart thumping, I was beginning to feel sick with pent-up nerves. I knew too much. My pretence had gone on too long already. I needed to get away before being found out. I could see my truck, barely five metres from where I was standing, but a glass wall separated me from safety. I could march straight out, through the canteen, office and reception—except then I'd be more likely to meet the health and safety manager, Brian Robertson or even the receptionist. They would all know that I had outstayed my welcome. I could continue the charade and slowly pretend to take measurements all the way back to the fire door that I knew wasn't alarmed, but that would take far too long. My truck was telling everyone that I was still on site.

I sent a long text to my aunt. I would call Issy and explain it all once I got back to the pickup. She would have the legal clout to enter Nicast and take statements from the employees who had spoken to me.

I was forgetting she could be in on it. My gut feeling said she was not.

I packed up my tripod, notebook in hand, and marched through the factory straight to the fire door. No pretence at surveying. No one stopped me. No one shouted. I breathed a shaky sigh of relief, pushed open the fire door and pressed the unlock button on the truck key.

Relief was premature. Relief shattered. Relief was forgotten as I was confronted by the criminal mastermind intent on silencing me.

Chapter 15
Meeting of Antagonists

"Good afternoon, Mr Rogers." Richard Sterling's designer suit leaned nonchalantly on the open door of the glowering, gleaming black BMW.

I couldn't miss it. It was parked side-on to my truck's bonnet. The BMW's silver door sill behind his charcoal-suited legs bore the blue and red stripe of power.

Immediately, I knew he was the mastermind. It was not some faceless bogeyman. He radiated malevolent force, control: a dictator. My heart pounded in my chest.

I squared my shoulders. "Good afternoon, Mr Sterling. Coincidence seeing you here today."

I proceeded to ignore him as he silently watched me open the rear of the truck and load the noise survey equipment.

It all fell into place. Why I had ever entertained the thought that Richard Sterling could be the victim was beyond me. He had targeted the newest high-efficiency turbine engines. I had thought he meant to make the market lose faith in the company, allow for a takeover on easy terms. Aunt Miranda's millions. But no.

The steel-grey eyes were cold, infinitely patient, calculating.

My mind raced. Richard Sterling's prize was to be the momentous crash of a highly publicised flight, bringing about a catastrophic ending for the company. Richard Sterling was going to bring down Sterling Ace tomorrow. My sister, the Prime Minister and a dozen other people were in mortal danger.

I shut the tailgate of the pickup with hands suddenly clammy. Richard Sterling was here for me, a threat to his plan. I thought fast. As a bluff, I continued to my driver's door.

Unsurprisingly, I was blocked.

"We have a meeting to attend, you and I." The threat, robed in civility, hung between us.

My mouth was dry. Pushing past him to get into the truck would have been futile; his car was barricading my exit. *Hal, you can handle this.* Let him work out the scale of my threat. Use him to cancel the flight.

"Indeed? How interesting," I stalled, dropping my keys and notebook. *Record it! The dictation app!*

I scrabbled under the protection of the pickup. Surreptitiously, I anchored the phone under my waistband. Internally I was thankful that Richard Sterling was the jigsaw piece in the turbine blade puzzle. Not so much a missing piece, but the driving cog in a hideous clockwork effigy.

It wasn't Issy after all! If only I could share with her the breakthroughs I had made at the foundry. I could imagine her face. I remembered her asking for proof. The phone dug into me reassuringly. This would be the evidence I needed to ground that plane. All I needed to do was to goad Sterling into indiscretion.

"Get up! What are you doing down there?" Polished black Italian shoes stepped towards me.

The sun was shining; people walked past; our vehicles were parked genteelly, not even touching. So why was my heart thumping as though I were about to cliff-dive?

Richard Sterling must have been alerted to my enquiries and theories a week ago, through overhearing Catrin mentioning foundry coatings on the phone to me. He had arranged for Brian to see me, to bring me here. It did not matter that he knew I'd been asking about the XRF gun—the flight was going ahead. No one would have tested blades already in the aircraft.

Brian must have called him while I was in the canteen. Taking a car with equivalent performance to my RS, the trip from Port Talbot to Dudley would have been made easily.

"Into reception," he said, adding a mocking, "please."

My mind was racing. *He's made this trip for me. To do what?*

Sickeningly, my dark-suited adversary got the receptionist fluttering with his urbane charm and thermistor-regulated smile.

She flushed. "Certainly, Mr Sterling, you can have the key to the conference room."

Turning to me, he said, "You realise by now, Nicast is one of my companies. It is mine to do with as I like!"

And what a shoddy, hazardous mess you're making of it.

The pantomime with the unsuspecting receptionist continued. *Isobel Fleming would never let him get away with that attitude!*

"Of course, Mr Sterling, I can arrange to have your car parked," she said, playing with her hair.

"Not a problem, Mr Sterling, I will make sure you are not disturbed," she murmured, eyelashes fluttering.

Maybe her job depended on a show of sexual subservience, poor girl.

Civility and normality belied the underlying threat. Danger pervaded the aura around the charcoal-suited, silk-tied man. I should have tried to leave at that point, while there were people in the office next door, but I was in too deep—and this was the best chance to collect evidence. Besides, I was hungry for the rest of the story. I had to know for sure why this businessman was planning to bring down a plane, to bring down his own engine company.

***

"Take a seat," Richard Sterling instructed, indicating a burgundy-upholstered wooden chair. It was at the end of the decoratively inlaid eighteen-seater conference table. Furthest from the door, I noted.

The room was chilly and smelled of a mixture of mustiness and chemical air freshener. Small sepia photographs of the original foundry building drooped on the white walls.

This was real life. People had meetings in real life; only in films did they result in bloodshed. So, why was I shaking inside?

Mutinously, I continued to stand. One dark, trimmed eyebrow raised an infinitesimal amount, amusement in the set of his mouth. He looked at me questioningly, a slight shake of the head. I felt childish in my rebellion, and embarrassed, I sat. The chair creaked, springs lumpy under me. No useful evidence-gathering questions entered my head. I waited to see what would unfold.

"How do you take your coffee?" He fitted a pouch into the coffee machine on the sideboard and waited, watching, assessing me as the machine growled and gurgled and dispensed the steaming black liquid. Still silent, his gaze on me but his focus on thoughts cascading behind his eyes, he operated the machine again. Playing for time.

This is not a man to go into battle unprepared. I'm the one unprepared, I thought, then, *I'm Issy's action man, I can wing it!*

I had uncovered part of his method. He had managed to co-opt the scientist who had shown me round earlier. Whether it was Brian's idea or Sterling had already known about cobalt coating weakening high-temperature blades, I did not know, but a batch of wax formers of aero-engine turbine blades had been dipped in double-strength cobalt aluminate, contaminated moulds made and weakened castings produced. The faulty castings had been identified and foundry records would show that they had been consigned to scrap. What really transpired was that the paperwork was swapped, and sound castings were scrapped in their stead.

The only person who had access to the chemicals, to the barcoding and the quality tests was Dr Brian Robertson. The serial numbers of the faulty blades would be known by Richard Sterling. Innocent companies like Gauge Precision unwittingly camouflaged the parts by machining and coating. Their quality checks added, the parts would arrive at Sterling indistinguishable from the sound parts. Only Richard knew the identity of the rogue parts masquerading in the stacks of trays.

The spanner in the works was me finding cobalt and aluminium milled from the forbidden coating in a CNC milling machine. He had not anticipated anyone understanding the consequence of using cobalt aluminate on an aero-engine high-pressure turbine blade. But why do any of this?

Richard picked up the condemning notebook. He would find how big a threat I was to him. Seeing the tanned, manicured fingers riffling through my pages, I couldn't breathe. My heart hammered in my head. Fight or flight, my senses were urging. *Oh shit, oh shit, oh shit,* my head added unhelpfully.

I concentrated on breathing slowly. Neutral expression; show no fear.

"You have been busy, manipulating my employees." Nostrils flared, and with force, he pushed the notebook down the table.

He didn't slam it down, but his anger gave such momentum to the book that it slid the length of the table and shot off the end to land by the door. I wiped my damp hands on my thighs.

The door opened. Over the book stepped the skinny jeans-clad legs of Brian the chemist, co-conspirator.

"Brian, we don't like people who make up stories, do we?"

I watched Brian. Had he fooled me with care for the environment? Did he really think he was just grounding aircraft? What did he get out of planning the deaths of innocent passengers and aircrew? The lab-man studied the patterns on the table, silent.

With an audience, Richard rounded on me.

"I've seen the likes of you in my factory," he sneered, baiting. "You play the part of a health and safety technician well. All you actors do is put out your pseudo-scientific measuring tools and disappear for the day. Your reports are nothing but plagiarised bullshit that have no relevance or meaning. You pretend to be scientists, but you know nothing. You sicken me."

I could not stand to have my profession kicked like that. "Hold on, I think it is you that knows nothing," I answered back. "The profession is occupational hygiene, not health and safety technician, and—"

"Profession?" he mocked.

"Yes, profession, chartered profession. It's a profession that saves lives." My palms dried. I could feel my face flush in the heat of defending occupational hygiene. "Here in your foundry, you are killing your employees with silica dust, refractory ceramic fibres, metal fumes."

"So?" came the careless reply. Amusement twisted his mouth, dispassion in his eyes.

I felt like a performing dog gratuitously jumping through Sterling's hoops, but still, I answered, "This foundry needs people like me to point this out and to show you how to reduce the risks to the workforce."

"Do you hear that, Brian?"

Brian looked uncomfortably down at his trainers.

"He thinks he can run a foundry now!" Sterling was openly laughing.

I refused to be belittled. "I know you are killing people at work."

"Someone like you can't possibly understand what we are doing, and if you did, no one would take your word for it. You are not a chemist, a metallurgist, an engineer." His lip curled. "Tell me, does anyone believe your cobalt... what shall we call it? Ah! Conspiracy?"

I thought of all the "It can't possibly happen" responses I had been fed. I looked down.

"Hmm, I thought not." His white smile was dazzling in triumph.

"Richard," Brian said warningly in a low tone, "we can't afford to underestimate him. He identified the additional cobalt in the first place and has followed the trail to this foundry and to your engine company. He is persistent, and I suspect far more intelligent and wilier than you give him credit for."

"But that's all he knows," responded Richard. "He doesn't know the plan and he hasn't had the opportunity to share his ideas with anyone that matters." He turned to me. "Your car keys."

I hesitated. I took a step towards the door instead. Lightning movement in my peripheral vision. A sudden impact to my diaphragm, expelling all breath, left me doubled over in shocked, surprised pain. The kick had come out of nowhere.

"What was that for?" I grunted. Sneering school bullies swam across my vision. Nerve endings remembered.

Looking up, I saw Richard studying me and caught a fleeting glimpse of intense pleasure on his face before he asked again. Without even waiting for an answer, he pivoted on his toes and brought his foot down on the back of my ribs in a measured Muay Thai fighting kick. I collided with the edge of the table and threw the keys across it. Let him get out of my face and fetch them.

I was shaken by the brutality of the moves. Bile rose at the arousal in his eyes. I needed to get mild-mannered Brian firmly on my side. I clung to the edge of the table.

"Brian, what did you think your cobalt dipping was going to do? Do you really mean for people to die?"

Brian, seemingly pleased to have a part to play, put on his explaining voice. "There will be no deaths. Only one batch of blades was dipped, and they will be mounted in ones and twos in new engines. When they fail, the broken parts will be thrown out through the exhaust. The engine will still be sufficiently operational for the plane to land safely. It will be a nuisance for the air company, and they will have to ground their fleet each time."

I was almost relieved to hear that. Brian was trying to ground aircraft, presumably for global warming awareness. He did not know that all the affected blades had been fitted into one doomed engine.

We had gone too far for me to pretend that I was no threat. Richard was not going to let me go. I had to appeal to Brian to have any chance of... of what? Of escape? Of survival?

Richard interrupted. "That's not all, is it Brian?"

Brian shifted the weight on his feet. "The blades were also cooled too quickly. They will fail within, um, eight hours of flying time."

The plane had been airborne for two of those eight when it came from Belgium. My voice was strained. "Brian, he is going to kill innocent people tomorrow. All the blades are in one engine." I could hear myself shouting and toned it down. "It will break up at thirty thousand feet. You don't want that."

Richard waved off my concerns. "It is nothing. Collateral damage is sometimes necessary."

At Richard's words, Brian blanched. Confusion and doubt clouded his blue eyes behind their wire-rimmed lenses. His Adam's apple rose and fell. Indecision, who to believe, made him fidget. The balance of trust was not quite in my favour.

"Please, Brian," I beseeched.

"Mr Rogers, your phone, please."

I made a show of patting my pockets. "Sorry, must have dropped it." Which was kind of true.

"Stand up straight," snapped Richard. "Check his pockets," he commanded.

I had no jacket. Hesitantly Brian patted my trouser pockets and shook his head. *He's missed it on purpose! I have a chance!*

Still in command, Richard ordered Brian, "Search the car. Phone, any documents. Bring a roll of duct tape."

Avoiding my eyes, Brian left the room. He was part of this, yet not part of it. Was he trying to save his job, his skin? How could I get him to act for me?

"Sit down." Just me and the sadistic martial arts BMW driver.

I sat. I could sense that inflicting pain, scaring me, was more arousing for him than foreplay. I would have to move his focus. I needed that confession.

I started with a question. "What, er, why did you become Chief Executive of Sterling?"

A glower in response. Disturbingly, I could understand the choices he had made.

"You never intended Sterling Ace to flourish, did you?"

Richard looked down at me, contempt twisting his mouth. I upped the ante, believing myself safe in the knowledge that Brian, a witness, would return shortly. "You were turning the tables on the family that spurned you, and on their company that should have gone to your father's aid, your late father."

Richard Sterling leaned forward. "You know nothing of my father."

"Your father is the whole point of this. You blamed the Sterlings for all the terrible things that happened. Did you not consider your own part?"

He went strangely calm. He was barely breathing but his teeth were clenched.

Nostrils flaring, eyes hooded, he ground out, "How dare you. Your father was a loser like you."

"You never knew my father." I stepped towards him, fists clenched.

He smirked, taking a seat, crossing those expensively trousered legs. He itemised on his fingers: "Dominic Rogers, trader, bet on futures, lost everything." Then, leaning forwards, enunciating each word separately, "The coward took his own life."

I felt the blood drain from my face. My heart was beating erratically. Pain flared in my chest. *He and my father were trading at the same time. No, no, no!*

He smiled at me, sure of the upper hand. "You think we are alike? Your father died; my father died." He looked me up and down. I stood over him, fists curling and uncurling. "Yet you dream of what I actually do."

"I am nothing like you," I replied heatedly. "My family supported me; they didn't abandon me like yours."

Contemptuously, he flicked lint off a cuff and replied, "You mean that lesbian journo? I wouldn't own up to even knowing her."

Aunt Miranda is a million times better than you! I could hit you for that! But I wasn't going to start a fight.

He picked at the skin at the side of his thumb, got up and paced, looking at me, considering, savouring. A wine connoisseur selecting a vintage bottle. It sent further shivers up my spine.

My pain had whetted his appetite. He couldn't harm me further in front of Brian. Would he dare do more with Brian expected back any time soon? He continued to pace, but more slowly as a thoughtful frown replaced the frustrated scowl. This did not bode well.

I needed to keep him talking. "How did you get Dr Robertson to agree to coat the blades?"

"I floated the idea of grounding planes. He did the rest." He eyed me suspiciously. "You knew this already."

The phone was digging into my waistband. I looked away, sure he would sense my thoughts, the phone, the dictation app, my plan.

"A very clever, essentially good man, Dr Robertson. You took advantage of him."

"A naive fool." Sterling shrugged, unconcerned. "He served a purpose." He looked at me, an idea giving him pleasure. Chillingly jovial, he said, "Perhaps I should thank him?" He took a step towards me.

This did not bode well. I willed Brian to return. Escape forefront in my mind, I swivelled towards the door.

I could hear the faint muffled noises of the office staff leaving for the day. No one could hear or see what was going on in the imposing room used to impress clients, subdue employees. *And frighten unwanted visitors.*

At that moment, Brian returned. I truly believed he was my only chance of escaping intact.

"No phone in the car, but I did find this." It was Issy's business card with the time I was to meet her in the morning scrawled on the back.

"You have failed—the phone must be there," Richard snapped at his partner in crime. "No matter, you have the tape."

Two rolls of grey duct tape were on the table.

The door was ajar. Richard Sterling was behind me, with only Brian between me and the door. *My chance!* I lurched round, intent on sprinting the short distance.

Less than a step, and Richard Sterling felled me neatly back down into the chair. My back was in agony, my legs tingling. I took shuddering breaths, unable to work out what had happened.

He gave a happy grunt, as if I had given him a pleasant surprise. The kick to my kidneys had certainly surprised me. And it wasn't pleasant.

"Mr Rogers. Hal. I am going to ask you some questions, and I suggest that you answer truthfully, or this could be a very long evening." He was threatening me. I did not know what he wanted. What would he do if I didn't answer? I could feel the uneven springs under my bottom. I tensed my legs, ready to jump up, but they remained inert slabs of meat, not responding.

This had the surreal quality of a dream, a scene from a cheap American crime film. This was the CEO of a major company, for heaven's sake. We were in a musty conference room in a proper working foundry in very real Dudley. Google Maps could find it. This wasn't fiction.

He leaned over me, breathing hard, searching my face. I could smell sour sweat, cologne and coffee. *Show no fear, show no fear, show no...* My arms were grabbed, held down, while Brian taped my wrists to the arms of the chair. Breath caught in my throat. I felt the rising panic of a trapped animal. I strained against the tape. There was no way I could remove the chair from my arms, even if I could stand up. There had to be another way out.

"That's enough," barked Richard at my wriggling. "How much do you know? Who have you told?"

I told them. I told them everything. I told them I knew that Richard was trying to close down his family's business. I told them that Richard had lured Brian with a false picture that would appeal to his ideals. I told them that they were going to be responsible for the deaths of dozens of people, including my sister the following day.

Chords in his neck stiff as hawsers, Richard's face flamed red. His eyes narrowed, jaw clenched as he stole jerky, uncontrolled breaths. The suave businessman had left. This was the raw, violent boiling magma at the heart of the man.

"Brian, leave now!" he ordered.

Brian, my last hope, closed the door behind him.

I felt light-headed and laughed, giggling inanely, at the puffed-up man in front of me. This was the end. I wasn't frightened. I was burning, shaking, coming down with a fever. I needed a wee. There was no way I was going to wet myself in front of him.

The man who loved to hurt pulled the chair and me away from the table. He circled me slowly. I was level with his crotch; I could see what this was doing for him. Staring, circling, circling, staring. His colour subsided; his gaze became more intense. He breathed deeply, inhaling the smell of my sweat, the salty seasoning of fear.

"Do you fear me?" he breathed.

"No," I said, not exactly truthfully.

"Then, you should." And with that came a karate chop across the bones and tendons of the back of my left hand. Intense pain shot into my elbow. I cried out. I tried to move my fingers, but all I got for the effort was a twitch of my thumb and smarting eyes.

"You don't fool anyone," I managed to say. "You're nothing but a common crook. A murderer."

Coming up on the other side of me, he murmured, "You saw me give Catrin the award. I knew her destiny that night. What do you say to that, hmm?"

Shocked, I raged inside but shook my head mutely. This time, a punch to the ribs rendered me breathless.

"Is this why—*uh*—you are not controlling—*uh*—your company?" Breathing hurt. "You don't have the," I panted, "self-control to be Chairman?" Foolishly, I goaded him, tearing the tyrant away from my family. "Your brain can't handle relationships."

Another punch to my chest made my body collapse forward. The chair rocked violently, taking the energy of the impact. I hurt. Deep down, I nursed a solid knot of terror, but I did not feel scared. I was in the moment, living the nightmare, dealing with it.

"Be quiet," barked the oppressor.

"Your own mother"—pant—"left you." Shaky breaths. "How many wives have you had?" Panting some more as I watched his beetroot face. "Do you hit them?"

As he snarled, "I told you—be quiet," he picked up a chair and smashed it over my already-painful left arm, a bomb exploding my shoulder. The world blacked out for a second.

"You are nothing more than a pawn to Beech Tree Investments," I choked. "They played you for a fool, using your vanity just to get your company." I stabbed him in his delusions.

Leaning into my face, the beast growled, "You know nothing about me," and purposefully, he pressed two thumbs down on my injured left hand.

Ice. Fire. Every sensation intense. I actually heard it crunch. Sweat sprang out on my face. I could not look.

People had seen me with Richard Sterling. The receptionist. Brian. I had to try.

"If I turn up dead, people know I'm here," I gasped.

He raised the broken chair again, breathing heavily, such hatred contorting his face.

"The HSE know I am here," I added, involuntarily cringing down.

He smashed the chair over my left side again. My left side was on fire, bursting. Unmoving. I wanted this to stop. I did not know how.

At that moment, the phone hidden in my waistband vibrated, a call for execution.

"What have we here?" Richard Sterling was suddenly amused. I had given him another reason to kick me, hit me, mutilate me. He pulled out the offending item, positively laughing at the dictation app. "You thought you would trick me, Mr Rogers?" He stared down at me, eyes crinkled in pleasure, eyebrow raised. "Very gratifying," he murmured.

His high spirits meant worse was to come. I was sure of it. I was not sure I could stand much more.

"Mr Rogers, you need to understand that you underestimate me," he said, his voice silky with threat. "So terribly sorry to hear that my visitor met with a terrible accident while he was prowling alone in my foundry. What can you expect?" A twitch in his eye, and a fat vein throbbed in his left temple.

I drooped. He pushed his hand into my hair and yanked upwards. I was forced to look at him. He licked his lips in anticipation, bunching a fist. I shook my head. His punch was aimed at my face. I threw myself and the chair backwards. A polished toe cap filled my view. *Shit!*

***

I awoke, if that was what this slow surfacing into reality was, into hot stygian darkness. I could not move. I remembered Richard Sterling, the kicks, the punches. I was sure I was still taped to the chair. The agony was intense. *I'm burning... I can't breathe... Don't pay the ferryman.*

I remained squashed up, pounded by torrents of irrational thought for God knows how long. Time had no meaning in that whirling, painful, black heat. *I can't see; everything is black, so quiet—am I dying? No light! No light!* Hot tears stung my sightless eyes.

Pictures from childhood floated into my head. Early ones: being seen but not heard, the feel of the thin brocade cushion on the carved chair. Later: climbing with Gareth, watching the stars with Carla, surfing with Catrin, Sunday lunch around the table. My family calling me.

My nose tickled. I rubbed it on the top of my arm. *I moved! Did I move?* I tried little twitches of my arms and legs. I could move my arms. Abruptly, I realised I definitely wasn't strapped to a chair anymore. I could feel I was sitting on my bottom with my knees tucked in front of me. I was squashed on all sides. It did not make sense.

I explored the darkness with my right hand. Warm metal sides with rough edges. I knew where I was. I was in a tin, one of the ones used for holding moulds, in an oven. An oven that could reach 1100 degrees. A pinprick of light shone in one corner. It swam in and out of focus. I retched. I closed my eyes, engulfed by waves of pain.

I was alive and had not expected to be and desperately wanted to stay that way. I fought down panic. I reached my uninjured hand forwards to the edge of the box. My ribs protested; I eased back. Tentatively, I leaned forwards and tried again. I pulled down on the edge of the box, the rough edge slicing into my fingers. Warm blood stuck my fingers together. Pulling myself out of the box was not going to be the best option. I reached down to the floor of the box and touched scratchy, thick padding. A picture of white refractory ceramic fibre wadding surrounding moulds came into my head.

Now I could visualise it, I tried to wriggle myself to kneeling. My ribs stopped me breathless many times. My head was pounding. I had to stop whenever I accidentally touched my useless left hand. Pain, whirling lights and nausea kept threatening me as I worked to get my feet underneath me.

It was so hot. I felt damp with sweat. The soles of my boots were tacky. *Everything hurts, I can't breathe, I can't get my feet under me! Just keep going!*

Eventually, I was in a squatting position, ready to stand up. How high was the roof? No use: jelly legs and the angles were all wrong. Wadding protected my hand when I tried to steady myself with the edge of the box. After much cursing, I managed, with one leg kneeling and one leg squatting, to lever myself above the rim of the box. Slowly, I straightened, anticipating a ceiling at any moment.

No ceiling. I felt around me with my good right arm and touched a rough concrete wall. I quarter-turned in the darkness and felt again. The wall continued round me at a stretch and full arm's length. Two more turns were needed before my questing fingertips found grooves for the hatch runners. There was no way I could reach the hatch without getting out of the tin, but I did not know what structure was below, holding the tin. Gravity and no strength—I could get trapped in whatever was there. I did not try.

I have to get out! I stood in the darkness, too frightened to move but too far from the hatch to find if it opened. I was wretched. Cursing myself, I felt the familiar panic welling up, tightening my breathing and scrambling my thoughts.

I was back on the Gower: surfing, seagulls, Catrin flying past on a surfboard. Catrin, her contagious happiness. I missed her strength and sense. Catrin always had friends. What would she think of Issy? I wished I could talk about Issy to Catrin.

Catrin, she was going to die if I did not get out and stop that plane. I didn't know how long I had been in the dark. Had her plane crashed already?

I stood there, a useless jelly, for an inordinate length of time, until a metallic rattle and clang vibrated into my enclosure. The pinprick of light now made sense. The light was coming through a temperature sensor hole! I had to be in the oven switched off for maintenance.

What was that noise? Was somebody there? If they switched the oven on, I would die. If it was Richard Sterling, he would have already switched it on and I would be dead anyway, but if the noise was from someone else they might open the hatch instead.

I tried shouting. Even to my ears in the echoing chamber, my voice was quiet. My ribs stopped me taking a deep enough breath to shout out. It was not just pain; the muscles simply did not work. Slowly and carefully, I bent down and with one working hand loosened a boot. I stood up, slid my foot partly out and raised my leg so that I could grab the boot.

Success. Tears streamed down my face. *For Catrin.* Sobbing with pain and effort, I hammered the boot on the hatch for all I was worth.

Chapter 16
Escape and Car Chase

Blinding light seared through the gap in the door panels as they swung open. Echoing clunks rang through my body; light swam in and out of focus. I dropped the boot and gripped the box edge as the world spun around me.

I had been more comfortable in the hot darkness. Now with the light came images that would not focus, I could not make sense of. Fresh, cool air brought new pain to my face. I could taste blood. My teeth. I had no teeth! Gingerly, I ran my tongue round; all the edges felt normal. But the pain in my face did not let up, despite my tongue proving it wrong.

An urgent voice called out, "Climb down, climb down."

Dazed, I wondered who was there and who they were talking to. I tried to see past the light. If I could see the people, I felt I would know, I would understand. I leaned to the side to look round the light. My body protested the only way it knew how: pain, spasm, immobility. I slowly breathed. I breathed slowly. Confusion started to clear. Body did not get the all-clear message, was still locked bent over the rim of the box.

"Hal Rogers, you have to get out," implored the voice. I recognised the voice. Come to help? Come to finish me off?

I had a plane to stop, I remembered. I had to get out from here to stop a plane. I would take my chances.

"Hal, it's Brian. I am trying to save you, you blithering idiot!" The voice rose in exasperated urgency.

My saviour! The shabby, skinny eco-warrior!

I went to swing one leg over the side of the box, but my body refused to work. I grunted in pain. I did not know how I could get down. It wasn't as though I didn't want to—I prepared for the pain, but my muscles just did not work together to lift my limbs.

"I can't get down. I can't move." My voice broke into a frustrated sob. *That sounded so bloody wet,* I thought. My father would never have said that. Miranda would have managed. Though she wouldn't have got herself in this predicament in the first place, I thought ruefully.

"Stay there. Stay there." Again, the urgent double instruction.

The cone of light inched closer, falling below my line of sight. I could see in the dim light of the foundry it was a forklift truck with forks raised to pick up the box. I half knelt and half squatted to keep my balance. The box, with me in it, was withdrawn from the oven and placed on the floor.

"Thank you," I muttered through teeth clenched in fresh agony.

I felt for my boot and tried to put it the right way up to slip my foot back in. The movement caused my head to swim, and I retched. This time, the contents of my stomach erupted out of my mouth and down my nose. Globs of black, congealed blood. The pain in my face intensified, and hot tears blurred my vision. My nose proceeded to pour hot, sticky lifeblood down my chin.

"Stay put, we'll have you away in no time."

I was handed a large, oily rag. I clamped it over my swollen nose and squatted further down in the box. I made sure I was leaning forwards because I knew that was what you did with a nosebleed. Familiar practice was comforting. I was regaining control.

With that, the burly forks raised the box and slowly jolted me through the shadows of the empty foundry. Brian had come back. Did Richard Sterling know? Was I going to meet him outside the door again?

Brian drove the forklift to the fire door by the knockout area we had visited a lifetime ago. I had found out what was going on. I had exposed the mastermind. I had found employees who could testify about the swapped batches of blades. Surely that was proof. That had to be worth the pain.

There was more to be done.

The motion sensor lights had come on. I looked at the rag. It was bright red over black oily stains. Dark red blood crusted my hands. My nose felt full, fat, painful and itchy all together. I dabbed it with my right hand and came away with a smear of half-congealed blood, but my nosebleed had stopped.

My left hand, which had felt so huge, looked disappointingly normal. It was swollen, with the skin stretched tight, and tinged purple and red, but in no way did its appearance describe the pain I felt.

The forks lowered, but I still had to climb out if I were to prevent the plane from taking off. With gritted teeth, I stood up on shaky legs. Leaning on Brian, I lifted one leg over the rim of the box and then the other. I had not put the boot back on. I looked at it in the box, as inaccessible as if it were on the roof. I gave an involuntary moan of frustration.

"Brian, please, would you mind?" I begged, indicating the boot. I stood straight, resting my cracked ribs.

Brian leaned over into the trampled, blood-soaked wadding. He retrieved the boot and with embarrassed tenderness, put it on my lifted foot and laced it up.

"What day is it?" I asked, fervently hoping it was still Thursday.

"Early Friday morning. It's about four," said Brian, looking at the huge, luminous, blue dial on his bony wrist.

There was still a chance. Life-saving adrenalin returned in overdrive. I could do it, I had time.

"Save that plane!" my unlikely saviour said earnestly, standing up. "Your keys." He handed them to me, and with that, he closed the door.

In the pre-dawn gloom, I looked around the deserted car park. My waiting truck was a joyful sight, glinting under the security lights. I was drawn to it as a drowning man to a rock. So many lights; the double images jumped in time with my heartbeat. Leaning on the cool, smooth wing, I waited for the dizziness to calm down. I knew I was in no fit state to drive, but the overriding thought in my groggy mind was that I had to stop the plane.

Opening the door, I realised I normally pulled up on the wheel with my left hand to get in. I scrambled in instead. Door closed, key in ignition. I focused owlishly on the dashboard lights. Mustn't turn the key until the heater lamp goes out. It was taking too long.

Tried my left hand to put it in neutral to start. Agony—it couldn't be done. Clutch down, I turned the key with it in first gear. Glass wall right in front. Slowly, I inched my sore body round to use my right hand to release the handbrake, left foot pushed on the clutch. Equally slowly, left foot jammed to the floor as hard as I could, I righted myself; I could not afford for it to jump forward and crash into the glass wall. Right hand turned the wheel, left leg released the clutch, right leg on the accelerator. Hadn't turned far enough; too close to the reception wall. Left leg raised up against the steering wheel to hold it, I changed my grip to force the wheel further. Not even a scuff: I'd turned the truck!

The truck rolled down the factory drive towards the barrier. Solid metal barrier. *It must open,* I prayed. At the last minute, the metal bar rose. Easy turn right, onto the road, over the roundabout onto the Dudley bypass dual carriageway. I crept along in first gear. Straight road; hands off the wheel to get into second gear, an easy flick, and then tricky dog-leg into third. Loud *Brrrrrrrr* as I took the wheel and veered off the edge-warning strip. I was concentrating so hard, so hard. Had to keep moving. Lights and roundabout ahead; I slowed but could not change gear. Needed my hand to steer. Prayed for green. No traffic about, so the lights stayed on green. I cleared the roundabout, steering, staying in third.

Two more roundabouts successfully negotiated, and I was beginning to get the hang of steering one-handed and juggling engine revs and speed with the accelerator, brake and clutch. I was going to catch the plane!

Next obstacle: left-hand turn at the lights by the Black Country Museum. Lights on green, sharpish turn to slow for, lights stayed green, I was going to make it, beating the lights. The lights changed; I saw red as I did my tight combined arm-and-leg turn: clutch and revs, clutch and revs, forcing it not to stall. And onwards up the Black Country Route and triumphantly onto the M6.

Faint hint of lightness in the east. No colour in the world. Black shapes of trees and banks alerted me to my junction. I had made it to fourth gear on the motorway but now had to come off the ramp towards Cannock. Top of the ramp—it was too slow, stalled; clutch down, I coasted onto the roundabout. Large tanker swerved, sounding his horn.

Tried for second gear while the truck was still moving and restarted the engine. Lurched forwards, pains through my chest, couldn't breathe, kept going. Kept steering. The protesting ribs subsided.

Too early for traffic, I made it through Cannock. Turned into the private drive to the large house and my flat. Shadowed fir trees masked the waiting enemy: a black BMW appeared in my headlights. Four exhaust pipes glared, M-decal threatened. A chained fighting dog awaiting its master. My toes tingled in shock. The steering wheel slid through my sweating right hand. *Richard Sterling is here! It's a trap! Is he searching my flat?*

A silhouette paused in the bay window then abruptly moved off. I stopped the truck short of the house, clutch down, let it roll backwards so I could escape out of the drive without changing gear. Back on the road, I had to keep moving; gear-change rigmarole back into third. What to do? *Think.*

Checked behind in wing mirror. Black car following, shining under occasional streetlamps, headlights off, menacing. Rising panic, engine screaming at me. I did sixty in a built-up area. I carried on breaking the speed limit, jumping lights. No saviours on the empty streets—where was a policeman when you needed one?

Back at the motorway roundabout, the BMW was waiting behind me to see which exit I was going to take, then I was sure it would force me over. I could not let it get abreast of me. I could not outrun it. Not on the motorway. I had a plan.

The L200 could go somewhere the BMW could not. Over the roundabout towards Wolverhampton, the gap closed. It was going to happen too soon. Only fifty metres to go. I weaved in desperation to keep him back, and then, passing the red turning triangle, with my right hand across the wheel, ribs tearing, I pulled the truck right into a single-track lane. Hedges on either side. *He'll never pass!* Down the lane, winding. BMW right behind but powerless to stop me.

Left turn at the windmill. Sky getting lighter; time was running out. Down the hill, prayed there was no one coming the other way. Blind bends, streetlamp by whitewashed school at the start of the village, sharp turn right away from the village. Narrow lane, silhouettes of curious horses and cows to either side, loose gravel on corners—*should not brake on corners*—down to the bottom of the lane. T-junction; which way? Right to the rough farm track or left to the main road? The main road was the riskiest part, but I chose left. Up another single-track lane, squeezed between hedges higher than the truck, right at the next bend, down another lane past the twenty-acre field, farms. Farms, farmers, Mick the angry farmer locked away from me by their front gates.

With fierce determination, the L200 careered right, onto the main road. Had to stay in front for two hundred yards. BMW tried to pass. *Oh no you don't.* A car was approaching up the hill. I veered towards it to cut off the BMW. Blast of horn from shocked Skoda driver. I continued weaving on the road for the length of the field on the right. Field gateway; I swung right across the road, foot down hard and rammed into the tubular metal gate. Twenty years ago, the gate was never fastened; it was held on with string for horse riders. It opened with a scream of scraping metal across the front of the truck. The risk paid off! *I am going to win this contest!*

The BMW had slowed but was still pursuing. Onto the grassy headland at the edge of the field, I slowed, unable to get four-wheel drive without stopping. The powerful but unprepared BMW was still following. The headland narrowed; I had one wheel on firm grass and one wheel in the plough trench a foot lower. Truck tilting, I slowed further. *Concentrate on keeping moving, keeping straight, not getting bogged down.*

As the headland widened at the end of the field, I looked behind. In the grey pre-dawn, the precocious black BMW had grounded, its rear wheels turning uselessly on grass and mud; its exhaust-pipe-striped belly resting on the edge of the grassy strip. *I had out-run a BMW!* I giggled inanely. The oppressive weight of responsibility to stop the plane soon swamped my jubilation.

If I followed the edge of the field, it would take me to the farm track leading to Aunt Miranda's old farm, the place where I had once been happy. She was no longer here, but I would be safe, while I worked out what to do. With a last look at the BMW, which had managed to free itself and was reversing back to the gate, I put the truck into four-wheel drive and continued to the farm.

The ticking countdown of the lightening dawn sky insisted that time was fast running out. I needed help. I stopped the truck at the side of an open barn stacked with bales of haylage wrapped in mint-green polythene. I knew the chocolate-box timbered farmhouse and brick barns; Cracker's stable was just the other side. Creaking out of the truck, I stumbled past curious chickens, along the muddy tractor tracks round the corner of the barn.

A black-and-tan mixed-breed farm dog approached me. It barked, warning me off. I took a couple of steps towards the farmhouse. The dog escalated its warning, stiff-legged, hackles raised, the barking replaced by a low guttural growl, lips showing sharp, white, dangerous teeth. I almost laughed. After the terrors of the last twelve hours, and to top it all, I was now faced with a dog! I looked at it in disbelief.

"You're not going to bite me," I told it. "Get out of my way." I took another step.

"Stop there, you bugger, or I'll shoot." Accompanied by the click of a shotgun catch, the old man's voice compounded the dog's warning.

I stopped, weary of threats.

"Mick, it's me, Hal Rogers—er, Henry," I called. I could feel myself swaying.

The farmer who used to throw brooms at school-boy-me came closer, loaded shotgun still at his shoulder, watery blue eyes alive in a brown, weather-beaten face. "By heavens, it is you. What is the matter with you? You look like you've been run over by a tractor." He aimed a kick in the direction of the dog. "Git away, you bugger."

The dog, used to his master's ways, wagged his tail and lay down in a pool of early morning sun.

"Good to see you, Mick," was my relieved reply. "Can you put the gun down, please?" I tried to smile but my face felt tight.

Mick stopped staring and shook his silver head. He broke open the well-worn double-barrelled shotgun and placed the cartridges in his pocket. "You can use the outside toilet to clean up. I'll get you a tea. It's none of my business what you've been up to, but you look like you have had a spot of trouble."

Shoulders rounded in age, he strode back to the house. Steadfast, never judgemental apart from when it came to animal cruelty, and maybe keeping small boys on task—I had a lot of respect for Mick.

I followed his advice and opened the battered wooden door. It had rat holes in the bottom nailed over with bits of rotting timber. Inside was a cubicle-size room of whitewashed breezeblock and a muddy concrete floor, with a thankfully clean white toilet and a sink bearing three dirty eggs, a nail brush and a bar of soap. Above the sink was a small mirror.

The image in the mirror was as stained and cracked as the mirror itself. Blood from my nose and gashed cheek had smeared across my face and down my once-white shirt. Both eyes were half-closed and bloodshot, and my nose looked fatter than it should be, tinged with blue and purple. My hands looked worse. My right hand was clawed, held in position by an obscene bandage of congealed blood and ceramic fibres, caked in blood, with dark red outlines on all my nails. My left hand was swollen to twice the size it should be, an abstract work of reds, purples, indigo, blue and yellow. I could feel just three of my fingers. Any movement was met with fat, painful resistance.

I took off my shirt—torn, bloody and coated in foundry dust—and squeezed it under the cold tap (the only tap connected). I dabbed the blood off my face, then set to work soaking and scraping the blood from my right hand. Only then did the need for a pee return. More blood splashed into the toilet bowl. I was making a mess of Mick's outhouse.

No reason to panic. I'm alive, a bit bloody, but nothing's getting worse. I guessed that I had a broken nose, broken bones in my left hand, cracked ribs and maybe a bruised kidney or two. If I were going to conk out from my injuries, I would have done so by now, or at least I would be dizzy and nauseous, neither of which I had felt since before sunrise.

Next plan: how to stop the plane, and how to get down to Port Talbot in time just in case last-ditch action was needed. There was no way I could drive that far. I had arranged to meet Isobel in a car park—perhaps she could come here, pick me up? But I had no phone to call her and no way to contact Catrin to convince her of the terrible threat to the plane and how the engines were going to fail.

"Shouldn't you be calling the police for something like this?" Mick gruffly suggested, holding out his old-fashioned mobile phone.

I dialled 999 and tried to explain to the operator there was a threat to the Prime Minister's life at Port Talbot. The plane he was to travel on had to be grounded. She wanted to know who I was, where I was calling from. Instead, I repeated my message and hung up.

When Mick brought out a chipped mug of sweet tea and a chocolate biscuit, I thanked him and explained that although it seemed improbable, I needed to catch a woman with a sports car in a pub car park in about twenty minutes' time so we could drive down the motorways of Britain to save an aircraft. Could he possibly give me a lift the five miles to the pub, please?

Mick nodded sagely through my request, as though I were describing nothing more abnormal than repairing a hole in a hedge. "You'll be needing a shirt," was all he said.

Off he stomped in his wellington boots, back to the farmhouse. I finished the tea and walked to Mick's muddy Nissan pickup truck, the equivalent of my L200. Handing me a light-brown check country shirt, he got into the truck. I gingerly put the shirt on and slid onto the black, waterproof-covered passenger seat. The dog jumped in the back.

I mulled over ways to ground the plane, but each option had its drawbacks. I could phone the company and tell them—but tell who? Who would believe me? Richard Sterling, CEO, was probably halfway back there now, and he would override any grounding instruction. I could try Catrin, but she had no seniority, no influence there. I could try Isobel, HSE inspector. Would she have the legal weight to ground the plane? I thought not. I had already called the police.

Maybe they thought there was a bomb on board. But the plane had been locked behind a perimeter fence for the last few days. The police were used to hoax calls, especially with environmental protestors actively rallying against air travel. Unless they found a bomb, the police weren't going to ground the plane.

There was nothing for it; I'd have to get there in person and make something happen to stop the plane.

The morning was brightening up and promising to be a fine, sunny day. Perfect for crowds celebrating the new aircraft. The aircraft, hiding its terrible secret, would be glinting, beckoning, inviting. I could not let it take my precious sister.

Mick drove slowly, his eyesight not the best. We approached the straight road to the pub. One car reflected the sun's rays at the side of the building. Mick pulled into the car park. It was empty apart from the publican's own estate car. My heart plummeted. I felt defeated. Everything relied on getting down to Sterling's airstrip.

"Are you sure this is what you arranged with the woman?" asked Mick, seeing my expression. "The right time and the right pub?"

I didn't know what to do. Mick would never get to Port Talbot. The furthest he ever drove was the local livestock market. I stared into space, mentally fighting defeat, cursing Richard Sterling.

I remembered the time written on the back of Issy's card. Brian had given it to Richard. Had Richard contacted her with a fabricated story? Maybe she thought I had called it off? Maybe she wasn't coming?

I was right on the first count, thankfully wrong on the last. A little white sports car drove into the car park with a slide and a scatter of gravel.

Chapter 17

Race against Time

Bundled unceremoniously into the black-and-red leather bucket seat in the open-top Fiat, I pleaded with Isobel to drive quickly.

Her eyes had widened when she saw me. I had cut off her questions by releasing all the important facts from my head: "I found out. It's Richard Sterling. The blades won't last another flight. He locked me in the foundry. I'm fine, but he's put all the blades in Catrin's plane. We mustn't let it take off!"

"Right, I'll call the factory. Tell them to abort the flight. What proof do I tell them?" Isobel had been so calm, decisive. Aunt Miranda would approve of her.

I had remembered that Stuart and Ste, influenced by Richard Sterling, had decided the plane could cope with engine failure. They did not know the entire high-pressure fan was designed to break up in flight.

"I couldn't get proof. No one will believe the urgency. We can't just phone up and tell them. It's up to us to stop it."

Isobel had not been surprised when I mentioned Richard Sterling's name. He had emailed her at hse-dot-gov-dot-uk, requesting her company at the inaugural flight of the Volantes Viktor XIV and saying that Hal Rogers, with whom she'd had the original invitation, had left them a message that he would not be coming to the event, being tied up elsewhere. I had spluttered at the impudence of Richard when she told me that.

I was immensely glad that she'd come to meet me.

"You have to drive faster." I carried on my urging.

"I am a civil servant; it is my duty to uphold the law, and being caught speeding would be somewhat against the law."

"Don't the HSE stretch to blues and twos?" I asked facetiously.

She laughed. "We will get there in time, trust me."

"What about traffic jams?" I retorted.

Did I trust her to get us there in time to stop the plane? I was used to depending on myself to get things done. Relying on someone else seemed alien, uncomfortable. I trusted in the honesty, the good nature of people, but rarely their competence, I realised ruefully. Maybe I looked at life the wrong way round. Richard Sterling's competence was never in doubt, but his honesty?

Isobel had the radio tuned to Radio 1—I'd thought she'd be a Radio 4 person. There was no mention of the Prime Minister's visit to Port Talbot. Maybe the Prime Minister was too trivial for Radio 1. Reassuringly, there were no traffic jams reported either. The disc jockey's chatter washed over me. Thankful for the side supports of the racing seat, I inched myself round on the slippery leather, easing pains.

I looked across at Isobel. Her expression was calm and serious as she drove. *Maybe she's right, we will get down to the plane before it takes off.* I recognised strength in the line of her jaw, determination in the set of her features. Her dark hair was pinned in an untidy bun on the top of her head, coppery, sun-bleached wisps dancing in the turbulent air. She was wearing a fitted white blouse today, with ankle-skimming khaki jeans. I had never seen any woman so beautiful.

"What are you thinking?" She threw me a glance with her dark-lashed hazel eyes.

"You are beautiful," I sighed.

"Uh oh, that's rubbish. You had a bang on the head. But thank you anyway." She carried on driving, a slight upward tilt to her mouth.

Now we were on the slip road joining the M6. The overhead gantries had no variable speed limits lit up. There was an urban myth that the speed cameras were operational only when the variable speed limit signs were on; I didn't know if it was true. I stole a look at the speedo. We still weren't exceeding seventy-five miles an hour. Would we really make it in time?

Her mouth twisted at the corner as unspoken thoughts flickered through her mind.

"Did you think you were going to die when you were trapped in the foundry last night?" she asked curiously.

Reliving the pain and confusion, I considered the question.

"I don't know," I finally answered. "I don't remember thinking I was going to die, but I did feel I was somewhere else, like another dimension for a while. I was most scared of dying when I knew I was alive and that Catrin needed me."

She nodded, overtaking a couple of lorries, and resumed a steady speed of seventy-five miles an hour in the left-hand lane. She looked melancholy now, as though something had evoked a memory of great sadness.

"What's up, was it something I said?" I suggested, keeping my eyes down.

Isobel's lips tightened as she thought. She waited until the car had manoeuvred onto the M5 before replying.

"It's nothing, really. Just the way you said it reminded me of the story Mama tells of escaping from Erbil," she finished quietly.

The memory looked private, and I did not want to pry. But Erbil... I racked my brain. Was it a prison? A town? Why would someone escape from a town?

"Sorry, what is Erbil, Isobel?" I asked.

"A town, in northern Iraq," she replied curtly, without glancing at me.

I remembered northern Iraq from the news. There had been fighting there for many years. As far as I knew, though, the fighting had been in my lifetime. Did this mean that Isobel was an Iraqi refugee and had escaped the shooting and bombing? Now was not the time to ask.

Pictures of bleeding civilians, child amputees, smashed buildings and dust travelled down the M5 with me. I remembered Ramon's real distress over his sister's danger. Did Isobel have family in Iraq?

Using Google Maps, the route that was fastest although longest was the M5 down to the M4 above Bristol, then along the M4 to Port Talbot. It was littered with average-speed cameras. That would not do. Isobel chose the route down the M5, M50 and A449. I considered it my route, as I travelled it often when visiting the family.

The sports car ate the miles down the M5 at a steady seventy-five miles an hour. According to Google Maps, we would arrive at Sterling at eleven o'clock with an hour to spare before take-off.

An hour later, just past Worcester, I was shivering despite the sunshine and the footwell heater. Isobel scrutinised me. "How are you feeling?"

"Fine thanks," I stuttered. My head floated and pounded at the same time, my left arm was a fireball, breathing hurt, and bouts of nausea came with waves of violent shivers. Stopping the plane was more important.

She frowned and cursed under her breath. Five minutes later, she pulled into Strensham Services.

"Talk to me, Hal," she demanded, facing me. Her eyes were flashing, her mouth tense. "If you are dying, there is no bloody point in taking a sodding corpse down to Wales." Wait—was she *angry* with me for not making a fuss. "Do I call an ambulance, or do you think you will make it to Wales?" She was serious. I was shaking.

"I'll have a hot drink," I conceded. "And maybe a Nurofen."

"Okay, out of the car, we'll get you sorted." She was brisk and no-nonsense, the HSE Inspector demanding unpleasant action.

The car was low. I had been seizing up for the past hour and a half, and just tensing the muscles needed to climb out brought waves of pain through my whole body.

"I can't," I said helplessly. "W-would you mind b-bringing me a d-drink and I'll wait in the c-car?"

Isobel Fleming, professional master of making people do things for their own good, opened the car door and bent down to help me out.

"No!" I shrieked in breathless panic.

Shocked at my reaction, she took a step back.

"Everything hurts," I said apologetically.

"All the more reason for an ambulance and medical help."

"No, we have to stop the plane from taking off. There are lives at s-stake. I am just getting stiffer, I am not g-getting any worse." I tried to ease her fears. "Please, I j-just need a drink and some pain k-killers."

Isobel left me in the car. I watched her walk across the car park. Her walk had determination, but the confidence of her poise had ebbed.

Quietly watching cars driving in, driving off, parking nose in, reverse parking, my mind calmed by trying to guess which cars would reverse park and which would make a meal of it. I liked Strensham Services. I tried to recall something important. Who had I told about Nicast? With returning clarity, it came to me.

Miranda—I'd told Aunt Miranda that Brian the chemist had doctored the blades for the Sterling engine. That's good. Was there another text? *Think, Hal.* Catrin. What did I text?

Just a few minutes later, Issy returned with a hot, sweet tea, a bottle of water, Nurofen and a couple of dark purple fleece blankets. *Universal panacea: hot, sweet tea.* Almost tenderly she pushed the blankets round me. She opened the bottle of water, gave me two capsules and then the water bottle. Gratefully, I swigged the water down. She put the tea in the central cup holder, where I could reach it with my right hand.

"I want to show you something." She angled the rearview mirror so I could see myself. A ghoul stared back. White face, blue lips, livid, swollen nose, dark red eyes with purple shadows, gaping gash across one cheek, hair spiked with encrusted blood.

"See?" She twisted the mirror back. "Just drink your tea," she said with a scowl.

She's frightened, I realised belatedly. Frightened for me. Like I was mad with anguish for my sister. It did not surprise me that she felt angry at me. She was doing her best to control an abnormal situation. I reckoned that if she was anything like me, the more information I could give her, the better she'd be able to cope. Maybe she'd be less angry.

"Issy, thank you for all you are doing for me, really," I started. "I am sorry I would not get out of the car. I have been punched and kicked and beaten with a chair. I think I have cracked ribs. I can still breathe, so they are not broken. I think I have bruised kidneys. I have no swelling in my abdomen, so I am sure I have no internal bleeding. I am sure my left hand is broken;

I am sure my nose is broken. I had a bang on the head, enough to render me unconscious, but I am not really nauseous or dizzy, so that is on the mend too. I have sat in your lovely car, I have seized up and I cannot move to get out. If you pull me up, I will scream."

"Okay." Issy let her breath out slowly. "That makes sense." She thought for a few ticking seconds. "You can't turn up to a public function looking like that. You'll be arrested or sent to hospital. The tea will make you want to empty your bladder, so you're going to have to move for that. You need food, to replenish blood sugar. I think we get you out of the car somehow, clean you up, get sunglasses and food." She looked at her watch. "All in the next ten minutes."

She was right on all counts. I tried moving again now the warmth, sugary tea and painkillers had done their best. I found I could roll sideways and forwards, but any stretching of my ribs jabbed me with vindictive pain. I saw it reflected in the sharp spasm of Issy's watching face.

"How about," she suggested, "you roll out sideways, so you end up facing the back, on your knees? You could stand up from there. If I sit by the car sill, you can lean on my shoulders."

I saw what she meant. There would be no pulling; my legs would push me up and I could uncurl to stand. "You're not just a pretty face," I joked lamely.

I dropped my new blanket on the floor for her to sit on. We managed the manoeuvre with a few grunts but no swearing, and I stood up at last. Mick's shirt flapped open; I had been unable to fasten the buttons. Livid red and purple welts showed up on the front of my ribs. Issy did not look pleased.

"It is a criminal offence, grievous bodily harm," she said. "May I photograph your injuries in case they're needed in court at some point?"

She took out her phone and lowered the shoulders of the check shirt so it was held by my elbows. I heard the fake shutter click of the camera and her indrawn breath. She moved round to photograph my left hand and then stood square in front of my face. Concentration and unwelcome thoughts sucked the softness from her expression. I stuck my tongue out.

"Idiot!" she laughed. That was better.

Slowly we shuffled down the wide brick path to the arrivals-hall-like glass vestibule. I turned off to the gents' toilets. My urine was still dark red. My back hurt. *Kidneys heal, don't they?* I washed my hands very gingerly and used unwound lengths of toilet roll to clean my face a bit better. I looked in the mirror. More colour, a lot more normal than earlier. *Phew.* I really did not want to scare anyone, especially Issy, even myself.

I found Issy waiting for me. The big question: "How are your kidneys?"

I lied with a smile. "Just pink."

She nodded.

Issy propelled me to the racks of miscellaneous clothing. She playfully stuck a bright red Ferrari baseball cap on my crunchy hair.

"Suits you, sir, and may I suggest sunglasses?" she said, selling clothing like a bad actor. She was trying to shake off the angst. I loved her for her efforts.

We settled on aviator-style reflective sunglasses (they were the lightest on my nose), the Ferrari cap, and an extra fleece jacket, this one black with Lamborghini logos. My card did its job, and I put the clothing on.

On the way back out, I bought more water, coffees, sandwiches and chocolate from the cafeteria area. I even managed to get back in the Fiat by sitting down and swivelling, feeling much better.

On time, the white sports car with its matte black bonnet flew down the M50 to Ross-on-Wye. We were going to get to Sterling before the plane took off. Exhausted and wrapped in blankets, I closed my eyes. I trusted her.

***

In a way, it was fortuitous that we were late, as there were no queues to get in. Onlookers' cars were parked along the verges of the concrete road all the way to the gates. Protestors with "Save the Planet" placards ranged along the fence line. There was an additional van parked up next to the gatehouse, a security company's logo on the side. Sterling had evidently paid for the event to go smoothly. Rather ironic, seeing as the threat was internal.

Security men in riot gear and armed with batons grouped in front of the gates. The protesters spilled over into the road, and we came to a halt. *We can't be stopped here—so near and yet so far!*

The barrier opened and we were waved through without checks. Controlling protesters was their focus.

The visitor centre car park was packed. The little car used up valuable minutes driving round and eventually found a space on the furthest edge. I rotated out of the car without mishap. It was going to take me forever to get across the car park.

Isobel turned to me. "I'll go ahead and find someone, explain to management. Will you be okay to follow?" She squeezed my right arm reassuringly.

Off she jogged, past the cars to the corner of the glass building. I followed as fast as I could, caught out by breath-stopping stumbling; I was too slow.

The public relations team from the factory were out in force in their matching company uniforms. I could see one of the suited ladies taking Isobel towards the visitor centre. I prayed she had enough influence.

Richard Sterling appeared in the doorway at just that moment. Horrified, I watched as the PR woman waved him over. Isobel spoke to him, then he took her arm and walked towards the plane.

Thunder, lightning; a storm in my head raged as I jumped to the only possible conclusion: Isobel was working with Richard Sterling.

I should hate her, but I couldn't. More reason to thwart that manicured Machiavellian monster.

It's up to me now to save Catrin!

I staggered towards the plane, intent on speaking with the pilot. Through the gate in the chain-link fence and onto wiry grass at the beginning of the airstrip, past celebratory barbecues and bunting. People, no doubt fearing I was a drunkard, hastily moved out of the way to avoid my staggering progress. The plane shone behind a temporary barrier in the late morning sun, an innocent casualty of Richard Sterling's plan.

I walked up to the airside barrier. "No Entry" signs stopped me, enforced by security men. Just the other side of the barrier, cameras were focused on a woman with a microphone.

"...will not be present, a change from schedule. Earlier, police were called by a man in Staffordshire claiming he knew of a bomb on board. This has been declared a hoax, after sniffer dogs and the bomb disposal squad spent two hours searching this plane. We believe the caller has been taken into custody."

The woman tapped her earphone and spoke with one of the cameramen. They all nodded.

"You find us today at the airfield of Sterling Ace Aerospace, on the occasion of the maiden flight of this beautiful aeroplane, the Volantes Viktor XIV..."

I walked right up to the airside barrier, determined to do whatever it took to ground the plane.

The plane was sleek, its sharp, narrow nose leading to the cockpit, the fuselage widening just enough for seven single seats each side with an aisle between. Six windows behind the open entrance door. Wide, tapered wings in front of two jet engines mounted on either side of the end of the fuselage, then the sloping T of the tail. Dark blue and grey curved lines served to enhance the sculptured body of the plane. A truly beautiful machine.

I could not see my sister. She was probably already on board with the other passengers, but not the PM. I waved at the plane in case she could see me. Heart stopping, I saw her outline in a window. Frustratingly, she wasn't looking at me. I forgot that I was wearing a red baseball cap over reflective sunglasses.

I didn't recognise anyone here to approach, to ask to stop the plane. Isobel had disappeared. Richard Sterling was nowhere to be seen.

A public address speaker erupted in static. "All visitors to leave the aircraft."

Half a dozen people in brightly coloured summer clothing descended the let-down steps from the plane. The unmistakable figure of Richard Sterling stood at the top of the steps, taking in the throngs of visitors, the success of the publicity ploy. His gaze swept round, over local dignitaries, over the invited friends and families of workers in the plant, the exhibition craft of the event.

Through the barbecue smoke and frying onions, unnervingly, he sensed me. His gaze stopped abruptly. He gave me a long stare. I stared back, hating that man. *Self-combust, throw yourself down the stairs, anything!*

He descended the stairs in frustratingly good health, sharing his charm with important visitors. The monster was certain there could be no disruption to his carefully laid plan.

Aircraft checks were made under the fuselage by blue-uniformed men and women: pilots and engineers from Volantes. Black-suited security accompanied the engineers. One security man remained in the plane doorway.

The plane, my sister and I were running out of time. As the visitors exited from the airside area, I pushed past them towards the plane. I staggered up to speak with the pilot or engineers. A security man barred my way, asking me to return to the visitor area. Forcing my way would achieve nothing, besides being physically impossible. I tried my best with words.

"Excuse me, I really need to speak with the pilot."

The burly security guard looked down his nose at me (he was six inches taller). "Sorry, sir. You must leave now," he repeated impassively.

"But you don't understand—the whole plane is in danger. My sister is on the plane. She has to get off!" I shouted, trying not to sound hysterical.

The security man looked unimpressed. Richard Sterling and the dignitaries had turned round at the fracas. The cameras pointed my way.

"Sir, I insist you stop this now." Taking me by my right elbow, the security man propelled me all the way through the chain-link gate back into the car park.

Richard Sterling caught my eye and ostentatiously flicked a piece of lint off his sleeve. His eyebrow raised and lip curled in a triumphant sneer before he turned away to his guests. I swore at him under my breath.

Fifteen minutes to go. The aeroplane door had closed.

Visitors enjoying the razzamatazz of a celebratory day were joined by workers in their grey polo shirts, given time out to see the fruits of their labours. The sun was warm; a radio was on low; barbecue smoke drifted under brightly coloured bunting. It seemed the world, unaware of the unfolding catastrophe, was happy.

The plane engines had started up. The sleek shape lumbered round in a circle, as unsuited to the ground as an eagle. There was no more time.

Marooned in the visitor car park, I racked my brain for inspiration to stop the plane, Catrin's plane.

A young Welsh voice said, "Uh, Hal?"

Ste was in the car park. He knew the story. I had to convince him about the latest development that the blades were bound to shatter on this flight. They had been on borrowed time since the short hop from Belgium.

"Ste, we've got to stop Catrin's plane. It's not safe."

His face portrayed a mixture of fright and horror, eyes wide, jaw slack, as I turned to face him. "Hal, what happened?"

"The plane. Richard. Turbine blades. Too many hours already."

"Slowly, Hal. Turbine blades and Richard?"

"Castings cooled too quickly and coated. Six hours left. In the starboard engine." I tried to get the information from my head into his as quickly as possible.

The shock in the young man's face turned to focused comprehension. "It's okay. I'm with you. How do we stop the plane?"

The familiar, flashy, green Dustco Transit van approached the gatehouse from the direction of the factory. At that moment, I knew how it could be done.

"No time to explain, Ste. Flag Dustco down. We need their van."

I waved at Darren, hoping against hope that he would see me. Ste joined in.

The van turned towards the visitor centre car park. I took off the sunglasses and carried on frantically waving.

"Righty ho, I'm coming over!" shouted the cheerful voice.

Ste sprinted along the glass front of the building towards the van. I followed slowly. A stationary black BMW leered over the footpath, its front spoiler shattered, grass snagged in the cracked remains. Unnerved, I skirted round it and stopped for the green van. Ste was already in it.

Darren leaned across. "Jesus! You look shit, mate."

"Darren, it's an emergency, I need you to drive like the Nürburgring all over again. That plane is going to explode if we don't stop it."

In my head, the turbine-blade-fracturing reality was usurped by the plane-will-explode story.

"He's right," Ste said. "We've gotta stop it."

"Yeah, let's do it!" Darren, game for excitement, inspired confidence in this last-ditch attempt.

I could hear engines, cheers from the crowd—the plane was taxiing up the runway.

I climbed up onto the passenger seat. It was even higher than my truck; much easier for me to get into than Isobel's little car.

"Belt up, you'll need it." And off we rocked, pausing at the gate, Darren taking precious seconds to use his fob, then bouncing left over the curb. We tore up the perimeter road running parallel to the concrete approach road. We were blind; the plane was on the other side of the factory. In my mind, it was already taking off.

Darren, foot to the floor, reached sixty miles an hour in third gear, the engine straining towards red on the rev counter. He flipped it into fourth, creeping to seventy, the tight bend at the end of the factory fast approaching. I held the edge of the seat. Pelting towards a bend with no bonnet in view between me and the road made my toes freeze.

Darren slammed it into third and down into second, van protesting with a lurch, then spun right, negotiating the corner of the factory. There was a thunderclap of tools rolling around in the back. I was thrown to the left, under Ste, pressing my left arm on the door. I may have screamed.

The plane was finishing its lumbering turn at the end of the runway, across the grass from us. It straightened up, accelerating fast.

Our green speed-machine raced through a chicane of bollards and onto the airfield road.

Over the sound of the straining diesel engine, I could hear the SFT 303 engines roaring. The Volantes Viktor XIV was gaining speed.

The Transit accelerated as though it too were about to take off. The plane accelerated. Too far away to overtake. We had to cut across its path to stop it taking off.

The plucky Transit leapt onto the rough grass, heading for the halfway marker on the runway—any further down and the plane would have already taken off. We bounced over the grassy tussocks, tools an ear-bleeding drum solo, Darren wrestling with the wheel.

The plane, nose still low, was gaining ground. I prayed it would see us and stop while it still had room on the runway.

"We've got company!" shouted Darren.

Security vans, headlights flashing, forced our van away from the rapidly accelerating doomed beauty.

The nose of the plane lifted. Rear wheels left the ground, just metres ahead of us. We watched it go, jet engines burning as it climbed into danger.

Chapter 18
Crash

Silver bird soaring to the gates of heaven. I had failed. Warnings unheeded, actions ignored. Head bowed, I closed my eyes. We had failed. I had failed.

Crushed grass scented the breeze, cooling engine ticking as the metal contracted. I opened my eyes. The van was stationary, but the tiny plane was climbing into the big blue sky. It hadn't exploded. Of course, what was I thinking? It had six hours—there was still time to get it down to safety.

Anger started a slow burn. Richard was still here. We had things to do.

Time to explain. "We did our best, thanks, boys. But we haven't finished."

The security vans surrounded us.

"What's this about?" Darren, flushed with exhilaration, was frowning uncertainly.

Security van doors opened.

"Yeah, Hal. You know something," Ste added.

"I met Richard Sterling with his tame chemist in Nicast, the foundry he owns, that supplies the blades."

"He beat you up?" Ste was first to ask.

The guards were walking towards our van.

"Yes, and locked me in an oven, but only after I learned that the blades were treated so they would break on this flight. Today."

Ste swore. "Catrin. We have to get the plane warned."

A grey-haired, rather portly security man in a black sweater with silver logos on the shoulder pads asked us to get out of the van. We complied. Darren knew him and spoke first.

"Alright, mate? Look, mate, I know you have your job to do, but we think the plane is in a dangerous condition. It needed more checks before taking off."

"You what?" The security man eyed Darren incredulously.

"He's right." Ste spoke up.

Darren continued, puffing his chest up in his most righteous manner. "Look, you know me. You've seen me working here for over five years. You know I would not do anything to harm the company." He pointed to me. "This young man's sister is on that plane. You know Ste here. You can trust us."

"There is something wrong with the starboard engine of the plane," I added. "We tried to stop it." I looked up into the sky, where the plane was a mere dot.

There was still a chance. The plane would last longer at low speeds. It had flown successfully from Belgium on Monday. The trouble was this was a flight specifically to prove how fast it could be, to show it would enable businessmen to have face-to-face meetings in different countries on the same day. I had to convince the pilot to land safely; he must not continue his flight.

I remembered the old engineering manager who could not be sacked. I had to trust my instinct that he was not involved in the plan to bring down the Sterling company.

"Ste, can you call Stuart Nicklin?" I asked. "He's the only one who can help now."

Both allies got out their phones. The security man looked uncomfortable and indecisive.

"I have to take you off the airfield and hold you for the police," he said. "Don't make this hard."

I tried again, as reasonably as I could, with a calmness I did not feel. "You could radio Stuart Nicklin and tell him that we are asking for him. Just see what he says."

We waited on the windblown grass of the airfield: warm sun, light breeze bringing with it the sounds of seagulls, the sky a perfect blue, no clouds, no planes. It seemed Sterling, security, sky and seagulls were all in denial of this life-and-death drama. My head pounded in synch with the throbbing of my arm. My ribs jabbed as I breathed, totally out of rhythm.

Catrin's face danced in front of me. I would not give in until she was safe, Richard arrested.

The handheld radio crackled into life. The security guard walked a couple of steps away and spoke into it. The reply floated back as jumbled static.

"He's coming over. He will talk to you in the gatehouse," reported the security man.

He consulted with his colleagues, and our small convoy, with the van sandwiched in the middle, drove like a funeral cortege back the way we had come and parked outside the gatehouse.

This was all taking too much time. The original flight plan was to take the Prime Minister to Edinburgh airport, celebrate Scottish exports of hydraulic systems, then fly off to meet the Prime Minister of Sweden in Stockholm to mark successful cooperation with the Swedish ES-19 electric airliner, and back to London City Airport.

The plane would be at thirty thousand feet over the Pennines by now. Bile threatened to erupt in my throat.

The gatehouse was a squat, dark, red-brick building, hot and stuffy with a locker-room smell. A shelf loaded with monitors ran the length of the gatehouse on the same side as the barrier. Battered stools covered in cracked vinyl were under the shelf.

"Take a seat," a thin, spotty young man in a black, ribbed security jumper said.

The three of us sat. Darren twisted the rotating seat round on its legs. "Not bad this, eh?"

Ste was ashen.

I looked through the window to see Stuart Nicklin striding from the factory towards the inner barrier, shirt sleeves rolled up, tie flapping at the speed of his walk. The young security man pressed a black button on a large control panel and the barrier drew back, allowing the engineering manager to pass without breaking stride. Stuart Nicklin waved his thanks. That looked like the action of a reasonable man.

All my hopes were pinned on Stuart being able to turn the plane around, to convince the pilot to reduce speed, to reduce stress on the engine. I needed to explain the whole situation to him. He had to believe me.

Stuart, frowning, stepped into the gatehouse. I stood up in respect, thereby catching sight of Richard Sterling striding from the visitor centre building. The CEO would just negate anything I said. No one would believe me once he got here. At least Isobel wasn't with him.

A police patrol car was driving into the car park. I was the villain they had come to arrest.

I felt the opportunity to save the plane slipping away.

I held out my hand. "Stuart."

"What the devil—" started Stuart.

Darren butted in. "That plane you let go has a serious defect in its engine, and it's likely to crash." Darren stared hard at Stuart. "Hal here can explain."

Ste took up the reins, looking to me for permission. "May I?"

I nodded.

"Stuart, you know we decided that our engines would safely eject a blade or two if they broke in flight?"

Stuart nodded.

"Hal has found out that all the blades in one engine..."

"The starboard engine," I supplied.

"... have been treated specifically to break on this flight."

"What treatment?" Stuart asked. "The cobalt aluminate would not work this quickly."

I took up the story. "The castings were coated and then cooled too quickly."

"How do you know?" Stuart looked puzzled.

"The metallurgist at Nicast told me."

"The foundry would never do that. We have the quality test information for every blade from the foundry." The grey eyes were serious. He was ready to listen despite the extraordinary circumstances. "Does Richard know?"

This was it. "Er, yes. He knows. It was his idea, his instruction."

"But Nicast isn't..." He tailed off.

"Yes, he owns Nicast. The chemist who sabotaged the blades was working for Richard Sterling."

Stuart's gaze took in me, Ste and Darren. He frowned uncertainly and worried at a broken nail.

That's it—he won't believe me now. No one sees Richard Sterling as a villain.

At that moment, a very angry, very red Richard Sterling himself entered the cramped room. His forbidding energy, like a thunder cloud, silenced everyone.

"You," he snarled in my face. "I shall have you convicted by the CAA for intent to crash my plane on take-off." He drew a breath. "I shall sue you for trespass." His eyes flashed, his tanned face grew rigid and the vein in his temple throbbed. He was dangerous.

He scrutinised the audience. "What fabrication has he been telling you?" He looked around at Stuart, Darren and the security men.

The security employees looked down. Darren, nostrils flaring, curling his fingers, looked ready to hit him.

Stuart, maintaining eye contact, spoke in a steady voice. "Richard, this young man has alerted me to a serious situation with the Volantes plane." He considered his senior colleague, assessing the man's volatility.

"And you believe him?" Richard Sterling said. "You, as engineering manager, know the quality procedures at every stage of the build. You of all people must know it is not possible for anything to go wrong with any of our engines."

Richard was the first to mention an engine since he'd come in—had Stuart noticed? I remained silent, watching this clash of powers. I willed the older engineer to act rationally, logically, with integrity.

Stuart maintained the even tone of his voice. "Richard, if we suspect a problem, it is our duty to inform the pilot. The pilot can do checks and make the decision."

A shadow of annoyance spread over Richard's face. He pointed at me mockingly. "But this man— look at him. How can you believe a wreck like this?" he sneered derisively. "Take off your sunglasses." He reached over and snatched the sunglasses off my face, purposefully swiping my nose as he did so.

He stared at me. The pulse in his temple quickened; small beads of sweat broke out on his brow as my nose started to bleed again. He licked his lips, savouring my pain. His eyes burned into my core, ridiculing my lack of backbone.

I could see no way to defeat him now. I stayed seated, looking down, trying not to antagonise him. I cursed myself for failing to stand up to this bully.

I needed Stuart Nicklin to believe me and do all he could to warn the pilot. What about Isobel? She'd been talking to Richard when she arrived. What did that mean?

Two uniformed police officers entered the doorway.

"Arrest him, officers!" proclaimed the lilac-shirted CEO, pointing at me.

Stuart did not defend me. I looked at him beseechingly, willing him to act. To stop this fiasco. Stop the plane.

Swiftly, he took Ste's arm and they squeezed between the police officers and marched back to the factory. *He's gone! Catrin's last hope, gone!*

The uniformed police constables removed their hats and took out notebooks. The spotty security guard gave me a sheet of kitchen roll. I sat looking down, the blossoming white paper now an artist's award-winning metaphor: defeat.

The red-haired police constable asked for the security guard who had called them out. The greying, older police officer read out the security man's name from his little black notebook.

Richard Sterling took this as his cue to take centre stage. "Richard Sterling, at your service. CEO of Sterling Ace Aerospace."

The older police officer wrote the name. He did not look impressed.

Richard Sterling, sickeningly, continued in his showbiz persona.

"Officers, what excellent timing you have." The brilliant white teeth flashed. "Sterling Ace Aerospace is, as you know, your region's major employer. We are integral to the local economy of Port Talbot. We support your local community with events like today. I am sure you know we are generous benefactors of the Police Support Fund?" He smiled his oily smile at the two constables, subtly intimidating them. They remained professionally impassive.

Isobel had disappeared. It was down to Stuart and Ste to contact the pilot. All I could do was wait. No news was good news at this point. I refused to believe that the plane had crashed already.

Richard Sterling was still talking at the officers. He indicated towards me. "We had an extremely unfortunate incident today when this member of the public tried to sabotage the plane we were showcasing." He put on a sorrowful expression.

I seethed, glaring and clenching my teeth at his dishonesty.

"Look at him." He pointed to my bloodied face under the red baseball cap. I wore the perfect makeup for his piece of theatre. What a farce.

"Thankfully," he carried on, "our excellent team of security guards managed to stop this criminal. They brought him and his associate to the gatehouse to await your arrest." I fully expected him to take a bow for this performance.

I hated this man so much. For fear of acting rashly, I kept my eyes focused on his shiny, pointed shoes. The plane was more important than Richard Sterling.

No applause greeted his finale. The police constables looked concerned and took a moment outside to radio their station for further advice.

Outside the window, Stuart reappeared and conferred with the police officers. They all squeezed back into the cramped room. Ste had come back and stood in the doorway.

Stuart cleared his throat. "Gents, your attention please."

We looked at him expectantly.

"The police will need to take statements from everyone." Stuart looked from Richard Sterling to me, his expression hard.

Richard nodded to himself, easing towards the door.

Stuart indicated the stream of visitors' cars leaving the car park, going over the raised zebra crossing. "We will be taking statements in the visitor centre. Please use the walkways and the zebra crossing."

Stiffly, painfully, I got up. I swayed dizzily. Darren grabbed on to me, keeping me upright.

The police officers accompanied me and Darren across to the painfully bright visitor centre. Ste followed. Richard Sterling peeled off towards his car. The murderer was going to escape. I was sure of it.

The BMW growled into life, defying anyone to challenge it. We stopped in our tracks.

Darren threw his van keys at Ste. "Don't let him get away!"

Ste sprinted back to the green machine behind the gatehouse. As the BMW peeled its broken fairing off the curb, he jumped into Darren's pride and joy. Enthralled by the noise and action, I watched the drama.

The Transit hurtled towards the visitor centre. The BMW had turned and was starting its run towards the car park exit. Ste performed a smoking handbrake turn and neatly blocked the exit. With a mighty bellow, the BMW accelerated past us. Desperate to escape, it rammed into the van. The black bonnet crumpled into the van's sliding side door, the pair of vehicles spinning on impact. Screeching, shrieking metal tearing at metal. Automotive black belts.

They came to rest with the black monster impaled on a barrier support barely fifteen metres from us. Darren looked on at the final curtain call of the machine that had taken him round the Nürburgring. A deafening silence. Darren sighed.

Steam rose; metal creaked. Ste walked away from the wreckage. Richard Sterling struggled to open the creased door of the BMW. Security guards swarmed around with fire extinguishers at the ready.

Darren finally spoke up. "Officer, that brute they just pulled out did this damage to my mate." He pointed at my face and left hand. "He's guilty as hell. You want to listen to what my mate has to say." To me, he said, "Tell them, Hal, about the engine and the beating."

I looked up at the empty sky. Standing in the sunshine on the pavement outside the tall glass windows, the police opened their notebooks again. "Sir?"

"Look, it doesn't matter right now. The plane must be warned."

I felt empty. Catrin grinning on a surfboard floated across the car park. I could have sworn I heard her chuckle behind me. I turned. No one was there.

"Sir, if you could..."

I interrupted. "The plane has to land. The starboard engine is running on borrowed time." I could hear my voice rise. "Radio it in."

With impatient frustration, I watched as the constables looked at each other. This was now out of their remit. They couldn't help.

With every second of high temperature and pressure, the stresses across those blades were straining them to breaking point. It was going to be too late. Must find Stuart.

I turned and entered the visitor centre. Stuart's face in the airy vestibule was white, shocked. His shoulders slumped. He looked older, worn. I knew something had happened.

The plane was down.

Chapter 19
Passed Out

Stuart revealed the fate of the plane, of my sister.

He had swallowed the bitter pill of the sabotaged engine and contacted the Civil Aviation Authority. The aviation authority told him that the plane was already down.

Stuart looked at us. The room was hushed. For a cruel moment, I could not breathe.

"The pilot had asked for clearance for an emergency landing at Leeds Bradford airport. The plane landed successfully."

A collective sigh of relief came from the room.

"Did they say why the pilot asked for an emergency landing?" I asked, relief flooding me at last.

"Our Katy, your sister, insisted that the starboard engine was faulty. The Belgian engineers listened, believed her, and told the pilot, all within the first ten minutes after take-off. It seems the sight of the van careering towards the runway convinced them all." Stuart seemed to be shaking as he told the tale, a reaction to the immense pressure and strain he had felt as he tried to get through to the aviation authorities. The pain of betrayal by his boss.

"That's not all," he added grimly. "As the plane was descending, flames and debris ejected out of the starboard engine. It was close."

Darren, listening in, said, "Your little kid sister saved the day then?"

I tried to smile. "I suppose she did, Darren."

"Because she saw my van," Darren persisted.

"Mmm," I agreed, unable to laugh because of my ribs. "I'll give you that."

Outside the window, a circus of emergency vehicles had appeared. Fire engines, uniformed police, even police backup in the form of two plain-clothes police officers in another black BMW saloon all parked haphazardly around the gatehouse. All on business with blue lights flashing.

The sober-suited man and woman got out of the BMW and walked across to the visitor centre. Stuart greeted them and showed them through the door to the presentation theatre.

"What happens now?" I asked when he returned. I leaned against a glass wall. I felt ill.

The adrenaline of the last twenty-four hours had completely ebbed away. Catrin was safe, so why wasn't I filled with joy? My whole being had been committed to saving her for the last twenty-four hours. What would happen after was something I had given no thought to. It was unknown, a void; a void through which I was falling.

Stuart indicated the door to the corridor. The toilets and the presentation theatre were familiar, comforting knowledge.

"The police and the HSE are preparing to take statements," he said. "Once they are happy with witness statements, you will be free to go."

HSE? Is Isobel still here? "What about Richard Sterling?" I asked.

Stuart shrugged. "I don't know, but the police have asked to have a word with him. I believe he is in the gatehouse."

Richard, power-crazed, assured, a talent for spotting opportunities. He had been gifted buckets of bureaucracy, different enforcement agencies to bluff. I sighed. My testimony had to join the dots for them.

"I'll give them a statement."

We waited. Stuart had a word with the receptionists, and they busied themselves making us drinks and bringing biscuits round. I downed a bottle of water and nauseously waved away a packet of shortbread. I would have preferred to munch painkillers. I asked for Nurofen, paracetamol, anything, but the company policy was to supply no medication in case of adverse reaction. Health and safety rule. Thank you very much, risk-averse health and safety.

Darren was enjoying his part of the drama. I could tell that this saga was going to be up there in his library of anecdotes alongside the Nürburgring.

"How bad is it?" I pointed towards the huddle of mangled metal outside the window.

"Write off. Chassis got buckled."

"Hey, I'm sorry, mate."

Darren shrugged offhandedly. "Had our times. Gotta get on with life. There's a new one I've had my eye on for a bit." He pulled his chin in and grinned at me as he and I realised how it sounded.

"And?"

"She didn't change. Nice dinner, a few drinks. I had to pick her up off the pavement. She was swearing and screaming like a hellcat."

"Yeah, well." *I told you so* remained unsaid. "Take a look at the engine over there. Catrin and Ste made it."

He got up and wandered over to the cut-away engine model, as I had just two weeks ago.

The model had put me on the trail of the sabotaged turbine blades. The awards dinner had been in a different dimension, another time. I looked round the empty atrium, remembering the fine dresses, tuxedos, perfume, canapés. I remembered the feeling of expectation and celebration. Catrin's pink glittering outfit, Catrin bickering with Ste. Ste showing me the model.

I also recalled Richard Sterling handing my sister the award and cringed as I remembered her pleasure. I wanted him in prison. Uncharitably, I'd have preferred him dead.

A receptionist wheeled over a typist's chair for me to sit on. Grateful, I perched on it, looking at the door through which Isobel might appear.

The most bizarre thing happened next. Skinny, ponytailed, jeans-clad Dr Brian Robertson came through the swing doors from the theatre corridor! I blinked twice, but still, the image of the metallurgist remained. I eased off the chair, determined to stop him.

But before I could do anything, he was followed by a tall, powerful woman striding in patent high heels, black trousers and a red cavalry jacket. *Aunt Miranda!* I'd sent her that text—I should have known she would act on it. *Now, what is she doing?*

Aunt Miranda marched past Brian and had thrust her hand out to stop two uniformed officers from handcuffing the chemist.

"That won't be necessary." She admonished the two men.

The ginger police officer turned beetroot.

"Doctor Robertson has given a full confession, and you are assured of his complete cooperation."

Brian looked as dumbfounded as the policemen as she continued, "Dignity, gentlemen!"

The police officers accompanied Brian towards the door to the car park and their waiting squad car.

Stuart came up to me. "They are ready for you now."

I flicked a glance over at Aunt Miranda. She mouthed, *"See you later."* I nodded to her.

Stuart walked with me to the theatre, where a plain rectangular table was set up. Three seats on one side faced a single seat on the other.

There was no vestige of the celebration that had been here two weeks ago. The dining furniture was absent; the empty room was dimly lit. A spotlight shone over the enquiry table. Issy's hair glowed beneath it. My breath caught.

The police officers and Issy were in shirtsleeves, jackets slung round the backs of their chairs. The two plain-clothes police officers got up and introduced themselves as Detective Sergeant Nick Brown and Detective Inspector Sharon Mackerby. Isobel rose too. I shook hands with the police and, after hesitating, Issy. So formal, so aloof. A wrench in my heart more painful than anything Richard Sterling had come up with.

Why is Isobel here? What is she doing with the police? Why didn't she come out to the gatehouse? Why is she behaving as though she barely knows me?

My beautiful lady frowned as the table tilted when I steadied myself. I sat down. Dizziness and pain made it difficult to understand what she was saying. I concentrated hard, so very hard.

"Hal, thank you for agreeing to give evidence," she said. "There will be justice, but industrial sabotage involves the powers of both the HSE and the police." She paused, looking troubled, before continuing. "I, er, I have to take your statement in the presence of DI Mackerby and DS Brown because I am already involved."

DS Brown prompted me. "Mr Rogers, Hal, do you feel fit enough to continue?"

One final hurdle, I told myself. Did I want to go over the whole thing? Could I face revealing my inadequacies? I looked at Isobel. Her face was drawn, lips compressed into a tight line.

"Okay," I said. "What do you need to know?"

DS Nick Brown wrote a note on his pad. The female police officer indicated a video camera pointing at us, operated by the Sterling audio-visual technician. "Your interview will be filmed, if that is acceptable. The alternative will be to write an account, for you to sign."

"That's fine," I said wearily. It would be quicker.

I outlined the trail that had led to me finding out about the sabotaged engine. They wrote it all down. I glossed over the threats and the pain of last night; I included the conversation in the foundry conference room. I mentioned the text from my sister that confirmed the suspect blades were all in the starboard engine of the plane.

Isobel asked for clarification on the steps taken to follow the cobalt trail. I was so tired, and this seemed so pointless. She already knew what I had done. Did I really have to explain it all again?

"I found excess cobalt and aluminium in the sump of machine seventy-six at Gauge Precision Engineering."

DI Mackerby interrupted for clarification. "That is the foundry?"

"No, it's the machining factory castings go to after the foundry."

"But you went to the foundry."

"Yes."

"Your samples weren't from the foundry?"

"No. Well, yes. The parts must have come from the foundry to start with."

I hadn't realised how much other people did not know. I would be the same about police procedures, I supposed. I was so tired.

Issy stopped the questioning. "We can carry on with this another day. Will that be okay, Hal?" She was looking at me with concern in her eyes. Was that concern for me, or just because I was taking so long to do this statement thing?

Brian's urgent shouts for me to get down from the oven, his tenderness putting my boot back on. They needed to know this.

I added how Brian had helped me escape.

As we were finishing, Stuart came back in.

"Have you finished with me now?" I asked wearily.

Isobel conferred briefly with the detectives before turning to me. "Thank you, Hal," she said, indicating I could go.

What had happened to the Issy from before? Did she exist?

Finished with me in every sense. The thought ricocheted through my pain-befuddled mind. I would not be returning with the woman I had come to think of as my friend, my future.

I'd expected to feel elation—Catrin was safe—but all I felt was overwhelming physical and mental pain. Like a wretched faulty turbine blade, I too had been stressed to my limits and had cracked under the strain. All of me hurt. My back hurt, my stomach hurt, my left arm was a torment, it hurt to breathe, my head was pounding. Issy... I did not know what to think. I slumped in a low, turquoise visitors' chair, counting my woes.

The golden sun. If I squinted my eyes, the mid-afternoon sun outside the atrium appeared like a golden, setting sun. Standing in the kitchen with Isobel, watching the sun going down over the trees. I remembered with a pang the happiness at the flat, of toasting teamwork.

I watched the sun; it was still there with my eyes closed. Strange. Beautiful, though. But now Isobel did not care for me. I had been a fool even to hope. Was it all a sham?

I continued to watch the shimmering golden ball. The muted murmuring of voices in the atrium was a steady background soundtrack.

"Hal, wake up!" Someone was calling my name.

I wasn't asleep. Silly of them to think I was.

"Hal, open your eyes," the voice was instructing.

The sun would go if I opened my eyes. I liked watching the glowing ball.

"He passed out about ten minutes ago. That's when I called you."

I opened my eyes. I was not asleep. I had not passed out. I could hear them. I was just watching the sun.

"Hal, you are okay?"

Silly thing to say. I knew I was okay. I opened my eyes.

"How are you feeling?" A green-uniformed paramedic was standing over me. She was a pretty girl. Sympathetic.

"Fine, thanks." Keeping the stiff upper lip going.

"I would like to check that you are like, er, fine," the Welsh girl said with a smile. "Can you see my finger?"

Silly question again. Of course, I could see her finger. I told her.

"That's great, Hal. Now I would like you to touch my finger." She put her hand closer, with one finger pointing towards me. I could see her finger quite clearly. I could see my own outstretched finger. Weirdly, I could not get them to meet. It was a very strange sensation.

"Hal, that's fine. Now tell me where you feel pain."

"Kind of everywhere, but mostly in my arm and my back."

The girl leaned closer. "I am going to put a needle in your arm. I am going to give you fluids and a pain-killer straight into your blood. This should make you feel more comfortable."

"I'm okay."

"You are dehydrated, you have toxins in your blood, and you have goodness knows how many broken bones." The girl sounded exasperated.

That just proved I was no good with girls. I sighed. They never believed me, and I always seemed to annoy them.

"Look, mate." It was Darren. "They're taking you to hospital. Just do as they say and let them get on with it."

A male paramedic came in with a trolley.

"I can walk," I protested. I tried to get up from the chair but failed miserably.

"Like buggery," swore Darren. "Mate, you have done all you can. Let them sort you out." He patted me on the shoulder.

"Henry, do as they say!" That was Aunt Miranda.

So that was that. I gave up all free will and let them wheel me away.

***

Patched up, plumbed in. Bed and breakfast with hospital food. No beer; a drip of saline and an efficient painkiller that might have been morphine—no one was saying. Attached to a catheter collecting blood-stained urine. My left arm was supported in a wodge of bandage. I was told the swelling had to go down before they could set the bones. I had been X-rayed and had four cracked ribs, as I'd thought. My nose, according to those who know noses, was not too bad and had been supported into shape with lots of tape and internal packing. It would heal up, same as the gash on my cheek, which had been stitched. As I had thought, nothing life-threatening. Just a pain.

Before visiting time, I had plenty of opportunity to lie in my white bed and let the thoughts and images of the last fortnight settle into order. One piece refused to fit.

Dark-haired, intelligent beauty, a heart-wrenching stranger. Isobel tentatively walked towards my bed. She was still wearing the white shirt and khaki trousers that she had driven us down in. Her expression was serious, her hazel eyes troubled.

"I'm sorry, Hal."

"What for?" I asked.

No hellos. *Is she using me again?* I did not know her.

She swept her hand over the bed. "For this, for everything."

She stood there, mute, eyes searching my face.

What does she want? What is she expecting? Gallant Hal to kiss her fingers?

"I... you... It was a mistake," she started.

"A mistake to come to dinner," I finished for her, almost choking on the words.

"Yes—no. No, not like that. That's not what I mean," she stuttered. "I should have told you."

"What?" I bit out.

"I work for the HSE."

"Like I didn't know."

"When your report mentioned there was a short spike in cobalt levels in that aerospace milling machine sump at Gauge Precision, my boss said it could be industrial espionage. He wanted me to keep an eye out for anything further. I thought it had to be one of those things he'd been trained on that never happens in real life."

"Oh," I said dispiritedly.

"That is what I could not tell you. We agreed you had to be acting independently."

"Oh," I said again. That did not make it any better. She'd used me, and she still came for dinner. Was all that playacting? I'd been so happy in the kitchen with her. Did that mean nothing?

"Why did you come for dinner?" I asked, accusing, hurt.

"I wanted to," she said simply.

"You mean you wanted to find out what I knew, without the courtesy of asking," I threw back at her.

"No, it's complicated."

"It looks straightforward to me."

She took a breath. "I came to dinner because you were interesting, not because of the turbine blades or Sterling..." She tailed off quietly. "I thought you liked me, that we might get on."

"Oh," I said again. *Dare I hope that she means it, or is she stringing me along again?*

It was the promise of an unchecked lottery ticket. I wanted to maintain my unrealistic hope unchallenged.

"I'm tired." I finished the conversation, closing my eyes. "I'll call sometime."

"Goodnight, Hal." I heard her go.

Eyes closed against the glare of hospital lights, I lay back, trying to find a comfortable position whilst a barrage of images from the day fired across my retinas.

***

Catrin and Ste arrived together, bringing "get well" wishes, a change of clothes from Gareth and apologies from Aunt Miranda, who had returned to Surrey. I had to insist I was not ill, that I was only staying the night. I felt a fraud. Neither took any notice.

Both engineer apprentices wore the uniform of youth in Port Talbot: designer-label tracksuits. I asked if they were going out. They thought it hilarious but did not say either way. The youngsters shared a look and smirked at some inner knowledge.

"Well done on your surfing move." I smiled at Catrin. She glowed with pride.

"Something special, isn't she?" Ste put his arm round her.

"You're no slouch yourself," I told him, referring to the green van exploit.

"Ste's not that good," said Catrin, and then her eyes widened in comprehension. She wriggled out of Ste's embrace. "This isn't about surfing. What have you done?"

"He only stopped the boss from escaping, with the most amazing handbrake turn."

Bewilderment crossed Catrin's face as she looked from me to Ste and back again. She pointed to my bandaged arm. "But didn't you get that in the van crash?"

"Nope."

She rounded on Ste. "*You* crashed Dustco's van?"

Mildly, I explained, "He stopped Richard Sterling escaping from the police."

Ste defended himself. "Strictly speaking, it was Sterling who crashed into the van."

Catrin stood away from the bed, her face a drama of different expressions as she thought through what she had just learned. No one had told her about Richard Sterling.

Ste and I looked at each other in dismay.

"So, if you didn't crash the van," Catrin asked me, "how come you're smashed up?"

"Richard Sterling," Ste and I said in unison.

"The turbine blades were his idea," I added. "He wanted Sterling Ace Aerospace to fail."

Catrin's eyes were puzzled, her mouth downturned, shoulders stiff. "But, why?"

"So it could be bought cheaply. He would have saved the buyer tens of millions of pounds."

"Oh. You sound like your Aunt Miranda."

"Yeah, what was she doing at Sterling with Dr Robertson?"

"Who's Dr Robertson?"

Ste answered. "Dr Robertson is the metallurgist at Nicast. He did the actual tampering. But he was told what to do by Richard Sterling."

"How does Aunt Miranda fit in then?" Catrin's colour had returned, and she returned closer to Ste.

It was my turn. "I'd kept Aunt Miranda up to date with my cobalt findings. My last text to her was from the foundry when I'd met Brian, er, Dr Robertson. So, she knew about him and the blades."

"If Dr Robertson is Brian, then who is this Mick that got arrested this morning and she had to bail out?" Ste asked with a frown.

Oh no! I had used Mick's phone. I could feel a smile breaking across my face at the picture this was creating. He must have called Aunt Miranda, and she had sorted it. She must have driven to Dudley and talked Brian into giving himself up. Well, well.

"Aunt Miranda's cousin. It's a long story."

I asked Catrin if she'd been scared when she was sure the engine of the plane was damaged. Her reply astonished me.

"No—aircraft can land with engine malfunction. It wasn't going to crash," she stated simply.

I recalled the fireball picture I had conjured up. I wondered if that was what health and safety work did to you—made you believe in the worst outcome. Maybe it was age and experience (of horrible plane crash headlines). I decided not to tell her about the accidents with uncontained engine failure debris rupturing hydraulic lines and forced crash landings.

"So, what did you do?" I asked her.

"I just had to tell Hans and Rudi to inform the pilot to go slow or to land." Catrin shrugged.

Ste took a dramatic deep breath, raising his eyebrows at her. He looked comical.

Catrin sighed. "Okay, I did have to pester them a bit before they would even do anything."

"Rudi told me that once the plane had levelled out, you stood in front of them in the aisle and would not stop nagging for a full five minutes!" Ste laughed, admiration in his voice.

"Yeah, well, it worked." Catrin grinned.

"Stuart said that you realised the danger when you saw Darren's van driving across the grass?" I offered.

Catrin sucked in her breath across her teeth, making a hissing noise. "That was the most stupid, idiotic, dangerous thing you could do to a plane," she replied, voice raised.

Ste and I looked guiltily at each other under the tirade.

"Don't you know that aircraft have a point of no return when they are taking off? They can't just slow down and stop!"

Heat rose up my cheeks when I realised I could have caused a far worse crash by intervening than the broken engine would have caused.

"I am sorry," I said baldly. "I am very glad you are alive and here to tell me off, though." I winced as my ribs protested when I tried to sigh.

Catrin put her arms round my shoulders in an awkward hug.

I whispered into her hair. "I am so bloody glad nothing happened to you today."

She stood up, blinking back tears.

"If you hadn't sent me the message about the blades, I wouldn't have known to stop the plane. And although you nearly killed us with that van, I realised how important it was to get the plane down safely, so you're the hero of the day really." She sniffed, giving my good hand a squeeze.

I smiled at her. "But you're the one that convinced the pilot in time."

Catrin dug Ste in the ribs. "You caught Richard Sterling."

"Teamwork!" we said together.

Catrin and Ste gave each other that look and smirk again.

I could not ignore it. "Tell me, what's that about?"

"The HSE lady, Isobel Fleming kept mentioning you. She said you were the best at teamwork," Catrin clarified knowingly. "Why don't you ask her out? She seems nice."

The raincloud of my doubts about Issy drifted away. Suddenly I felt lighter and happier. *That'll be the morphine, Hal!*

"Maybe. And how was your week with the Belgians?"

It seemed that they had enjoyed explaining processes to the engineers and had been invited to spend a week in the Volantes factory in Belgium. All was good in their world.

***

Issy came to see me again the following afternoon. She was wearing a summer dress and sandals. She looked and smelled gorgeous, feminine. I was off the drip and drainage and had finally had a wash, though I still had bloodshot eyes and pirate stubble. I felt bad about how offhand I had been with her the previous day.

"Hiya. Nice of you to visit me again. You didn't have to."

She looked tired, with shadows under her eyes. "S'okay."

I wanted her to smile, to make things right between us again. "Look, I'm sorry I was such a stupid, rubbish person yesterday. I was unreasonable. I'm sorry."

She just smiled tiredly and shrugged it off. "Doesn't matter. You were in pain."

"Isobel, how are you? Are you okay?"

She tucked a strand of hair behind her ear. "I'm fine, just tired from non-stop meetings and reporting."

I considered her, my head on one side. I stood up and offered her my arm. "I know of a special little coffee house." Then I added, like from a black-and-white film, for good measure, "Could I tempt you to a little light refreshment?"

The sad hazel eyes glimmered. Hope blossomed in my heart.

"Certainly, sir." She took my arm.

I shuffled down the hospital corridors dressed in a knee-length hospital gown, boxers, and Gareth's cardigan. Issy stepped lightly at my side. An old couple passed us, tutting sternly.

I laughed. "They must think we're out of the theatre. The princess and the pantomime dame!"

"Shh, they'll hear you." Issy leaned close, realising the funny side of our attire.

The old couple paused in their walk. We looked at them, then each other and burst out giggling, trying to hide it, holding each other up.

"Come on, I think we need a drink now," I said, once we had calmed down and Issy had wiped her eyes.

In relaxed good humour, we continued slowly to the hospital cafeteria.

***

That evening, Stuart called in to see me at the hospital. The man looked older and more tired than I had ever seen him, but he still retained the aura of honesty, of integrity. He still worked at Sterling, but the CEO had been arrested and the company's finances were floundering. He was not the youngest of men to face battle.

I invited him to sit down, but he remained standing.

"All this..." He waved his hand over my bandaged arm and my taped nose. He looked very uncomfortable, steeling himself to say something.

"If you are going to say it's your fault, then that's rubbish," I told him. "The only person to blame is Richard Sterling, and maybe me for acting without thinking."

Stuart looked slightly relieved. I could tell he had the weight of the world on his mind. There was the company's uncertain future, the relationship with Volantes to mend, the board of directors and shareholders to appease. If the company were to be salvaged, he would be facing an uphill battle. I wondered whether he would retire now, bow out gracefully.

"Are you okay?" I asked him.

"Yes, yes," he answered distractedly.

"Are you going to retire?" I asked him point-blank.

"What? Good gracious, no!" He ran a hand through his thinning hair. "Do I look that bad?" He raised a fighting grin.

"What are you going to do?" I asked.

"I have been asked by the chairman to take on the position of temporary CEO."

"Will you?"

He looked up at the ceiling. "I think I shall. I know what it needs. The fiasco with the foundry proves that we need to move with single-crystal blades, bring in XRF checks, give the R and D department more strength. We have the right people here, right now."

"What about funding?" Years of testing were required for new engines before they could be certified.

The old engineer's face creased into a smile. "Your sister has seen to that. The Volantes engineers were impressed with Katy. Volantes have proposed to provide funding and resources for a joint venture for a new plane and new engines. The whole of the aircraft industry is working on reducing global warming emissions. The new plane will be up there with them."

I nodded. "Stuart, everyone at Sterling likes and respects you. I am sure the company will do very well under your guidance now," I tried to encourage him. At the top, there would be no one to remove his doubts.

"Thanks, Hal."

With a loosening shrug of his shoulders, he grinned at a recent memory. "Warn me next time I think of going to a pub for food with Darren. He's a lunatic!"

I snorted with laughter.

He turned. "Before you leave for the Midlands, call in at Sterling, would you? I have a proposition."

Off he went, leaving me intrigued.

Chapter 20
Proposition

Three nights in a white metal bed. Enough! The new week was definitely time to get out of hospital and get on with life. Doctors on the new shift gave me the green light. Not properly fixed, but nothing left that couldn't be done in Outpatients.

I could not believe it had only been a fortnight since Isobel Fleming inspected Gauge Precision a long, livid lifetime ago.

My mind flitted between concerns and plans, pausing only for a surprisingly good hospital-issue egg mayonnaise sandwich and a bizarrely bright neon-orange jelly.

Had Barry managed to decorate his grandson's room? Philip would have to be careful about reintroducing him to production work. Maybe he suited precision toolmaking. I should work on a plan to get him back to production just in case.

Nicast—should I tell Isobel about the standards there? It just wasn't right that employees were being exposed to hazards unnecessarily. Something needed to be done there.

And Isobel—call her, ask her out properly.

Half-past two approached. I managed, one-handed with taped ribs, to get into Gareth's jeans and baggy brown cardigan. With distaste, I pushed bare feet into stiff, bloodstained work boots, socks stuffed into my pocket.

A bubbling blonde tornado ruptured the calm antiseptic of the hospital ward. Catrin showered the nursing staff with smiles and grateful thanks. On me, she showered packages and instructions.

"Hal, you can't meet everyone like that! We've got to get you tidy!"

Everyone? I had the awful feeling that she had arranged a party or something. I had promised Stuart I'd see him.

"Catrin, look, it's really thoughtful of you to bring me clothes and the shaver, but I've said I'll see Stuart before going home. If you've arranged something... I'm sorry, but I can't go."

Catrin's lips pursed, and her jaw clenched as I was speaking. She scowled at me. She looked as though she wanted to tell me something.

"Hmm, so you want to go to Sterling first, to see Stuart? Does he know you are coming? He might be busy." She made an odd noise, ending in a cough, hair falling over her face.

"It'll be okay, Catrin. He probably just wants to touch base for a couple of minutes. Let's just go."

Catrin avoided my gaze while I changed and shaved. She busied herself collecting my stuff as I got the discharge letter and painkillers. We walked in silence through the fantastic fresh air of the car park to a small white Citroen van with Sterling signwriting. *Have I upset her? What have I done?*

Catrin's shoulders and neck were rigid with tension on the drive to the factory. A small smile twitched at her mouth and was quickly repressed. She stopped the van in front of the visitor centre and jumped out, leaving me to struggle.

"Ste!" Catrin ran up to the curly-haired engineering apprentice in the open doorway. She flung her arms round him, shoulders heaving.

The young man laughed, then calmed the histrionics. I realised they were laughing at me. I'd been set up! I had to see what this was about.

Then I noticed the little Fiat. *She's here!*

With a smile, I entered the visitor centre, thankful for my tidy shirt, chinos and slip-on shoes. Inside the atrium, a group of suited businessmen were engaged in discussion with Stuart Nicklin. Stuart, still an engineer in shirtsleeves and a loosely knotted tie, left his guests and approached with his hand out.

"Hal, good of you to come."

I shook his hand. It was firm and dry, decisive. The man himself seemed to be bursting with energy, eyes glinting, so different from the defeated shell here on Friday.

"Let me introduce you to the MD of Volantes and his senior engineer." We made suitable noises, shaking hands with the dark-suited Belgians.

"You know Philip Wheatley, I believe?"

Philip turned round with a smile in his grey eyes and shook my hand as well.

What is all this about? I looked for Catrin, but she had disappeared.

"Gents?" Stuart ushered us to the theatre.

The room was dominated by a shining model engine mounted on the raised podium. Exhibition stands held drawings, specifications, graphs. The stand closest to the door boasted the ownership, "Volantes-Sterling-Joint-Venture". Catrin's and Ste's grey polo shirts each sported a navy and turquoise 'VSJV' logo. They bounded up to me. I hugged Catrin and shook Ste's hand.

Across the room, two women were talking by an information stand, their heads close. Both were tall and slim, one in a purple-and-black dress suit, the other's familiar curves in a khaki shirt with tan, slim-fit trousers. *Aunt Miranda! Isobel!*

Miranda typed notes onto a handheld tablet and looked up with a smile. "Henry!"

Isobel was already watching me. I tried to guess her mood, if she was happy or sad. What were they talking about? I smiled at them both.

Stuart cleared his throat, a signal for silence.

Catrin grinned at him and stood in front of the group, saying, "Welcome to the Volantes Sterling Joint Venture." She rattled off a short speech, explaining the information posters. I smiled and nodded, very pleased for her and the company, and again, very proud of her.

The serious, bespectacled, dark-haired Belgian MD spoke. "Today we sign the joint project agreement between our great companies. Without your actions, Mr Rogers, this day may never have come.

"You made a difference. No one else could have done what you did. You had the presence of mind to act. You understood the relevance of the results you found. Without your tenacity in following that up, without your intelligent grasp of what had happened, without your action to stop the plane, our plane would almost certainly have crashed, and many lives been lost. You made a difference. You, Mr Rogers, not any-one else. Believe it."

The man's expression was earnest and not in the least embarrassed at giving such an embarrassing speech. He reminded me of Brian when the scientist had talked about climate change.

I didn't really do any of that. I just didn't understand the results. I didn't really know what had happened until I was told in the foundry. Then it was too late. And I didn't actually stop the plane. A fraud.

I looked around. People I knew, respected and believed in smiled and nodded.

"Er, thank you." I smiled, suddenly glad that I had followed things up. Maybe I *had* done what he said.

As we shook hands, a photographer, answering to Miranda's instruction, took photos.

Then the real work of the afternoon began. Interviews for Miranda's scoop, and the most amazing carte blanche opportunity to make a difference with occupational hygiene.

The proposition was for me to lead a team from VSJV with Philip Wheatley, and advised by Isobel, to set standards in occupational hygiene for global suppliers of Volantes Sterling Joint Venture, to audit all suppliers and advise on improvements. This is what I had dreamed of. No—it was beyond anything I had dreamt. For as long as I had been an occupational hygienist, work had been my life, but I had felt strangely unfulfilled.

Isobel caught my eye over the meeting table. She smiled. *Just one more step, Hal.*

***

Issy had insisted on driving me back to the flat after the meeting. She had changed into trainers with jeans and a hooded sweatshirt. With her hair in a swinging ponytail, she looked the same age as my sister.

We had driven in silence for an hour. It had given me time to realise that I needed to do something if I wanted to keep this amazing, clever, practical, wonderful woman in my life. My heart seemed to ache, just looking at her as she drove.

At the Goodrich Castle sign, I asked to turn off the main road and try the castle for a cup of tea. Isobel looked at me with a frown of concern. *Is she replaying Friday's drive down?*

"I just thought it would be nice to have a quiet cuppa with you, after this afternoon's excitement."

With a little smile, a "Hmm," and a shrug of slender shoulders, Isobel flicked on the indicator, and we left the main road.

I watched Isobel's expression change as she drove the short distance down narrow lanes.

Concentration compressing her soft lips, she pulled in for a car to pass. A twitch of those lips, a crinkle around long-lashed eyes as she flicked a glance at me. *Happy! I am so light, I could laugh out loud, turn cartwheels! Today is the day I ask her out!*

"What are you grinning at?" Isobel laughed.

"Just happy!" I replied as the little car turned into the quiet, tree-lined car park.

With strapped-up ribs, I struggled to get out of the low-slung sports car and ended up on my knees on the gravel. Issy came round to help me up.

Pointy gravel dug into my knees. I took her hand. Delaying standing, I looked up into her deep hazel eyes.

"Would you, Isobel Fleming..." I paused. "...have dinner with me tonight?"

As I had hoped, she laughed. I stood up. She continued to keep her hand in mine. Electric tingles ran from her fingers up through my arm into my chest, my core.

We stood so close, barely breathing. Her hair, so beautiful, so soft... a strand blew across her smooth, warm cheek.

I let go of her hand. Gently, I caught the stray hair and stroked it back into place. I inhaled. She smelled of evening flowers, sun-warmed grass. Summer.

Her eyes held little flecks of gold, amber, bronze, autumn leaves. I felt the feather-light touch of her body against mine. I pulled her to me, and we kissed long and deeply in the dappled green light under the trees.

Author Profile

Leila Kirk is a working chartered occupational hygienist. She started her own consultancy in 2006, after surviving a close brush with death. Because she believes people come first, the company was named Workforce First. Its aim is to help small businesses manage their own health risks. Work has taken her across the UK and into Europe. She is a guest lecturer at the University of Birmingham.

She is a proud mother and stepmother of seven amazing adults. Her spare time is spent with her husband shooting clays, growing veg and cooking.

She replaced her pickup truck with a van in 2016.

What Did You Think of Cast Doubt?

A big thank you for purchasing this book. It means a lot that you chose this book specifically from such a wide range on offer. I do hope you enjoyed it and found it useful and informative.

Book reviews are incredibly important for an author. All feedback helps them improve their writing for future projects and for developing this edition. If you are able to spare a few minutes to post a review on Amazon, that would be much appreciated.

Publisher Information

Rowanvale Books provides publishing services to independent authors, writers and poets all over the globe. We deliver a personal, honest and efficient service that allows authors to see their work published, while remaining in control of the process and retaining their creativity. By making publishing services available to authors in a cost-effective and ethical way, we at Rowanvale Books hope to ensure that the local, national and international community benefits from a steady stream of good quality literature.

For more information about us, our authors or our publications, please get in touch.

www.rowanvalebooks.com
info@rowanvalebooks.com

Printed in Great Britain
by Amazon

84585643R00161